LOVING THE HIGHLAND WARRIOR

Highland Destiny
Book 2

by Michelle Miles

ARE YOU SIGNED UP FOR DRAGONBLADE'S BLOG?

You'll get the latest news and information on exclusive giveaways, exclusive excerpts, coming releases, sales, free books, cover reveals and more.

Check out our complete list of authors, too!

No spam, no junk. That's a promise!

Sign Up Here

www.dragonbladepublishing.com

Dearest Reader;

Thank you for your support of a small press. At Dragonblade Publishing, we strive to bring you the highest quality Historical Romance from some of the best authors in the business. Without your support, there is no 'us', so we sincerely hope you adore these stories and find some new favorite authors along the way.

Happy Reading!

CEO, Dragonblade Publishing

CHAPTER ONE

CHLOE SINCLAIR SAT on the edge of the ambulance with a scratchy blanket wrapped around her shoulders. The paramedic insisted she remain there while they stitched her up. A bullet had grazed her upper arm, but it was nothing serious. She was lucky. Luckier than some of the guests in the museum.

Six masked men with guns had invaded the Edinburgh museum during the gala event, the one she had planned for months as a major fundraiser. Her sister, Evie, had traveled from the States to join her and visit for a few days. Then, all hell broke loose. Chloe frantically searched for Evie in the ensuing chaos when the men forced them from their chairs and made them lay face down on the floor.

Someone had managed to call the emergency number to alert the police to their dire situation. The moment that happened, Chloe had started looking for Evie.

She had excused herself to go to the ladies' room and hadn't returned. Worry gnawed at her. When she saw Evie sprinting up the staircase to the next level, her heart had rammed in her chest. One of the men had followed her, tried to grab her on the stairs, and capture her. But Evie…she hiccupped a breath, remembering. Evie had kicked him in the face!

She couldn't believe it when she saw her sister do that. Then Evie ran up the rest of the stairs.

When the sirens sounded, the man upstairs ran back to rejoin

1

the others and then they left as quickly as they had arrived, leaving wreckage in their wake, exited through the front door and into the night before the police arrived. When the officer asked her if there were any more people left in the museum, she told him her sister was still in there.

Now, she waited impatiently for the officers to return and tell her the results of their search. Her leg bobbed up and down in a nervous tick as she waited, chewing on her thumbnail. If Evie were here, she'd tell her to stop it.

When she caught sight of the officer emerging from the museum, alone, her heart sank. She knew instantly something wasn't right by the look on his stoic face. Chloe jumped to her feet, tossing off the scratchy blanket.

"Where is she?" she demanded, trying to keep the emotion out of her voice.

"I'm sorry but there isna anyone inside the museum," he said.

His gaze cut to the front of the museum as another officer emerged, carrying two things she recognized. A pair of shoes and a black satin handbag. Hot pinpricks of fear broke out all along her body as she watched the woman approach carrying the personal items.

"We found these," she said when she arrived next to the other officer.

"Those are Evie's," she said, her voice wobbling with emotion.

The officer handed them to her. "I found them in the loo."

Damn it all. Where the hell was Evie? Why had she taken off her shoes? Maybe because she'd heard the gunfire and thought she might have to make a run for it. She couldn't do it in four-inch stilettos, so she had left them behind.

Chloe took the shoes and the handbag from the officer. Inside the handbag was her small wallet, her cell phone, and a little drawstring bag in blue velvet. She pulled out the bag, but it was empty. She had no idea what it was. She had never seen it before.

It was unlike Evie to leave her cell phone behind. But then, things had been chaotic.

"Are you *sure* she wasn't in there? I saw her go to the second level. There are cameras in the museum."

The officers exchanged a look. "The cameras weren't working," the woman said.

Chloe blinked as she glanced from one to the other. "What do you mean they weren't working?"

"We're already checking for the footage. There isn't any," the male officer said.

Her stomach turned over, a sick feeling creeping through her as she stared in disbelief at the two officers. She didn't understand what was happening. The intruders hadn't taken anything from the patrons or the museum. What was there to take? Why come to the museum? It didn't make sense. Still, she was convinced her sister was inside.

"But, Evie—"

"There is no one left inside, miss," the male officer said, his tone one of patience.

"But—"

"You should go home and get some rest," the woman said. "There's nothing more we can do tonight."

Panic began to set in. "My *sister* is missing. If she's not in there, then one of the men took her."

"Did you see them take her?" the man asked.

Chloe sank to the edge of the ambulance, the cold metal biting into her bum. "No."

"Then how do you know she's missing? Likely she got out with everyone else and returned home," the officer said.

But Chloe was shaking her head hard. "No. She doesn't know the city. She wouldn't leave without me. I'm telling you, if she's not in there, then something is wrong."

The female officer reached for her, wrapping an arm around her shoulders. "Why don't I give you a ride home?"

It was a suggestion to appease her, she knew. But something niggled at her. Told her not to leave the scene of the crime.

Surely, Evie was still in there somewhere and she would emerge any second now, barefoot and angry she was left behind.

"I can't leave without my sister," she said, hot tears threatening her eyes.

The two officers exchanged a glance. Then the woman said, "We've checked the place several times. There is no one left inside."

She didn't believe them. Evie wouldn't have disappeared into thin air.

"Come on, now. Let's get you home."

She hated the thought of leaving without her, but the officers gave her no choice. She allowed them to drive her to her flat. She sat in the backseat clutching the handbag and shoes with a death grip, her knuckles white. When they arrived at her flat, the female officer walked her to the door and saw her safely inside.

She dropped her sister's shoes on the floor, then placed her handbag and the small blue velvet bag on the coffee table.

As soon as the door closed behind her, she reached into her own handbag and brought out her phone. She punched in the number and waited for her boyfriend, pacing the small length of the apartment. Finally, Bruce's sleepy voice answered.

"Chloe? It's late. Is everything all right?"

"No, Bruce." She said his name on a breath. "Something terrible has happened."

THIRTY MINUTES LATER, a knock sounded on her door. It was nearing three in the morning. She peered out the peephole to make sure it was Bruce. When she saw it was, she opened the door and ushered him inside. As soon as the door was closed, she fell into his arms. He held her, holding her tight.

"What is it? What's wrong, lassie?" he asked. He pulled back, holding her at arm's length and noticed the bandage on her upper arm. "Ye're hurt."

"I-I don't know where to start. It's all so awful!"

He wrapped an arm around her shoulders and led her to the sofa where they sat together. He held her close, his muscular arm reassuring around her. She tucked her head under his chin as she fought off the tears.

"Ye said something happened at the museum tonight? Was the gala not a hit? How did ye get hurt?"

When she heard that, she burst into tears.

It took several minutes for her to get her sobbing under control enough to tell him what had happened.

"Everything was going so well," she said and sniffed. "Then these men came. Masked men with guns. Oh, Bruce, it was horrible!"

"Men with guns?" he repeated, sounding horrified. He glanced at her bandaged arm again. "Were ye shot, lass?"

"It's nothing." She wasn't concerned about her arm. The pain had subsided. "I don't know what they wanted. They stormed in and made everyone get on the ground. They didn't take anything like wallets or purses. It was as though they were looking for something. But nothing was stolen from the museum, either."

She sniffed again.

"What about the police? Did they come?" He continued to hold her close.

"Yes, but it was too late. They must have known the police were called because they all left the museum before they arrived."

"I'm sure they have a lead, aye?" he asked. "There are cameras in the museum."

She sat up straight, meeting his gaze. "That's the other weird thing. The cameras weren't functioning."

Something flickered in his sharp blue eyes. She didn't understand what it was. Was it relief? But why? Her gut clenched tight and she got a strange sense from Bruce.

What was it Evie said?

Always trust your gut. It's never wrong.

Her gut was telling her something was off about Bruce. It was a feeling she had never had about him. Until now.

"Someone cut the cameras. Likely that someone was one of the intruders." His voice was dead calm as he said it. Then he glanced around the flat. "Where's Evie?"

She sprang to her feet and paced the small area in front of the sofa. Tears threatened again. "I don't know."

"What do you mean?" he asked.

"She disappeared. I don't know where she is. She never came out of the museum."

He stared at her in silence, his face devoid of emotion. Finally, he said, "I'm sorry, Chloe."

She spread her hands in defeat. "I don't know what to do."

Bruce got to his feet and walked over to her, wrapping her in his arms once again. The odd sensation that something was wrong dissipated. It was stress and worry making her question everything. He kissed her forehead.

"I should have been there," he said, the guilt lacing his tone.

But he had had a gig at the pub and wasn't able to make it. She understood, of course. She had been elated Evie was with her. Now, she was missing.

"Where could she be?"

"Ye need to get some rest, lass. In the morn, file a missing persons report. I'll go with ye, if ye like."

"Yes, please."

He walked her to the bedroom where she kicked off her shoes. She sank onto the bed, still dressed in her evening gown and clutching his hand.

"Stay with me tonight?" she asked. "I don't want to be alone."

He brushed the back of his hand over her cheek. A faint smile flickered over his face. "All right. Rest, now. I'll make ye some tea."

When he left the room, she kicked off her shoes and curled on her side, still dressed. But it wasn't long before exhaustion took over and she was fast asleep.

BRUCE MACDONALD RETURNED to the bedroom, a steaming mug in his hand. Chloe, though, had fallen asleep. He placed the mug on her bedside table and then did a cursory glance around the room, looking for anything out of place or different. He took long, slow, quiet steps through the room, examining the top of her dresser, the bedside tables, the top of her chest. He kept his hands clasped behind his back to keep from disturbing anything.

When his search turned up nothing, he stepped out of the room and slipped his phone from his pocket to make a call.

"Well?" John, his brother, answered in a terse tone.

"She doesn't know anything," Bruce said.

As he stood outside her bedroom door speaking in a hushed voice, he saw it then. The blue velvet bag rested on the coffee table next to Evie's black handbag.

"I did find something interesting. The bag."

He walked over to the table as he spoke and picked up the bag. There was nothing in it.

"No stone?" he asked.

"It's empty. I'm telling you, the lass disappeared before my own eyes. She used the keystone."

He had chased her up the stairs and almost caught her, but the lass had kicked him in the head. It still throbbed. She had scrambled up the stairs to the second level where he found her hiding behind a samurai statue with her hand clutched into a tight fist. He had been certain she had the keystone. Plus, he had heard the humming coming from the small thing.

"Then it's already in the past." John heaved a sigh of annoyance. "We need the other piece of the keystone to follow her. Keep an eye on her sister. She may have it and not know it."

"I doubt that, but I will," he said.

As he ended the call, he stuffed the bag in the pocket of his jacket on the off chance he'd find the other stone. Another quick glance around the room yielded nothing.

Chloe stirred then. He reached for the mug as she rolled over, her eyes blinking open as she looked up at him.

"I brought the tea, lass."

She waved it away. "Come to bed."

He replaced it on the bedside table, then slipped off his jacket and his shoes and crawled in bed beside her. He took her in his arms as she snuggled against him. If the other piece of stone was here, he'd find it.

CHAPTER TWO

S UNLIGHT STREAMED IN through the opaque curtains pressing against her eyes, waking her. Her head pounded as though she were hung over. Her throat was raw. Her eyes were gritty. Her bandaged upper arm throbbed. She sat up with a start as the horror of the previous night came crashing back to her.

Oh, God, Evie. Where are you?

She rubbed her temples, trying to make the headache go away. When she placed her feet on the floor, she realized she still wore her red sequin evening gown. She also realized Bruce was gone. He had left a note on the bedside table beside the mug of tea that was now cold. The hastily scratched note said he had returned home to shower and change and to call when she was ready to file the missing persons report.

She padded to the kitchen for a glass of water. She paused in the living room where she saw Evie's shoes still on the floor and her handbag on the low table. She stared at it a long moment trying to make her fuzzy brain work when she realized the blue velvet bag was missing.

The only person who could have taken it was Bruce. Why would he take it?

Shaking her head, she continued to the kitchen where she got a glass of cold water and downed it. She had to pull herself together.

First order of business was to shower and dress, then get to the police station and file a missing persons report. That's what Bruce had said he'd help her do. He'd said he'd go with her but now she wasn't sure she wanted him to go.

She thought back to last night when he had arrived. Something was off, but she was unable to put her finger on it. Why did she have a bad feeling about him? What was bothering her?

He seemed…relieved when she told him the cameras weren't working. And then he had said… She tapped her finger against her chin, thinking. He had said someone cut the cameras and he suspected it was one of the intruders.

Was he guessing when he had said that? Or was there something more?

She shook her head to clear it, pressing her cold fingertips to her forehead and massaging.

Get a grip, Chloe.

Bruce was not the enemy. The men who had attacked the museum were. She refilled her glass and took another sip of water before going back to her bedroom. On her way there, she halted at Evie's guest room.

Her suitcase was still open on the floor, the pieces of clothing scattered as she had tried to find her black cocktail dress. She had tossed the clothes out in a frenzy looking for the bolero jacket that went with the dress.

Chloe stood in the doorway, remembering their exchange with such clarity, her heart hurt.

"I can't find it," she said as she furiously dug through the small carry-on. "Those TSA agents stole it."

Chloe laughed. "Why would TSA want your bolero?"

Evie stopped to look up at her sister, her brown eyes shining with frustration. When she realized what she said, she laughed, then. "You're right. I probably left it at home."

"We better get going. I can't be late."

Evie hopped up, her bare feet pattering on the floor behind Chloe as she followed her into her bedroom. She headed right for the closet and started going through her clothes.

"Do you have anything I can borrow?"

"No. Eve..." When she said her nickname, Evie turned to face her. Her wild fiery red hair framed her face as question etched along it. "You'll look beautiful without it."

Evie took one more longing glance at her closet. "Are you sure?"

She moved toward her sister, and grasped her by the hand, squeezing. "Yes. I'm so glad you're here, Eve."

She gave her a winsome smile. "I'm glad I'm here, too."

"Good! Now go get dressed!"

"Okay...*Mom*." She rolled her eyes as she left the room and headed back to hers.

Sometimes, she had to be the bossy one. The one who made sure Evie was taking care of herself. The one who made her go to bed early when she looked exhausted from working all day. The one who made sure she got her fruits and vegetables and harped on her about drinking enough water.

It was because she cared. And because she knew what sacrifices Evie had made to allow her to go to college and graduate with honors.

And where was Brianna, their older sister, during all that time? Sipping piña coladas on a beach in the Caribbean with not a care in the world or a thought about them.

Chloe shook herself to come back to the present. She didn't need to dwell on their older sister right now. Right now, she needed to find her twin and her best friend. She needed to find Evie.

AFTER SHOWERING, SHE dressed and made her way to the police station to file a missing persons report. She told the officer everything that had happened the night before and that her sister had seemingly disappeared into thin air. He looked at her like she was crazy.

She wasn't crazy. She hadn't dreamed it. Her sister's belongings were still in her flat.

The officer took down the report though he didn't give her much hope.

Her next stop was the museum. It was closed. Police tape still barred the entrance. The shattered glass door was boarded up. She was unable to get inside, which made her heart sink. Her logical mind told her Evie was no longer inside, but shouldn't she at least check?

As she stood on the steps of the museum trying to decide what to do next, her cell phone rang. It was Bruce.

"I was calling to check on ye, lass."

"I appreciate that. I'm just...out of sorts. I filed a missing persons report."

There was a long silence, then, "I thought you wanted me to go with you."

Her hand tightened on the phone. She didn't want to tell him she didn't want him with her. She opted to tell a trivial lie. "I got up early this morning to go. I didn't want to bother you."

Another beat of silence. "How about I pick you up and take you to lunch? To take your mind off things for a while."

She glanced at the parking lot, her heart in her throat though she was unable to explain it.

"I ken ye're worried about yer sister," he said, his voice full of sympathy and concern. "I would be, too, if I were in yer shoes."

"I am worried. She had a blue velvet bag. It was collected with her shoes and her handbag from the museum bathroom. I've never seen it before, and I have no idea where she got it."

The bag that was missing after he left last night.

"Perhaps a jewelry bag?" He acted as though he knew nothing about it.

She shook her head as if he could see. "She doesn't wear jewelry."

Chloe knew this to be a fact. She and Evie had gotten their

ears pierced when they were twelve, but Evie had had trouble with hers and ended up removing the studs and letting the holes grow in. She never wore earrings or anything else.

"Oh, well, perhaps for something else, then?"

"But what?" Chloe insisted. And why was she so determined to find out?

"I have to be at the pub this evening. How about an early dinner?" Bruce asked, changing the subject.

It irritated her. "I don't know."

"It will help you take your mind off yer sister. I'm sure the police are doing all they can to find her," he said.

Were they? The officers last night didn't seem too concerned Evie was missing. They assumed she had gotten out of the museum with the rest of the patrons. But if she had, then she would have been at the flat when Chloe returned home, and she wasn't.

If the police weren't going to do anything, then she would have no choice left but to go to the embassy and see if she could get help there.

"What do you say?" he said.

Maybe Bruce was right. She needed to go to dinner with him to take her mind off things. Worrying was doing nothing but making her sick to her stomach.

"All right," she finally said.

"Good. I'll pick ye up at six."

He hung up before she could object.

WHEN CHLOE RETURNED to her flat, she went straight to Evie's guest room. She started going through all her things, looking for clues about what might have happened to her. She placed the clothes in a pile on the bed and then searched the zippered compartments of the suitcase. On the outside, there were two pockets. One small, one large. Her passport was in the large one. When she slipped her hand inside the small one, she felt something.

She pulled out a white business card with embossed gold lettering reading *Mystic Treasures*.

"*Where the past meets the present,*" she read aloud.

There was one name below that line. *Moira.*

Who was Moira and what was Mystic Treasures?

There was no address or phone number. She got out her smartphone and did a quick search for Mystic Treasures. Nothing came up. No shops in the area. She tried another search for the area near Evie's apartment back home in the States. Again, nothing.

She stared at the card for the longest time, wondering where and how Evie had gotten it. If she hadn't brought it with her, then where would she have gotten it in Edinburgh?

The airport seemed unlikely.

And then she remembered something about the day they were out shopping on the Royal Mile. When they were going to have lunch, Evie had seemed distracted as she peered across the street at…something. What was it? She had told her and Bruce to go ahead, and she would catch up. That she would only be a moment.

Bruce had taken her by the hand and turned Chloe toward the restaurant, so she hadn't seen where Evie went.

By the time she had joined them for lunch, her face was flushed, and her hands shook. She'd seemed nervous. Chloe had never asked her about it because they were still with Bruce, and she didn't want to question her in front of him.

None of this made sense to her. The only way to figure out where Evie had gone that day was to try to retrace her steps. That's exactly what she was going to do.

A quick glance at her watch told her it was nearly time for Bruce to pick her up. She frowned. She didn't want to go to dinner with him, but she had agreed, and she didn't want to cancel at the last minute. She slipped the business card in the back pocket of her jeans.

In the bathroom, she brushed her auburn hair and swiped fresh lip gloss over her lips. Staring at herself in the mirror, her normally bright emerald eyes were glassy with bags under them. Fatigue lined her face. Though she had managed to sleep some last night, it was restless, and she was still exhausted. She used a bit of concealer to hide the shadows, but it didn't seem to help.

She had to get through this dinner with Bruce. Once it was over, she told herself she would head to the Royal Mile to see if she could find the mysterious Mystic Treasures.

A knock sounded on the front door. She grabbed her purse and headed to open it. As she passed through the living area, she glanced at Evie's small handbag on the table and her shoes on the floor. A pang of worry went through her.

"I'm going to find you, Eve," she said. "I swear it."

Then she whisked open the door to see Bruce standing on the other side.

"Hi," he said.

He acted like he wanted to come in, but Chloe pushed past him, pulling the door closed behind her and locking it.

"I'm starving," she said, trying to sound like her bright and sunny self. In an effort to seem as though everything was situation normal, she hooked her arm through his. "I realized I haven't eaten all day."

Confusion flickered over his face as she ushered him toward the car. "How about the tavern then?" he asked. The tavern was a favorite of theirs.

"On the Royal Mile?" A glimmer of hope flickered through her.

He nodded. "If that's what ye'd like."

She pasted on a bright smile. "Sounds wonderful."

And if she were lucky, perhaps she could give him the slip to look for Mystic Treasures.

CHAPTER THREE

CHLOE WAS A nervous wreck all through dinner. It took everything in her to sit still, to pretend everything was great and she was having the time of her life. Bruce didn't seem to notice and for that she was grateful. She managed to have the appropriate responses to his questions as they chatted through dinner.

As they left the restaurant, she tucked her hand in his elbow.

"I feel like an evening stroll," she said glancing up at him. Hope curled in her chest.

"All right."

They headed down the street, the lights of the early evening blinking on. The walking tours were getting started as they strolled down High Street. Chloe thought of the gold-embossed card in her pocket and kept an eye out for the shop. Her gut told her it had to be on the Royal Mile and, like Evie, she had to listen to her gut.

Then she spied the small shop between a cigar merchant and a shop specializing in cashmere and lambswool. The name, Mystic Treasures, was in gold letters over the door. She had never noticed it there before and thought it was an odd place for a shop.

How was she going to get away from Bruce long enough to go into it?

"Are ye feeling well tonight, lass?"

"Yes, I'm fine." Though she knew it was a lie.

"Maybe I should take ye home. It's been a long few days for ye."

That sounded like a great idea to her. She nodded. "Yes, I think you should."

As they headed back to his car, her mind raced with what to do once he dropped her off. She decided to return to the Royal Mile and go to the shop and hope it hadn't closed for the day yet. It was a long shot, but she had to try.

"I have to stop for petrol on the way," he said.

She nodded agreement, trying not to be annoyed about the delay as she got into the passenger seat. They headed back to her flat with the one stop on the way. He got out to fill the tank.

While he stood outside the car, she was overcome with emotion when she thought about Evie and getting back to that shop on the Royal Mile. As her eyes welled with tears, she popped open the glove box in search of a tissue and stopped cold.

The blue velvet bag was stuffed inside the small compartment.

The same blue velvet bag the police had retrieved from the ladies' room with Evie's handbag and shoes. She stared at it, dumbfounded, as she confirmed the theft.

She had left it on the table in her living room, but it had disappeared. Here it was in his glove box. Why would Bruce take the velvet bag from her table? There was no reasonable explanation she could think of for him to take it.

He finished filling the tank. Chloe slammed the glove box closed and dried her eyes with the sleeve of her sweater. She placed her hands in her lap, trying to keep them from shaking, when he got back in the car and started the engine. He must have sensed something was off.

"Are ye all right? Ye look white as a ghost."

She pasted on a bright smile. "I'm a bit tired. Like you said. It's been a long few days."

"Well, then, I best get ye home."

When they arrived at her flat, she hopped out and hurried to the door, leaving him behind. Still, he followed. At the door, she turned to face him.

"Thank you for dinner. I appreciate it." She kissed him on the cheek. "Good night."

And then she pushed inside and closed the door before he managed to reply. She flipped the lock, leaned against the door, and blew out a breath, her hands still shaking. She stood there for a long moment, staring at her sister's handbag on the table and wondering what had been in that blue velvet bag. Why would Bruce want it?

Chloe headed to her bedroom to change into her favorite jeans, sneakers, and a long-sleeved cable-knit sweater. She pulled on her light jacket as the nights were chilly. After swiping a brush through her long auburn hair, she headed for the door and paused there, staring at it. Wondering if she had given Bruce enough time to drive away.

She checked her watch. It was nearing the time for him to be on stage at the pub. Confident he was long gone, she pulled open the door and stepped into the night.

When she arrived at the Royal Mile, she made her way through the street looking for the small shop she'd spied earlier that evening. She reached into the pocket of her jacket and pulled out the card, staring down at it in the light from a streetlamp. The embossed letters shone in the lamplight, sparkling in a way she hadn't noticed before.

Just when she was about ready to give up hope, she saw it nestled there between the two other stores she had seen earlier. It seemed strangely out of place here, but she was determined to get to the bottom of the mystery. The name on the door—Mystic Treasures—was in the same shimmering gold letters as the business card in her hand.

The bell on the door signaled her arrival. The moment she crossed the threshold, a strange pull pounded through her, as though she were meant to be there. She stood a moment in the doorway, taking in the small store crammed full of antiques with everything from trinkets to furniture. A sense of calm washed over her.

"Hello, there," a woman called with a bright smile as she approached. "I was about to close for the night but something told me I should wait."

Chloe stuck the card back into her pocket. "I can come back tomorrow."

The woman halted in front of her. She was striking with long pale hair and bright-blue eyes that sparkled in the light of the shop. When she smiled, it showed off her dimple. Her name tag read Moira. Like on the business card.

"Nonsense," the woman said. "I've been waiting for you."

That gave Chloe pause as she remained rooted in place at the door. What did that mean? Cold pinpricks danced up her spine and pooled at the base of her neck. But it wasn't alarm she felt. No. It was more like…anticipation. Like she was about to get all the answers she needed to find her missing sister.

"If this is a bad time…" Chloe began.

"Not at all." She smiled at her, a warm, congenial smile that was meant to put her at ease. "You're the last customer of the evening. I'll let you have a look around."

She disappeared through the maze of clutter, leaving her standing there with unanswered questions. What did she mean she'd been waiting for her?

Chloe moved deeper into the small shop, the musty smell of antiques wafting to her nose. In all the time she had been in Edinburgh, and all the time she'd spent on the Royal Mile, she had never seen the shop before.

"Have you been here long?" she called.

"Not long," the woman answered. "As long as I need to be."

Chloe's brows drew together. She didn't understand what

that meant either.

"Have a look around," Moira said. "I'm sure you'll find something you'll want, Miss Sinclair."

Gooseflesh erupted on her arms underneath her sweater as she stared at the woman who busied herself dusting a shelf of knick-knacks. How did she know her name? She hadn't told her.

"I don't...how did you..."

"Och, I know you have questions. They'll be answered in time." She paused her dusting to meet her gaze. "But first, look around."

There was an oddity about the shop and the woman proprietor. Chloe almost turned and dashed for the door until she heard a faint humming. She turned to look around for it, tipping her head to one side and listening.

Chloe stepped deeper into the shop as the humming increased as though there were a force pulling her toward it. Normally, she didn't believe in all-powerful things, but there was something about the thrumming of the sound, drawing her closer and closer, until she stood in front of a glass case with all sorts of trinkets inside.

There were small items with Celtic symbols on them. A mother-of-pearl necklace. A Celtic cross. Intricate knotwork that wove through what appeared to be an old faded bookmark. A silver circular brooch adorned with Celtic knotwork and two amber stones on either side of it. She caught herself staring at the brooch for a long moment, admiring it. It was a beautiful piece of jewelry.

But then another item in particular caught her attention. It was a small, odd-shaped stone with faded lines across it. The stone looked at though it were part of a bigger piece. As if it had been broken or split in two. She was certain she had heard the humming coming from behind the glass from that stone and pressed her hand against it, confident she'd feel the vibration. She didn't.

Her heart drummed hard against her chest. Her pulse quickened. A vision flashed through her mind of a castle against the inky backdrop of night and a tall man with a thick beard, long hair plaited on either side of his face, and eyes like the sea after a storm.

She dropped her hand from the case and stepped back, her heart in her throat.

"Ah, I see you've found it. Or, rather, it found you."

Moira was at her side, which made Chloe jump. She hadn't heard the woman approach.

"Found what?" Her voice was a rough whisper.

Smiling, Moira opened the case and picked up the strange little stone. She held it out to her. Chloe stared at it, her hands clenching into tight fists. The impulsive side of her wanted to take it. The logical side of her told her not to.

"You'll be wanting this, lass," the woman said.

"What is it?"

"Your future and your past."

Chloe's head snapped up and she met the woman's starry-eyed gaze. That didn't make sense to her at all.

"I don't understand."

"It calls to you, doesn't it?" Moira asked, a pleasant expression on her face.

Chloe managed to nod, her hands loosening at her sides. Her fingers twitched with the sudden need to take the stone from the woman's palm.

"How does it…why does it do that?"

"It senses you and knows who you are."

Finally, Chloe reached for the stone, plucking it from the woman's palm and holding it in her own. The lines were faded to almost nothing but she was able to discern that they were once engraved. There was an arch with another line going through it.

Chloe was familiar enough with the Celtic symbols to imagine what it was—part of a triquetra with a circle going through. An ancient symbol of the trinity knot that meant different things. Such as the three stages of life—youth, adulthood, old age.

Perhaps that's what Moira meant when she had said it was her future and her past.

But the symbol also had ties to the Maiden, Mother, Crone, symbolizing generations. Her gaze flickered back up to the woman. When she had said her future and her past, was she referring to Evie? Or something else?

"It looks like it's part of something bigger," Chloe said.

Moira merely nodded. "It is. And it's yours."

"Oh, I—"

"I must insist." She waved for her to follow toward the back of the shop.

Chloe stood there for a long moment, watching her walk away, dumbfounded and unsure if she should follow. She stared at her back, the way her long silvery hair fell in soft waves. She closed her hand around the stone and headed for the shopkeeper.

Moira stood behind the cash register waiting for her. As Chloe approached, she noticed a picture of a castle on the wall behind her. She gave it a quick glance, then looked back up at it. It sat on a craggy hill. Its high towers were shrouded in mist. Behind it, a placid loch under an overcast sky. A sense of familiarity flickered through her as she looked at it, as though she had been there before. In her short time in Scotland, she hadn't had time to explore castles.

"That castle…"

"Dundale," the woman replied. "You'll see it soon enough."

Chloe blinked in confusion as she looked at the woman. "Isn't Dundale on the Isle of Skye?"

"Aye, it is. Once the seat of Clan MacLeod," she agreed and held her hand out to her. "Let me package that for you."

The eerie feeling did not leave her as she dropped the stone into the woman's hand. She rustled about under the counter.

"How much?" Chloe asked.

"Free of charge."

When Moira handed her back the stone, it was inside a blue velvet bag.

CHAPTER FOUR

A SORT OF numbness pressed through her when she took the blue bag. It was like the one Evie had had with her that was retrieved from the museum bathroom. The same one Bruce had stuffed in his glove box.

Bruce had taken the blue velvet bag from her flat.

Chloe stood a moment at the counter across from the woman trying to make sense of it all. Then she asked, "How did you know my last name was Sinclair?"

Moira gave her a little smile. "I know your sister."

Hope exploded through her as her chest tightened. "Evie. Did you give one of these to Evie?"

"You must be Chloe," she said, ignoring her question. She walked around the counter. "You'll want to be careful with that. It's a powerful thing."

Chloe gripped the bag tighter in her hand. "Someone else wants it?"

Moira's face turned serious then. "There are those who would kill for it. Never let it out of your sight." Then she changed the subject and motioned her toward the door. "I must be closing for the night now."

"Oh," she breathed. "Yes, of course. I'm sorry to keep you."

Chloe followed her to the front of the shop. As the woman reached for the door, she turned back to her. She looked her over, as though she was memorizing her face.

"Good luck to you, Sinclair."

Then she opened the door and stepped aside. Chloe's only response was to nod as she stepped out into the crisp evening. Moira closed the door after her and flipped the lock.

She stood on the sidewalk, gripping the bag with that eerie sensation still piercing through her. It was the oddest conversation she had ever had with anyone.

Chloe put the bag in her pocket as she headed for her car.

THREE HOURS LATER, she perched on the edge of her sofa staring at the bag sitting next to Evie's handbag. The stone rested on top of the bag as it continued to quietly hum.

Her mind was so befuddled she hadn't thought to ask Moira what the stone was. All she knew was that it was part of something larger. Another piece perhaps. But the way it was broken indicated to her that it must be part of two larger pieces.

Did Evie have one of the pieces? She must have. She must still have it, wherever she was, because her bag was empty.

Which made her wonder why Bruce was so interested in it.

Exhaustion pounded through her. She lay on the couch, tucking her legs up. Her eyes became heavy as she stared at the humming stone, the bag, and her sister's purse. The strange vision she had had in the shop came back to her. The one of the castle and the man she had never seen before.

It was the last thing she thought of when she drifted off to sleep.

The dream started immediately. The man had chiseled features with the most incredible sea-green eyes she had ever seen. Firelight flickered over his face as he sat with his massive forearms crossed over his chest. The expression on his handsome face was pensive. His gaze flickered to hers and his expression softened as he looked at her. He held his arms out to her in invitation.

She slid into his arms as he wrapped them around her, surrounding her in his warmth.

"Och, lass, I cannae resist ye."

His words were sweet as they rumbled through his broad chest. She tilted her head back and looked up at him. As his lips met hers, she startled awake. She sat up, her mind foggy, as she peered into the shadowy darkness of her flat, feeling a bit off kilter.

Who was the man she dreamed of? He was the same one in the vision she had had in the antique store.

She pressed cold shaking fingertips to her lips but the kiss wasn't real. It was merely a dream.

The humming of the stone had grown louder, drawing her attention. She reached for it, picking it up and saw the lines on the stone faintly glowed. Her brows drew together as she peered down at it.

As she was about to run her finger over the stone, there was a pounding on her front door, startling her. She clasped the stone in her hand as a gasp escaped her and she shot to her feet. A quick glance at her watch told her it was nearly one in the morning.

Who would be at her door at this time of night?

Her heart raced as she stared at the door. There was silence. Had she imagined it in her post-sleep haze? She took a deep breath and expelled it, trying to calm her ragged nerves. She needed to go to bed and sleep.

Chloe turned toward her bedroom. As she did, there was a loud crack, like wood splintering. She spun to face her front door as it flew open. Two masked men rushed inside. She didn't have time to react as one of them grabbed her, pulling her to him and wrapping her in his arms.

She thought of that night at the museum. These men were dressed like the ones who had invaded the night of the gala.

"I'll hold her. Ye look for it," he said.

The second man went directly to her bedroom. Her heart

rammed hard in her chest as she stood there, shivering with fear. Sounds of things hitting the floor and drawers opening came from her room while the first man held her clutched against his heated body. His shallow breathing shuddered in and out, as if nervous and on edge.

The second man came out of the bedroom, halting in the doorway and something about the way he stood there holding his head sent a shudder of familiarity through her. He turned his head in the light in a way that she got a glimpse of his bright, piercing blue eyes.

She sucked in a sharp breath.

"Bruce?" His name quivered from her.

Across from her, he stiffened. His entire body went rigid.

Behind her the man holding her barked, "Keep looking."

"It's not here," the other replied.

As soon as he spoke, she knew she was right.

"Bruce, why?" was all she could think to say.

He stood motionless for a heartbeat, then reached up and pulled off the mask, revealing his familiar face. Those piercing blue eyes met hers and her heart sank to her shoes.

Evie had sensed something about him, something she didn't like. She had tried to tell Chloe but she wouldn't listen. She had thought she was in love with him. She had thought he might be the one. Now she knew he wasn't.

He was the one who had stolen the bag off her coffee table. He was the one who had hidden it in his glove box. Was he also the one who had chased Evie up the museum steps that night?

"I know it's here, lass," Bruce said.

She didn't know what he meant but she had a sudden suspicion he was looking for the stone. The one Moira gave her. The one clutched in her hand, the jagged edges biting her palm.

"What are you talking about?" She tried to play dumb.

The man holding her twisted then. He looked down at the table and saw the other blue velvet bag. "There's the bag." He turned back to Bruce. "Find it."

"I don't have to. She has it." His gaze flickered to her clenched hand by her side.

Hot, wild fear pumped through her as she stared at the man she had thought she loved. He took two steps, closing the distance between them.

"Let her go," he said to the one holding her.

He didn't ease up on his grasp. "Are you mad? If I let her go, she'll bolt."

"She's not going to," Bruce said, his gaze never leaving her face. "Are you, Chloe?"

She decided there was only one way out of this and that was to comply. Moira had told her, though, to never let the stone out of her sight.

There are those who would kill for it.

Her words rang back to her. But if she didn't comply, was she risking her life? She didn't think Bruce would hurt her, but now she wasn't sure.

"No," she finally said, her voice weak and rough.

The man released her and stepped back. Bruce motioned to the sofa for her to sit. She kept her hand clenched as she perched on the edge of the cushion. She placed her hands in her lap. Her fingers were still tightly clasped around the stone. He sat next to her. How many times had they spent in her flat doing that? She didn't want to think about that. Not now.

"You have something in your hand, don't ye?"

"What if I do?" she asked.

"I need ye to give that stone to me. That's what ye have, isn't it? A wee stone?" he said.

Her heart pounded harder. She tried to ignore the flat door that was wide open. It was her only escape route and the other man stood between it and her. The chilly night air spilled inside.

"It calls to us," he said. "We can hear it."

In her palm, the stone hummed a little louder.

"I don't know what you're talking about," she said.

"Christ's sake, Bruce, take the bloody thing from her, will

ye?" the second man said, his tone laced with annoyed impatience.

"Don't be like yer sister, lass," Bruce said.

She straightened a little. "Where is Evie? What did you to do her?"

He chuckled. "I did nothing to her."

"Then where is she?"

Now she was convinced Bruce had something to do with Evie's disappearance. Had he taken her? Or, worse, killed her? Where was she?

"Give me the stone and I'll tell ye where she is."

A trade. She clutched her hand tighter around the stone. Did she dare trade the strange looking stone in her hand for Evie? He wasn't giving her a choice. Likely, he knew she would do anything to get her sister back. She tipped her head down to look at her clenched fist.

"Och, this is taking too bloody long," the other man snapped.

"Patience," Bruce replied, his tone hard and unforgiving. Then to Chloe, he said, "I know ye want to know where she is. I can help ye find her."

She wanted to believe him, but she didn't.

There are those who would kill for it.

She had to think and quickly. She cut a glance at the other man who was edgy as he stood near the door. If she was fast enough, she could bolt around him and out the door. She still had on her sneakers. She could make a run for it. But then what? Where would she go?

She decided it was worth the risk. One step at a time. She'd jump to her feet, make a mad dash for the open door, and pray she'd make it.

"All right," she said, as though she were agreeing to hand over the stone. *Never let it out of your sight.*

She took a deep breath, expelled it, and then gathered all her courage. She shot to her feet and turned in one motion, taking two steps toward the open door. The second man tried to block her but she used her fisted hand to deliver an uppercut. Her hand exploded in pain but she managed to keep her grip on the stone.

He was so surprised by her punch, he stumbled back a step and crashed into the bar, knocking over a vase of flowers. That gave her enough time to go for the door again. But then she was tackled from behind. She lost her balance and started to pitch forward. Bruce had his arms wrapped around her, holding her upper torso in his muscular arms, arms that had once held her with tender care.

She started to go down, taking him with her. She crashed against the floor, narrowly missing the coffee table, jarring her and rattling all her teeth. Her elbow cracked against the floor, the thin carpet not much cushion. He was on top of her now, reaching for her fisted hand and trying to claw her fingers open.

With her other elbow, she jabbed him backward as hard as she could. It connected with him and he emitted a muffled oof. He refused to let go, though.

Bruce flew backward off her. She clawed her way to her feet and glanced back in time to see the second man had had enough of Bruce and was coming after her himself. Bruce shoved him out of the way. He stumbled, fell, landing on the coffee table with an audible crack. Chloe bolted outside, running down the street, her leg muscles screaming in agony. His feet pounded the pavement behind her.

She didn't understand why he wanted the stone or why it was so important. She didn't understand why it continued to hum in her hand. Bruce caught up to her, grabbing her from behind and dragging her to him. They stumbled backward into the shadowy night, away from prying eyes in case anyone happened to look out their window. He held her against him, his breathing heavy and his heart pounding against her back.

"Give it to me," he panted, "and I'll let you go."

She glanced down at her hand and saw with some shock light seeping from around her fingers. She didn't know what to make of that. A burning sensation pierced her palm. She opened her fingers enough to see the lines on the stone lit up. She sucked in a sharp breath as a sudden need to touch those lines pounded through her. She swiped her forefinger over the lines.

The world fell away from beneath her feet and then she was falling. Cold wind sucked the breath out of her lungs and for a moment she was unable to breathe. It was as though she were drowning. Bruce was no longer there as she tumbled into a free fall.

Then there was nothing at all.

CHAPTER FIVE

MALCOLM MACLEOD SAT in his bedchamber with his arm cradled against his midsection, brooding. He'd come out of the battle with the MacDonalds mostly unscathed, save for one cut on his upper arm. Dougal had wrapped it as soon as he and his brother, Jamie, staggered back into the keep after the fighting was all over.

That was nearly a week ago.

He recalled the end to the battle with clarity. Frustration had edged through him when he had stood on the bloodied field and watched Rory MacDonald and his men ride away in defeat into the night, leaving behind the aftermath of their skirmish. Dead men and dead horses had littered the ground. Men he had recruited from Clan Sinclair to fight against their rival clan. Good men. Men who were now dead.

But they had no choice, did they? They had had to rally the banners to fight the thousand-strong army MacDonald had brought with him. They hadn't had the numbers to fight and both he and his older brother, Callum, knew it.

The only thing that had saved them was his brother's new bride, Evie Sinclair. She had used the piece of the keystone as a weapon, a weapon that had killed many men and stopped the onslaught. If it hadn't been for her, they would have all been slaughtered.

The fire blazed in the hearth as he stared at it, a restless feeling sweeping through him. He was not one to sit around and do nothing, especially after a battle like that.

He hadn't slept all night and now that morning was upon him, there was no reason to go to bed. In a fit of frustration, he stood, leaving the warmth of the fire and his bedchamber behind.

He had to do something or he'd go mad.

He needed vengeance for the death of his da. He needed to kill Rory MacDonald.

He headed to the great hall where Jamie, his younger brother, was breaking his fast. He had a stack of oatcakes in front of him and a pint of ale.

"Angus Sinclair is leaving today," he announced as though that were the most pressing news of the day.

Malcolm took the seat opposite him and poured himself an ale. Then he stole one of Jamie's oatcakes. His brother scowled at him about the theft but said nothing.

"And this concerns me how?"

"I thought ye'd like to know since ye brought him and his men," he said. He guzzled the rest of his ale and thumped the tankard on the wooden table.

Malcolm broke the oatcake in half and popped it into his mouth. "It doesna matter to me."

"Och," his brother said and shook his head. "Fine then. Be that way. Callum was hoping ye'd escort them back to their home."

He lifted a brow. "Callum wouldna ask that of me without a good reason."

"Aye, ye have the right of it, brother," Callum said as he made his way into the great hall. Under his tunic, the bandage was still visible. During the battle with MacDonald, he had been stabbed in the shoulder.

"And why do ye wish me to go with them?"

"I want ye to scout the area," Callum said.

"Och, so I'm no banished anymore, is that right?" Malcolm couldn't help the sarcasm lacing his words. He leaned back in his chair and crossed his thick forearms over his chest, staring up at his brother.

After their da was killed by Rory MacDonald, Malcolm had taken it upon himself to retaliate by raiding one of the MacDonald's villages and burning it to the ground. He had made sure there were no injuries or deaths when he did it—all were ushered out of their beds that early morning and forced from their homes. He'd merely wanted to put the fear into MacDonald and let him know what the MacLeods were capable of. When Callum had learned of his night raid, he punished him by sending him away from Dundale.

He understood why he had done it. It was his right as laird. It hadn't lessened the sting of fury, though.

However, when he had ridden away from the keep with no destination in mind, he had seen the MacDonald clan heading toward Dundale with his army. It was then Malcolm had made the decision to ride to the Sinclairs, knowing he would answer the call for help because he thought Evie was one of his kin.

Mayhap the lass was, but it was hard to know for certain since she was from the future.

"Ye've been brooding around here for a week. I ken yer restless," Callum said. "So, I'm giving ye this task."

"Why?" Malcolm asked. "Aren't ye afraid I'll burn down another village?"

Fire flashed in Callum's eyes. "If ye do, then expect a harsher punishment than banishing."

His brother's piercing blue eyes settled on him with a look that said he wanted no argument and he meant what he said. The threat was real.

If that's the way his brother wanted to do things, then he would pack up his horse and escort the Sinclair clan back to their keep as well as scout the area.

"When do we leave?"

MALCOLM RODE IN solemn silence next to Angus Sinclair as they headed back to his keep. He hadn't had much to say along the way and wasn't interested in conversation. Sinclair wasn't interested in conversation, either. He'd lost men at the battle. He rode stiff and tall in the saddle. Despite the silence, Malcolm felt as though he should say something.

"Did my brother thank ye for coming to his aid?" Malcolm asked.

Angus gripped the reins tighter in his hands, his eyes forward. "Aye."

He didn't seem to want to elaborate, which made it difficult for Malcolm to continue on. Still, he tried. "Good. I want to thank ye, too."

"'Twas a strange thing to see," Angus said, as if he hadn't spoken.

Confused, he drew his brows together. "What was a strange thing?"

"The lass." Angus turned to him and gave him a pointed look.

He didn't have to explain for Malcolm to know what he meant. He referred to Evie. He thought back to the way she had stood on the battlefield with her hand glowing, that feral look in her deep brown eyes, and her fiery red hair whipping around her face in the wind, the way she knelt on the ground with her fisted hand and how it had rumbled. There was something mystical about it.

He, of course, understood what it was. She had held the keystone in her hand, the stone they were prophesized to protect. He didn't know if Sinclair would understand that.

"Is she a witch?" Angus asked.

Malcolm managed to suppress the chortle that wanted to erupt. "She is no witch."

"Then what is she?" Angus gave him a glance that was full of curiosity tinged with fear.

"She's no to be feared," he replied.

But Angus had more questions. "What did she have in her hand that MacDonald wanted? What trickery did she use to subdue the men? There was a flash of light and—"

"Aye, there was a flash of light," Malcolm agreed with a nod. "But it was nothing more than lightning."

Angus gave him a sour look. "Och, laddie, do ye think me daft? Dinnae tell me falsehoods for I ken the truth of it. There was no lightning that night. What was it the lass did? Tell me truly."

He cut him a glance and saw the man was not going to leave the subject alone. He wanted answers and he wanted the truth. Dare Malcolm tell him the truth? Would he believe in the prophecy as he and his brothers did? Or would he think *he* was the daft one?

He took a deep, cleansing breath. "There's an old story about a keystone. One that was split into three pieces by the Goddess of the Present herself. One that controls all of Time. It's powerful and dangerous."

Angus stared at him a long moment as they rode on, then he threw his head back and laughed. "Ah, lad, that's the best story I've heard all day."

"No, Da, he tells ye the story true." Duncan Sinclair rode up next to them, slowing his mount to a trot as he did so.

Duncan was the spitting image of his father. Red hair kissed by the sun, a full, thick beard covering his face, and cool gray-blue eyes that missed nothing.

Angus glanced over at his son and shook his head. "Dinnae tell me ye believe in this falsehood of a story?"

"Have ye never heard the story?" Duncan asked, as he peered around Malcolm to look at his father. "The story of the goddess who shattered time to save it."

"Och, 'tis nothing but a myth." Angus dismissed the idea with a wave of his hand.

But Malcolm knew it was no myth. It was the truth. And Evie

held one piece of the ancient and fabled keystone. One piece that belonged to a larger piece. One piece that MacDonald would kill to get his hands on.

"No a myth," Duncan said. "It is said the Triple Goddess shattered the Chronos Stone into three pieces to keep it safe from those who would use it for evil."

His father lifted a faded red brow. "The Triple Goddess?"

"Past, Present, Future," Duncan said, sounding as though he was sure of his answer.

Malcolm nodded, though, because he knew the younger Sinclair was right.

"And what happened then, lad?" Angus asked, the light of amusement flickering through his eyes.

"They sent the three pieces to the far reaches of Scotland," he said. "Only to be found when it was needed once again."

This was a part of the story Malcolm had not heard. He listened in rapt fascination.

"Then, when the time came, the Goddess of the Present would find a way to give it to the one clan who would be able to protect it," Duncan continued.

"And what clan is that?" Angus asked.

"Clan MacLeod." The younger man gave Malcolm a pointed look.

Angus snapped his head in his direction. "Clan MacLeod."

"Aye," Malcolm said, nodding agreement. "But I've heard it as two bloodlines, one destiny. The Sinclairs' and the MacLeods' destinies are intertwined. The lass is a Sinclair."

There was a long silence and then Angus burst into laughter. "Aye, then, the lass is the protector of this magical stone?"

"Aye," Malcolm and Duncan said in unison.

That stopped Angus's laughter. He clenched his jaw, the muscles flexing there and turned his attention back to the road ahead. His mannerisms indicated he didn't believe the prophecy. Callum hadn't either for the longest time until Evie convinced him that she was the one to bring the keystone back in time to protect it from the MacDonalds.

"We best make haste, boy," Angus said. "Yer mam will be waiting for our return."

Then he kicked his horse into a gallop, putting distance between Malcolm and Duncan and the rest of the men. The younger Sinclair cut a glance at Malcolm.

"He doesna believe," he said.

Malcolm took in a deep breath, exhaled it. "Then mayhap it's up to ye to convince him."

In the distance, billowing smoke caught his eye. The gray-and-white column curled into the sky. Ahead of them, Angus halted his horse, his gaze on the smoke ahead.

"Da, what is it?" Duncan called.

He cut a glance back to his son. "The village."

Then he kicked his horse into a gallop in the direction of the smoke. Malcolm and Duncan exchanged a glance before doing the same. Behind them, the men followed. It didn't take them long to come upon the village.

It was burned to the ground.

CHAPTER SIX

I T HAD TAKEN some time to go through the village to count the dead. There weren't many, so it looked as though most of the inhabitants had made it out. Once the men had buried the dead, they continued on to Angus Sinclair's castle. The men scattered and returned to their own homes, leaving Malcolm and the two Sinclair men.

Seeing the acrid smoke, the burned-out homes, and the dead made Malcolm think of his own raid on the MacDonald village. The one which had gotten him banished from Dundale. He, however, had made sure no one perished in the fire.

Angus's face was hard, his jaw clenched and his lips in a thin line. It was clear he was angry about the raid and even angrier that people had perished. Malcolm followed him through the gatehouse into the bailey.

"I should return to Dundale to report this to Callum," Malcolm said.

"Ye will stay," Angus said, his eyes flashing.

He dismounted his horse and handed the reins off to his stable hand. Duncan did the same, not looking Malcolm in the eye. Since he didn't seem to have a choice, he followed. The last thing he wanted was to witness Sinclair's fury over the death of his people and the burning of their village.

When they arrived in the great hall, they found Lady Fiona Sinclair distraught, having already heard the news from a messenger who had arrived before them. She clutched the rolled parchment in her hand until it crinkled. Her bright emerald eyes were shiny with unshed tears and her thick auburn hair was plaited in a single braid that rested over one shoulder.

"They had no warning," she said. "Thankfully, most of them made it out."

Angus swiped a hand down his face, a look of exhaustion replacing his fury. He lowered himself into one of the chairs at the great hall table.

"Who would have done such a thing?" she asked.

Angus heaved a sigh, his gaze flickering to Malcolm, his expression grim. He understood in silent communication that they both knew who was responsible for such an atrocity. It was in retaliation for the battle they had lost at Dundale, the battle in which the Sinclair clan had lent their aid.

"There is only one clan who is responsible," Angus said. "Do ye agree, laddie?"

The question was directed to Malcolm. Lady Fiona looked at him, her tawny brows drawn together as she waited for the answer.

"MacDonald, no doubt," he finally said.

Her shoulders drooped as if in defeat. "Then I take it things did no go well for him."

She referred to the battle they had endured to keep Evie and the keystone safe, though Lady Fiona didn't know that. Angus said nothing. When she gave him another questioning glance, he nodded.

"Aye, to be sure. Rory MacDonald and his men were defeated at Dundale," Malcolm said. "But it appears they dinnae rest for long."

A range of emotions creased her face—worry, guilt, fear. She was the one who had encouraged them to fight against them. She tossed the parchment on the table and then took the seat next to her husband. She placed her hands into her lap as she sat straight, her face a map of regret.

"I shouldna have insisted ye go," she said.

Angus's bright gaze flickered back to her. His features softened as he reached a hand to her. She placed her fingers in his hand.

"Dinnae blame yerself, wife. Fighting with the MacLeods was the right thing to do. I dinnae regret it." He squeezed her hand. "Ye would have been proud of the lass."

A tingling of surprise went through Malcolm as he realized what Angus was about to say.

"Oh?" She tipped her head to one side.

"I'd no seen anything like it. She saved us all," Duncan said before his father replied. Lady Fiona glanced his way, question lingering in her eyes. "She used the fabled keystone. Her hand lit up with the power of it."

"Och, laddie, that's no what she used." Angus's tone was full of disbelief.

"How can ye say that, Da, when ye saw it with yer own eyes. She was there with the keystone. I dinnae ken what else it would be," Duncan said.

The lady's gaze turned to Malcolm then, as though she were waiting for him to confirm or deny the story. He cleared his throat and shifted from one foot to another.

"Is the story true, then? Does the lass possess this keystone?"

Malcolm glanced at Angus, who still appeared as though he didn't believe. "She does."

"'Tis nothing more than a story." Angus huffed and released his wife's hand and pushed up from the table. He stalked off, leaving the great hall, the muffled steps of his boots on the rushes.

Silence descended. Lady Fiona slowly got to her feet and turned toward the two of them. She clasped her hands in front of her.

"Well," she said at last, her voice quiet. "He doesna believe the story is true. But I do."

Malcolm did his best to hide the shock rolling through him as he stared at the woman. "Ye ken the tale?"

"Of course I do. We've all heard the story. Even Duncan." She nodded to her son. "We've heard the tale about the fabled keystone that can control time as well as the intertwining of the two bloodlines. Why do ye think I sent my husband to fight with ye?"

Two bloodlines. One destiny.

The words leapt to Malcolm's mind. For the first time, he wondered if Evie was the only Sinclair who would arrive from the future.

"The hour is late," she added. "Mayhap you'd like to dine with us and stay the night?"

Malcolm thought of the promise he had made Callum—that he would scout the area to see if MacDonald was making any moves to attack again.

"I best be making my way home, my lady, but I do thank ye for the offer."

He bid her farewell and headed for the great hall door to exit into the bailey and retrieve his horse. Duncan followed.

"I'll see ye off, then," the lad said.

As they headed out of the great hall and toward the stable, Malcolm was surprised to see Angus there as though he had waited for him to arrive. He glanced at Duncan, wondering if he was surprised to see his da. He wasn't. When he came to a halt outside the stable, Angus gave him a nod of greeting.

"Malcolm. Ye cannae be thinking of leaving already?" Angus crossed his forearms over his chest, his sharp eyes assessing him. As though he had something in mind for him to do.

"Aye, I am. I made Callum a promise to scout the area."

"Och, by God's blood, laddie, did ye no see what happened to the village? I think we ken Rory and his men are still out there marauding." There was fire in his words.

"And what will ye have me do?" Malcolm spread his hands in question.

Angus looked to his son who stood rigid next to Malcolm. Silent communication passed between father and son. Then his gaze flickered back to him. "Come with us."

A skittering of apprehension went through him. He understood what Angus meant. He also understood if he participated in an event like that, it would raise the ire of his older brother, the laird of Dundale, once more. He had forbidden him to do anything rash again, especially after the last time he had taken matters into his own hands.

"Ye mean to retaliate," Malcolm said.

"What kind of a laird would I be if I dinnae?"

He raked a hand through his hair and heaved a sigh. "I cannae—"

"Ye must," Angus insisted. "Are ye a MacLeod or are ye no? If what my son and my lady wife said, our clans are to unite to defeat our common enemy."

So, despite his claim he didn't believe in the prophecy of the keystone, he appeared to have embraced it all the same. Because now it meant something and he was out for blood.

"It's the only way to make sure they understand we protect our people," Duncan added. "No matter the cost."

He understood that, too. He understood, more than anyone, especially after Rory MacDonald killed his da in cold blood. He had felt he same as Angus and Duncan. He wanted vengeance. His jaw clenched with his indecision as he glanced from father to son and back again. There was a light of desperation mixed with fury in Angus's eyes.

"When do we leave?"

IT WAS A mistake. He knew it was a mistake and yet he went along with it. He had to show Sinclair that a MacLeod was not a coward.

The three of them headed out of the keep after sunset. Darkness shrouded them in shadows. The plan was to raid the nearby

MacDonald village. The Sinclair laird wanted to take prisoners and ransom them back—retribution for killing his people and burning his village—but Malcolm was less than enthusiastic about that plan. He tried to talk him out of it, but Angus held firm.

They approached the village in the dead of night. All was quiet and still in the area. There was no candlelight in any of the windows, indicating all the inhabitants slept. Angus motioned for them to stop at the edge of the tree line. He dismounted. Duncan followed suit. He produced a torch. The striking of a flint was heard and then it flared to life. Malcolm remained in his saddle.

"Come, laddie," Angus whispered and motioned for him to follow.

Reluctantly, he dismounted and brought up the rear. Duncan held the torch aloft as they approached the village, closing the distance between the tree line and the first house. But as they did, a crack of what sounded like thunder sounded.

They halted, glancing up at the night sky. But if there were clouds, the inky blackness concealed them. Malcolm peered at the sky, his heart beating wildly. He had heard this cracking boom once before. The first time, he hadn't realized what it was until his da came to fetch Callum to tell him about the lass who fell from the sky—Evie.

But hearing it now raised all the hairs on the back of his neck.

The boom sounded again and then the space in front of them split in two with a slash of light exploding in a bright flash, as though the air in front of them was sliced open to reveal another world. For a moment, he was blinded by the light. He lifted his hand to shield his eyes. A shadowy figure tumbled out of the light, plummeting to the ground in a violent fall. To his surprise, it was a woman. She landed on the ground with a muffled oof, rolled to all fours and started to crawl away as if something or someone was following her.

Seconds later, another figure emerged. Malcolm saw right away a man followed her who was on her in an instant, as if crossing through the strange light was an everyday occurrence.

Just as quickly as the light exploded, it disappeared, leaving him blinking to clear away the glow burned into his eyes.

The man snatched her by the hair and jerked her upward. She shrieked, her fisted hand waving in the air as she reached back for him with her other. Angus and Duncan were frozen in place. Malcolm glanced between the two of them as they gaped at the woman struggling in the grasp of the much-stronger man. She tried to fight him off, but he held firm and clawed at her fisted hand.

"No!" she shouted.

Something ignited within Malcolm, some force of will that pushed him into action. He bolted toward her, intending to take out the man. The stranger dragged her to her feet, one arm around her torso. His free hand wrapped around her wrist, pressing hard enough to make her cry out.

Malcolm reached the two of them. As he neared, he saw they were both dressed strangely. Instantly, he understood they were not of this time and the flash of light he saw was them coming through time.

Like Evie. His da had said the sky split in two and she fell through the light.

Malcolm reached the man and grabbed him with both hands, giving him a wild jerk. Startled, he released her. She stumbled away as Malcolm gave the stranger a shove backward. He placed himself between the two of them.

"Get away from her," Malcolm snarled.

The man gaped back at him. He was dressed in a black tunic and trousers and stared at him with wide, unblinking blue eyes.

"She's mine," he said, his voice gravelly as he took a step toward her once again as if to reclaim her.

Behind him, she sucked in a breath. Malcolm unsheathed his claymore and held it pointed at the man's throat.

"I dinnae think the lass will agree with ye," he said, his tone one of warning.

The man's gaze flickered to her, then back to him. By now,

Angus and Duncan had joined him, forming an impenetrable wall between her and the stranger.

"She has something that belongs to me." The stranger pointed to the lass, a fierce look on his face.

"It doesn't belong to you." Her voice was low and raspy. As if she'd screamed until she couldn't scream anymore.

Malcolm turned and gave her a once over. Color had drained from her cheeks. In the flickering light from Duncan's torch, sweat gleamed on her brow. Her auburn hair was wild about her face and her eyes were wide and glassy with fear. She still had her hand clenched into a tight fist, clutching her wrist and holding her arm against her torso, as though she were in pain. Her gaze met his and, in that instant, he understood she was on the run from the stranger. In that one look, her gaze implored him for help.

He turned back to the stranger, still clutching his claymore and pointing it at the man's throat.

"Ye best be on yer way, laddie," Malcolm said.

"But she has—"

"Or shall I run ye through?" he interrupted.

He snapped his mouth closed and took two steps backward, his hands up in surrender. He looked from Malcolm to the lass cowering behind him.

"This isn't over," he said before he turned and ran into the darkness.

Malcolm sheathed his sword. It was only when he heard Angus do the same did he realize the man had wielded his own weapon. He turned to the lass, who blew out a breath of relief as she watched the stranger disappear into the thickening gloom. When he was gone, her legs gave out.

She tumbled to the ground so quickly he didn't have a chance to catch her. But he was there in an instant, scooping her slight weight into his arms and pulling her to him. She looked up at him with wide, emerald eyes. Eyes so dark green he had never seen the like. A small smile formed on her quivering lips.

"Thank you," she whispered.

And then she fainted in his arms.

※ ————— ◦ ————— ※

CHAPTER SEVEN

"WHO IS SHE?" Angus asked. "Where did she come from?"

"She's from the future," Duncan declared, a hint of excitement in his voice.

"Och, lad. I told ye no to believe in those falsehoods," Angus snapped.

But Malcolm held the woman who resembled Evie, his brother's wife, and was certain she had fallen through time. When she had fainted, her fist relaxed and her fingers half opened. An object nestled against her palm. Gently, he pushed open her fingers and saw the jagged little stone. The stone that had similar markings to the one Evie possessed.

His heart clawed its way to his throat as he plucked the stone from her hand and held it up in the firelight of the torch.

"What's that?" Duncan asked, moving closer with his torch, which was what Malcolm needed to see the stone clearer. Duncan leaned down to get a closer look.

"It's a stone," Malcolm said.

"'Tis nothing but a jagged piece of rock," Angus said with a snort.

Malcolm lifted his gaze to Duncan, who shook his head, dismissing his da's explanation. Knowledge twinkled in the depths of his eyes.

"We best get back to the keep," Malcolm said. He pocketed the stone in his sporran, then lifted her into his arms, cradling her against his chest.

"What about the lass?" Duncan asked.

"She's going with me." There was no way he was going to let her out of his sight. He suspected he knew who she was and what she held. "We'll stay the night at yer keep, if ye permit it, my lord. And then be on our way to Dundale in the morn or as soon as she's ready to travel."

Angus lifted a brow as he eyed the lass in his arms. "Aye, I permit it."

He stepped a little closer, eyeing her as the light from the torch played along her features. She was a bonnie lass, to be sure. High cheekbones, much like Evie. Porcelain skin, smooth and perfect. Emerald eyes fringed in dark lashes. Freckles dotted her nose and cheeks. Thick auburn hair fell over Malcolm's arm as he held her.

A flicker of recognition went over the laird's face as he gazed at her.

"She...seems familiar, though I cannae say where I've seen her."

"She looks like Evie, Callum's wife," he said.

"Aye, that must be it." He brushed away the thought as he headed for his horse. "We best be on our way if we're to make it back to the keep before morn. We have a long night of riding yet."

Knowing he was right, Malcolm followed Angus. Duncan fell in step beside him.

"I think we ken where she came from, don't we?" he asked, his voice low. He had a knowing grin on his face.

"Aye," was all Malcolm said.

Wouldn't Callum and Evie be surprised when he arrived at Dundale with her?

WHEN CHLOE CAME to her senses, the first thing she noticed was the pungent animal smell accosting her nose. The second the thing she noticed was the warm, solid body next to her. And the third thing she noticed was the soft rocking to and fro as though she were on a…horse.

That must be the animal smell.

She cracked one eye open to see that she was cradled against a man who smelled a lot like leather and musk. He held her in his lap. His hands clutched what appeared to be reins.

The first signs of panic pounded through her. Where was she? Who was he? What the devil was going on?

She had to think to keep her wits about her. What was the last thing she remembered?

She was in her flat. Bruce was…oh, God, Bruce! He had attacked her, tried to take the stone from her. But she had held onto it and the thing was humming and the lines were glowing. He had clawed at her hand, trying to get her to release it but she wouldn't. He had gripped her so hard, he hurt her.

Deep desperation pounded through her as she hung onto the stone. Then… what…what had happened? She swiped her thumb over it and—

Oh. *Oh!* There had been a terrible free-fall feeling as the ground collapsed under her. The breath had been sucked out of her. Her lungs burned with the pain of it as it had hit her hard. Bruce was still near her as they had tumbled through the bright light together. He had tried to grab her but she managed to kick him away.

The world had split open in the strangest way. As though there were a rip in space. And she had fallen through it and he fell with her.

And then she had landed on the ground, her bones rattling with the force of it. Bruce had been right behind her, grabbing her by the hair—yes, that was it. Her scalp was sore from how hard he had jerked. He had pulled her to her feet, still trying to claim the stone and then…

And then he had released her and she had fallen forward. She had been on the ground when she looked back to see the broad-shouldered man with a beard standing between her and Bruce. He had held a sword, firelight glittering along the edge.

But firelight didn't make sense. She had climbed to her feet, her legs wobbly and her muscles quivering from the intense fight. She had still clutched the strange little stone in her fist and met Bruce's terrible eyes. Eyes that were once full of love now gleamed with hate.

When her savior had spoken, he had sounded…Scottish. He was protecting her? Then there were two more men moving to stand between her and Bruce. One held a torch. And the man, the first man, had told Bruce to leave. Bruce had said it wasn't over and she believed him.

The man who had saved her turned toward her and she met his sea-green eyes. In that moment, the recognition had hit her. She'd seen him before in her vision when she was in the antique shop. Or was her mind playing tricks on her? Her legs had been no longer able to hold her up and she collapsed to the ground.

He had been there in a flash, pulling her into his arms. Such strong arms. As she'd looked at him, she confirmed he was not a figment of her imagination. He was real and he was holding her. All she had thought to do was say thank you.

Now, she jerked upright in his arms, her eyes wild and her heart pounding as she looked around. She was indeed perched in the lap of the man who had scooped her off the ground. He chuckled, a sound rumbling deep in his chest, his gloriously broad chest.

"Awake, I see." There was a smile in his voice.

The morning light glinted across his face, illuminating it in a pale-yellow glow. His features were hard, chiseled. His cheeks and chin were covered in a beard. His mouth was thin and unforgiving even though his lips held a smile. His eyes…oh, those eyes. They were a sea-green—or were they? In the morning light, they changed color from bluish to greenish, like a stormy sea churned by gales of wind. He was fierce looking and yet, she was not afraid of him.

"Who—" Her voice cracked. Her throat ached. Her mouth was parched.

"Och, lass, dinnae try to speak. Ye've had a bit of shock, I'd wager. We're almost to the keep."

That voice. It was dark and deep and thrummed through her, making the hairs on the back of her neck stand on end. Not in a bad way. In a way she had never experienced. In a way that told her he was not to be trifled with and yet he would fight to protect her with everything he had in him.

She glanced around again, trying to get her bearings. They were, in fact, riding a horse. The two men she had seen earlier were ahead. In the distance, a castle. Dawn glinted off the ancient stone, the high turrets, the wide curtain wall. The portcullis was up.

But, no, this was no ancient castle. This was someone's home. The man's? She didn't know.

Her hand throbbed. She looked down to see the lines from the stone burned into her palm. Her skin was red and angry.

"The stone!" she gasped.

"Safe, lass," he said, his tone reassuring.

She looked at him, but his eyes were straight ahead, never wavering. "And Bruce?"

His gaze flickered to hers. "He was the one who attacked ye?"

She nodded, afraid to say it aloud for fear she would break into sobs. Bruce was the man she had thought she loved. The one she had told Evie she thought was the one. But he wasn't, was he? He had betrayed her. He had tried to take the stone from her.

Her savior's gaze hardened as though the mention made him angry. "He willna bother ye again."

Hot tears pricked her eyes. Emotion clotted in her throat. She *trusted* Bruce. She had been sure it was love at first sight with him. He was charming and witty and handsome and she had envisioned spending the rest of her days with him. And now…now he had tried to hurt her. Had he tried to hurt Evie? Did he...no, she shoved that thought away.

She had to believe Evie was alive and well somewhere. But where? Where was she? Why was Chloe unable to find her? And why did Bruce steal the blue velvet bag?

The blue velvet bag like the one Moira had given her.

With the stone.

Oh, God. Did Evie have a stone like hers?

"Are ye well, lass? Yer shaking." Concern edged his features.

"Am I?" Her voice was still rough. It hurt to talk.

His arms tightened around her. "I swear to ye, by my sword, he willna touch ye again."

Chloe melted a little against him as she met his gaze. The way he looked at her told her he meant every word.

But she had trusted a man before. She had trusted Bruce. He had betrayed her. He had attacked her.

"Ye have my word," he added, his voice low and rumbling and delicious.

She said nothing as they rode toward the castle and the sun rose higher into the sky. The castle was nestled among a rugged and weathered landscape. The wind was cold and sharp with a hint of dampness in it. It reminded her of Edinburgh on a brisk fall day and she wondered where—no, when—she had landed.

It was clear she was no longer in Edinburgh. In the year she had lived there, she had ventured out of the city only once and that was to visit Inverness.

Now, she was certain she was in the Highlands. And she was no longer in her own time. The historian in her wanted to pause and take in all the sights, the sounds, the everything. The woman in her, though, wanted to remain nestled in her savior's arms.

They trotted through the portcullis and halted behind the thick, tall curtain wall. Before her was the most magnificent castle she had ever seen. Not that she had seen many. She hadn't. It sat on a cliff with the azure sea glistening in the morning sun behind it. The castle itself was a tall, square building of at least three stories with rectangular windows and two chimneys rising up on either side like bookends.

Two young boys ran out to greet them as the older man stepped down out of his saddle. He handed the reins off to one of the boys. The second man did the same. As he handed off his reins to the boy, he turned to the two of them.

Her savior had come to a halt as the second man headed toward them.

"This here is Duncan," her savior said. "He'll help ye down."

She cut him a glance and he gave her a wink and a nod of encouragement. Duncan held his arms up to her. She slid out of the saddle. He caught her and helped steady her feet as her savior dismounted. The older man made his way over to them, eyes the color of a wintery morning piercing her.

Eyes that reminded her of her older sister, Brianna.

He had a shock of red hair, graying at the temples.

But that shock of red hair reminded her of her fraternal twin sister, Evie.

If she were truly in the past, she had the strangest feeling she was looking into the face of one of her ancestors. That couldn't be right. Could it?

His face was covered in a faded red beard. There were crinkles at the corners his eyes. He assessed her as he approached.

"Well? Have ye learned who she is?" the older man asked, his hands fisted on his hips.

Her savior moved closer to her, the warmth of his big body radiating over her as he gazed down at her. His sea-green eyes softened. She moved closer to absorb his warmth. Her hand slipped into his. Surprise flickered through his gaze for a moment, then it was replaced by delight.

"What's yer name, lassie?"

"Chloe," she said, and her voice was a little stronger this time.

"Well, Chloe, this is Angus Sinclair, laird of this castle."

Upon hearing the man's full name, she sucked in a sharp breath. "Sinclair? You're..."

Her stomach lurched and her knees gave out, her hand slipping from her savior's. The next thing she knew, she was crumpling to the ground as blackness overtook her.

CHAPTER EIGHT

MALCOLM SAW HER eyes flutter closed moments before she fainted. He managed to catch her, scooping her into his arms and holding her close to him. It was the second time she had ended up in his arms. He was starting to enjoy it far too much.

"We best get her inside," Angus said.

He and Duncan followed him into the keep where Lady Fiona paced the length of the great hall, her hands clasped in front of her. When they entered, she halted, the worry on her face collapsing into relief.

"Angus Sinclair, where have ye been?" she demanded of her husband. "I was worried all night and now ye turn up—oh! Who's this?" She halted her tirade when she spotted the lass in Malcolm's arms. She hurried over and peered down at her. "Where did she come from?"

Malcolm wasn't sure how to answer. He had seen the flash of light, the rip in space and time with his own eyes. But explaining it? That would be difficult. Thankfully, Angus and Duncan had witnessed the event, too.

"She's from the future," Duncan exclaimed, his eyes bright with excitement.

"Och, laddie, ye dinnae ken that," Angus said, his voice laced with annoyance.

Lady Fiona glanced from her husband to Malcolm, one dark brow raised. "What happened to her?"

"She fainted," he said.

He couldn't say why she had fainted, but he assumed everything that had happened to her since her arrival was too much for her to handle.

"I saw it with me own eyes. Ye did, too, Da. She fell through a rip in time."

Angus grunted is disagreement. "I'm going to bed."

"Well, from the future or no, she's a guest here. Let's get her to a bed so she can recover," Lady Fiona said. "And then ye can tell me exactly what happened and where she came from."

She motioned for him to follow her through the keep. Duncan fell in step with him, too. Malcolm glanced down at her as he walked and admired the way her lovely face seemed to be in repose. The resemblance to Evie was unmistakable.

Lady Fiona led him up the stairs and down a long corridor where she pushed open a door to one of the bedchambers. She hurried to the bed and pulled back the blankets.

"Put her here. Duncan, get the fire going in the hearth."

As Malcolm placed her gently on the bed, Lady Fiona eyed her strange attire. She wore dark blue breeches that hugged every curve from her hips to her thighs to her calves. She wore strange looking white shoes. An oversized tunic in a fuzzy material that also hugged her every curve.

Not that he'd noticed.

"I'll find her some suitable clothing," she said. "After ye tell me what happened."

Duncan finished placing logs in the hearth, then brushed his hands together. "It was incredible, Mam. It was like the world split open for a moment and then, there she was."

Lady Fiona gave Malcolm a curious but questioning glance, as if she wanted to confirm what her son said. He nodded.

"Aye, 'tis the truth of it." It also did not escape his notice that Chloe had the same big emerald eyes as Lady Fiona.

"Da saw it, too, with his own eyes," Duncan said. "And yet he still doesna believe."

"I'll speak to him," she said waving away the thought, as though her husband's beliefs didn't matter. "Do ye ken who she is, Malcolm?"

"She said her name was Chloe. She fainted when she heard the name Angus Sinclair."

Lady Fiona chuckled. "Most bonnie lassies did when they saw my husband in his younger days. However, I dinnae think that was the case this time."

She moved closer to the bed to get a good look at her. Chloe's hair was the same deep auburn as Lady Fiona's.

"She's a Sinclair," she announced, as though she knew this for certain.

"From the future?" Duncan asked from his crouched position in front of the hearth. He finally got the fire going.

"Aye," she said. "She must be. 'Tis the only explanation."

"There was also a man who followed her through," Malcolm said. "He attacked her."

"And ye saved her," Lady Fiona said with a faint smile.

He nodded. When the man had jerked her up by her hair, something inside him snapped. But Lady Fiona didn't grasp how much the strange man had wanted to get his hands on Chloe. There had been fierce determination in his eyes. It was why Malcolm had remained between the two of them with sword drawn.

"Well, ye must be famished. Duncan, run along to the kitchen and fetch Malcolm and his guest some food. I'll find her something to wear."

Duncan followed his mother to the door.

"I do thank ye, my lady, for the hospitality," Malcolm said.

She gave him a nod and a smile as she exited the room, closing the door behind her.

WHEN CHLOE AWOKE, she was surrounded by cozy warmth. She burrowed deeper under the blankets and opened her eyes to an unfamiliar place. She blinked, trying to remember where she was and what had happened to her.

The last thing she remembered was her savior introducing her to Angus Sinclair.

Sinclair.

Had she fallen into an alternate dimension? Was she in some strange twilight zone? Or had she truly been transported back in time?

She didn't know the answer.

She took inventory of her aching body. Her bandaged arm still throbbed from the gunshot wound. Her elbow hurt from when she had bashed it on the floor in her flat. Generally, her whole body ached from head to toe.

Now, looking around, she realized she was in a stranger's bed. Likely in a stranger's home. She managed to sit up to take in her surroundings. Her pulse thundered as her gaze darted about the room, dimly lit stone walls covered in tapestries, wooden beams overhead, and a fire flickering in the hearth. The strange room was as alien to her as the earthy scent of the fire.

A horrible thought pounded through her. This wasn't home. This wasn't even her century. Reality settled over her as her chest tightened.

Sitting by the fire in a chair was her savior. His chin was on his chest as he dozed. In front of him, a table with a tray of food—bread and cheese. Upon seeing the food, her stomach rumbled.

She slid from the bed, her sock feet landing on the cool stone flooring. She paused there a moment, keeping her eyes on her savior who hadn't moved and continued to snooze. Then she pushed the rest of the blankets away and rose, walking on wobbly legs toward the tray. As she reached it, he inhaled a deep breath and lifted his head.

He pinned her with his sharp, assessing gaze that was definitely like a stormy sea. She froze where she was, staring back at him with her heart in her throat. She reminded herself she didn't need to fear him. He had rescued her from Bruce, after all.

"Och, awake, I see. Hungry?" He waved to the tray.

He was a man of few words. She nodded and moved toward it, unsure what her voice sounded like. Her throat felt better, but she was still thirsty and didn't trust that she wouldn't sound like she'd been in a bar all night drinking shots and smoking cigarettes.

The bread and cheese were sliced into thin strips. There was even a bit of dried meat. Like jerky. She picked up a piece of bread, deciding to start with that. A tankard of what looked like ale sat next to the bread.

"Have some ale," he said, motioning to the tankard.

She picked it up and sniffed. It smelled like a weak version of beer. She took a sip. It tasted awful. She scowled, dropping the tankard back to the tray. He chuckled.

"Is it no to yer liking?" he asked, a smile on his lips.

"Sorry, no," she said and was glad to hear her voice was almost normal. She munched on the bread as she gave him a wary look. "You know my name. What's yours?"

"Malcolm," he said.

She picked up a piece of hard cheese next. "Are you a Sinclair, too?"

"Och, no. I'm a MacLeod."

She froze, holding the cheese halfway to her mouth as she leveled him with her gaze. "MacLeod?"

He nodded.

"Not MacDonald?"

His brows drew together as he shook his head. "MacDonald is our sworn enemy."

Relief flooded her. "Oh, thank God," she whispered.

"Why do ye thank God for that, lass?"

She popped the cheese in her mouth, chewed. "Because the man who attacked me is a MacDonald. I didn't want to be in enemy hands." She picked up another piece of bread and considered it. "So, Malcolm MacLeod, what are you doing here with the Sinclairs?"

He stared at her a long moment in consideration, as if he were deciding how to answer. "I think the real question is, what are *ye* doing here, lass?"

She flushed and turned away as she held the piece of bread in one hand. She glanced down at her hand with the burned image of the stone. How was she to answer that? Finally, she turned back to him and held up her hand.

"I suspect it has something to do with this."

He stared at her hand, running his over his bearded chin, the coarse hair bristling against his palm. She wondered what it would be like to kiss a man with a full beard. And then she quickly shoved away that silly thought.

She wasn't interested in him.

Even though he was gorgeous, especially with those sea-green eyes that pierced her soul.

He reached into his sporran and brought out the stone, holding it up between his thumb and forefinger. "This did that to ye, didn't it?"

Chloe closed her hand and dropped it to her side. "Yes, I imagine it did. It was humming and the lines were glowing at the time."

There was little she understood about the small piece of stone. One thing was clear though—it appeared to be a time traveling device and Bruce MacDonald wanted it.

To her surprise, Malcolm held it out to her. "Ye'll be wanting this back then."

After a moment of hesitation, she reached for it. Their fingers brushed. His left a tingling sensation in his wake. She flushed again, her cheeks burning as she stuck the stone in the front pocket of her jeans.

"Thank you for keeping it safe," she said.

He regarded her with a curious glint in his eye. She finally popped the piece of hard cheese into her mouth and looked away, feeling self-conscious under his expressive gaze.

"What do ye remember? Anything?" he asked.

"I remember everything."

She shuddered and leaned against the mantel, soaking up the warmth of the fire. There was a chill in the room. Despite her sweater, goosebumps rose on her arms. She expected him to ask more questions, to press her for details about what had happened and how she had ended up here, but he didn't. She appreciated that. She wasn't ready to talk about it.

But then he said, as if he knew the answer already, "He attacked ye because he wanted the stone, aye?"

She nodded, aware of his presence so close to her. "And the stone brought me here." She cut him a quick glance before turning back to the fire to watch the flames flicker. "Where is here?"

"I thought that was clear. We're in the keep of the Laird Sinclair."

She understood that, of course, but… "Which is where, exactly?"

Malcolm leaned forward, his elbows on his knees. "Lass, do ye believe ye time traveled?"

It was an odd question and one that made her look at him. "Why do you ask that?"

He kept his gaze focused on her face, searching it as though looking for the future in her expression. Finally, he leaned back into his chair.

"Ye are in the Scottish Highlands in the year of our lord thirteen hundred fifty-seven."

Every muscle in her body clenched as she stiffened while staring at the fire. She didn't want to believe she had time traveled. She thought this was all merely a strange dream or a weird figment of her imagination. But, no. Her savior—Malcolm MacLeod—confirmed otherwise.

He pushed up from the chair. "I'll fetch Lady Fiona. She'll bring ye…" He paused, looked her up and down. "Proper clothing. Then, we'll be on our way back to Dundale."

Dundale? She recognized that. It was the name of the castle Moira had mentioned. The woman's words came floating back to her.

You'll see it soon enough. Once the seat of Clan MacLeod.

"Dundale?" she repeated.

"Aye. My brother, Callum, will be wanting to meet ye. And so will his bride, I should think."

He gave her a knowing grin. What was so special about meeting his brother's wife? There was something unspoken in his words that seemed to give an edge of significance.

Before she could press him further, he strode to the door and pulled it open. "Rest while ye can. We'll leave soon."

He opened the door and left, leaving her alone with whirling thoughts.

CHAPTER NINE

WHEN MALCOLM LEFT, Chloe forced herself to eat more of the bread and cheese. She nibbled a piece of dried meat even though her appetite warred with the tangle of knots in her stomach. Her hands trembled as she tried to process the impossible.

The stone had ripped her from everything she knew and tossed her into the fourteenth century with a stranger. A man who had come to her rescue, saving her from Bruce's vicious attack. She dropped the half-eaten bread as the realization pressed down on her.

Bruce.

Bruce was here, too. He'd followed her through the portal. Where had he gone? What was to stop him from searching for her? Worry gnawed at her as she thought about the light of determination in his eyes when he had looked at her and told her it wasn't over. She knew what that meant. He would find her and try to take the stone from her no matter what.

The questions churned in her mind, colliding with the overwhelming truth—this was really happening.

Thinking of the stone, she reached into her pocket and brought it out. It was quiet now, the lines faded once more. She lifted her other hand and stared at her red, angry palm. The lines were burned into her flesh, leaving a mark she wasn't sure would ever go away. How could something so small and insignificant be so powerful? She didn't understand it.

And she had spent the majority of her life understanding things—specifically ancient things. She was a lover of history. Her degree was in ancient history. She was lucky enough to land the job at the museum in Edinburgh to become their youngest Director of Public Programs. She was proud of that distinction. The gala she had spent months planning, making sure every detail was perfect, turned out to be a disaster.

She had been so distracted by the disappearance of her twin, she hadn't thought about the fallout from the invasion during the gala. She sagged against the chair, clutching the stone in one hand and putting her head in her free hand.

Evie's whereabouts took top of mind. She hadn't even considered what was going on at the museum. It had never occurred to her she would still have a job after what had happened, though it certainly wasn't her fault.

And now she was stuck in the fourteenth century. A stranger in a strange land.

But she wasn't going to let that deter her. She would find a way back to her own time and when she did, she would resume her search for Evie.

A swift knock on the door sounded. She stood and turned toward the door as it pushed open. A woman with bright green eyes and auburn hair stood on the other side of the threshold. She gave her a pleasant smile as she bustled into the room, a younger woman on her heels carrying an armload of material. Chloe pocketed the stone as the two women entered.

"Ah, good to see ye up, lass. How do ye feel?" the woman asked.

"I, ah…" Chloe watched the girl behind her struggling to hold the armload of what appeared to be gowns. She moved toward her, holding out her hands. "Can I help you with that?"

Surprise flickered over the girl's face, then she glanced up at the woman in front of her. The woman's dark brows rose.

"Elaine, put the dresses there. I'll help the lassie."

The girl scurried to the bed and dumped the material, then did a quick curtsy and hurried out of the room. The lady remained, clasping her hands in front of her and giving Chloe a winsome smile and a good once-over as she took in her appearance.

"She's a bit shy," the woman explained. "I'm Lady Fiona Sinclair."

"Chloe," was all she managed to say.

Lady Fiona lifted one brow as she regarded her. "Sinclair?"

She stiffened as she stared at the woman, trying to decide if she were friend or foe. "Perhaps."

Lady Fiona's smile broadened. "Ye have nothing to fear from us here. After all, we are yer kin."

Chloe tipped her head to one side as she gazed at the woman. Indeed, she did look much like her own mother who had passed away when she was a teen. But what she didn't understand was why she thought they were related.

"Perhaps we are distant relations," Chloe said.

They stared at each other in awkward silence for a long moment. Fiona looked as though she might have something else to say, but then decided against it.

"Well, I ken Malcolm is waiting. Let's get ye dressed, aye?"

Chloe eyed the pile of material on the bed with apprehension. She wasn't too keen on getting rid of her modern clothes. At least not yet.

"I'm good, thanks." She backed away from the bed, edging closer to the fire.

"Och, it isna proper for a young lass such as yerself to be wearing…" She paused as she eyed Chloe's blue jeans, her fuzzy sweater, and her sock feet. "Well, it's no proper."

It was clear to her Fiona didn't understand her attire and that was fine by Chloe. She remained rooted in place. Evie used to tell her she was stubborn as the day was long and she was right. When Chloe made her mind up about something, she rarely changed it. That was why Bruce's betrayal had come as such a shock. She'd made her mind up that he was the one. Turned out, he wasn't.

"I do appreciate the offer," she said, "but I'd rather not change, if it's all the same to you."

"But—"

"I think she's dressed just fine."

It was Malcolm's voice coming from the doorway. Lady Fiona stepped aside and turned to look at him. He leaned against the door jamb on one shoulder with his arms crossed over his chest.

Seeing him there Chloe thought it was disarming how handsome he was as he gave her a faint smile behind that full beard. His long hair was plaited on either side of his head, the braids pushed back behind his ears. One stray lock fell over his forehead as he peered at her with amusement in those depthless sea-green eyes.

Question and confusion flickered over the lady's face. "Ye said she needed proper clothing."

"She doesna wish to change."

He pushed off the door jamb and stepped into the room with a lazy sort of movement that sent shivers down Chloe's spine.

"Mayhap merely a cloak for the journey back to Dundale," he suggested, his gaze never leaving her face.

"As you say." Lady Fiona motioned toward the pile on the bed. "I'm sure she will find something suitable there."

Then she excused herself and left the room, leaving the door open. Malcolm made no other move to enter the room. They stood several feet apart, Chloe feeling awkward where she was by the hearth, the warmth of the fire radiating through her.

"I don't mean to be a problem—" Chloe began.

"Och, dinnae worry, lass." He waved away the thought as if it meant nothing. "But I need to return to Dundale." He cut a glance to the pile of clothing on the bed. "There's a chill to the wind. Ye'll be wanting a cloak. I'll wait for ye by the stable with the horses."

He left. Chloe heaved a sigh, sure she had insulted Lady Fiona and that amused Malcolm.

She walked to the bed and rifled through the clothing until she found what appeared to be a fur-lined cloak with a hood. She pulled it on over her shoulders to test the size. It fell to the floor, dragging a bit behind her as if it were too long. That would have to do. She stuck her feet in her sneakers. Satisfied, she headed out the door to meet Malcolm.

CHAPTER TEN

CHLOE MADE HER way outside the keep with the cloak tightly wrapped around her. She garnered a few strange looks as she walked across the yard looking for Malcolm at the stables. With no clue where he'd be, she paused to scan the area, trying to ignore the curious glances.

Then she spotted him. He stood with one hand on the reins of a horse speaking to the older Sinclair, Angus.

Duncan spotted her then and gave her a jaunty wave and a broad smile. He was younger than Malcolm, clean-shaven, with bright, intelligent eyes. He trotted over to greet her and was not at all bothered by her attire.

"Did ye sleep well?" he asked.

She nodded, though, truthfully, she was exhausted. Traveling through time had taken a lot out of her and she wasn't certain she would ever recover. Duncan seemed pleased with her answer though and offered her his arm.

"I'll escort ye to the stables."

He seemed so eager to please, it was hard to turn him down. She placed her hand on his arm and off they went through the courtyard.

"It appears I'm not suitably dressed," Chloe said as they walked and she continued to notice the surreptitious glances.

"Och, dinnae fash yerself about that, lass. They dinnae understand where ye came from." He gave her a sheepish glance with a coy smile. "But I do and it doesna bother me one whit."

She wasn't certain why hearing him say that made her feel better, but it did. "I think I may have insulted your mother by not changing into her offered clothing. Please tell her thanks for trying."

He chuckled, a little sound deep in his throat. "My mam can be somewhat pushy. But I will be sure to tell her."

They arrived at the stables where Malcolm turned to give them his full attention. His gaze first went over her, then to Duncan. Chloe thought for the briefest of moments she saw a hint of jealousy flash through his eyes before he managed to conceal it. He held out a hand to her.

"Thanks for escorting her," he said to Duncan.

She started to reach for Malcolm's hand, but before she was able, Duncan grasped it and kissed the back of it. It was probably the most chivalrous thing that had ever happened to her, and she flushed hot.

"'Tis been a pleasure, my lady. I hope to see ye again some-time."

Malcolm seemed less than amused by that and reached for her, taking her free hand in his and pulling her toward him.

"We'll be on our way." He turned to Angus. "I thank ye for the hospitality."

He gave a nod of acknowledgment. "Farewell and Godspeed, lad." Then he bowed to her. "My lady."

Angus and Duncan left them and headed back to the keep. Chloe didn't deny how awkward she felt standing in the presence of a man she hardly knew and yet was willing to ride away with.

"How long will it take us to get to Dundale?" she asked.

"A few hours. Can ye ride?"

She glanced at the large horse with a bit of apprehension. The one and only time she had been on a horse was when she woke up cradled against his chest. She didn't recall much about that ride other than how much her throat had hurt and her head ached.

"Ah, so, ye never have, eh?" he asked, as though he read her thoughts.

"No, never. Well, except for when I rode with you yesterday."

His face was devoid of any sort of expression. At least, one she was able to read. She was sure he must think she was inept for not being able to ride a horse.

"My brother's wife had never ridden a horse, either," he said. "She does fairly well now."

And she needed this information why? She lifted a brow at him. "Does she?"

"Aye. Ye'll meet her when we arrive," he said, a twinkle of knowing in his eye. A small grin appeared on his bearded face. "If ye prefer to ride with me, I dinnae mind."

She realized the horse he held onto was meant for her. "Oh. I'm sure I can manage."

She wasn't sure she was prepared to ride with him again. It was much too close to him, after all.

Sensing her hesitation, he held a hand to her and gave a "come on" nod toward the horse.

She reached for the reins, taking them from him. She could do this. She'd seen enough movies about riding a horse. Taking a deep breath, she stuck her foot into the stirrup, which felt uncomfortable at best. Her knee was to her chest as she tried to lift herself up. While she had never done it before, she had a working understanding of how to do it. She managed to swing her right leg over the horse's back and settle into the saddle. He seemed satisfied with that and walked around to his own, which waited next to hers.

His horse was far bigger than her little brown one. A large black steed, she was certain it was a war horse with its long thick mane and tail. By the time he was in the saddle, he sat at least a head taller than her.

It was a bit intimidating.

But she was not to be dissuaded.

He assumed she knew what she was doing and started off, heading for the portcullis. The distance grew between them while she tried to figure out how to get her horse to move. Finally, she gave it a little kick with her legs and the horse started to move forward.

Then stopped.

She jerked the reins and whispered, "Come on. Please?"

But the horse remained in place. Ahead of her, Malcolm came to a stop and turned to look at her. There was a wide grin on his face as he walked the horse back to her.

"Trouble?"

"No," she said quickly. When he chuckled, she blew out a breath. "Yes."

"Ye can ride with me, then."

But she didn't want to. Being that close to him did things to her. Made her feel things she didn't want to feel.

Malcolm made a motion to one of the stable hands. When the boy rushed over, he said, "Help the lass down and stable the horse. She'll be riding with me."

"Aye, my lord," he said with a nod.

The boy was at her side then, looking up at her and taking the reins out of her hands. She swung her leg over and slid down to the ground in a most ungraceful way. She stumbled, but the stable hand was there to keep her on her feet. She gave him a grateful smile while Malcolm chuckled again from his mount.

She flashed him a glare. A smile hid behind his thick beard.

He waved her toward him. With reluctance, she made her way to his side. The stable hand was there once again, helping her onto the horse. She managed to settle behind Malcolm, wrapping her arms around his waist.

Without another word, they headed off at a slow walk through the bailey toward the portcullis.

Chloe didn't want to notice how solid and warm he was next to her. The cold wind pressed through her, her jeans doing nothing to keep her warm. She managed to tug up the hood on her cloak and cover her head but it didn't help much. She ducked her head and pressed it against his back, inhaling the leather scent of him. A sigh escaped her.

As they rode, she tried to keep her face out of the wind. But every now and then she'd peek out to see the magnificent scenery. In her present, there were winding roads and cars frequenting them. But here, in this time, the landscape was untouched by modern man. There were no concrete roads or cars.

Towering mountains shrouded in mist were outlined against the cloudy, moody sky. While in her time, there were small villages nestled against the rugged landscape, here there was nothing more than a vast, untamed wilderness.

"Not long now, lass," he said over his shoulder.

It was a relief to hear, but she did wonder what his definition of not long was. An hour? Two? It seemed as though they had been traveling for an eternity. The sun, hidden behind the clouds, dipped closer to the horizon. She was sure it had been higher in the sky when they left the Sinclairs.

He seemed unconcerned with the way she huddled against his back. As though it didn't affect him in any way. Maybe it didn't.

"Och, there it is now, lass." There was a smile in his voice and perhaps a little relief.

She lifted her head and saw the castle rising in the distance. It looked as she imagined it would—a formidable medieval fortress. The exterior featured battlements, turrets, and gray stone walls surrounding it to keep invaders out. In the center of it all, the keep. Beyond it, a glistening loch.

The familiarity of it swept through her. This was the castle in the picture in Mystic Treasures.

He nudged the horse into a gallop. She tightened her grip around his waist as their speed increased. The wind was still cold in her face but curiosity won out as they trotted past the portcullis and into the inner bailey. There, he slowed to a stop and immediately dismounted. He turned, holding his arms up to her. She slid off the back of the horse, falling into him. He caught her, his smile evident behind his beard, and held her a moment to steady her wobbly legs.

"Thanks," she muttered.

Without a word, he took her by the hand. She was grateful for his steady presence and didn't try to pull away. A stable boy arrived to take the horse by the reins and lead it off to the stables. Malcolm gave him explicit orders to make sure the horse was fed and brushed since it had been a long journey.

He led her from the yard toward the keep where he pushed open a heavy door. The hinges groaned as they entered the great hall.

It was a large room with a soaring ceiling and a long table in the center. Chairs were on either side, at one end, a hearth with a blazing fire to warm the place. Two men and a woman were seated at the table. When she and Malcolm entered, they all rose.

A gasp escaped the woman. Chloe's gaze fixed on her and for a moment, she didn't recognize her. Then she realized who she was. It couldn't be? She stared across the room, still clutching Malcolm's hand, into the face of her missing sister.

"Evie?" Her voice was a roughened whisper.

Evie hurried around the table, her fiery hair pulled back in a braid and her eyes shining with a joyous light. Before she reached her, though, it was all too much for her. Her knees gave out, crumpling underneath her, as she crumbled to the ground, releasing Malcolm's hand.

"Chloe!"

Her sister bounded out from behind the table and ran to her, her face lit with happiness and her eyes shimmering with tears.

Relief mixed with confusion flickered through her as Evie fell to her knees and wrapped her into the fiercest hug she had ever felt.

"You're here!" she said against her hair. "You made it."

She said it as though she'd been waiting for her arrival.

Chloe wrapped her arms around her sister, holding her tight, never wanting to let go. Relief sputtered through her. Relief Evie was alive and well and hugging her hard. Relief they were together once again. When she finally pulled back, she held her at arm's length.

"What are you doing here?" Chloe asked.

But it was Malcolm who answered with a chuckle. "Och, lass. This is my brother's wife."

CHAPTER ELEVEN

"WIFE? YOU'RE MARRIED?"

Evie flushed, her cheeks turning pink, as she helped her to her feet. Chloe cut a glance to the men standing at the table. One was clearly younger than the other one.

"Sorry I didn't send you an invitation to the wedding, but you were a few hundred years in the future," Evie said with a sheepish grin.

She took her by the hand and led her way from Malcolm, who remained where he stood.

"Chloe, this is my husband, Callum MacLeod." Evie beamed with pride as she introduced him.

He stepped forward with a nod of greeting. "We've been waiting for ye, lass."

Her brows drew together. "What does that mean?"

"It's a long story. And this is Jamie MacLeod."

As he approached, Jamie's grin deepened, two dimples carving into each cheek as he reached for her hand. His fingers were warm and sure against hers as he lifted it, brushing a delicate kiss across her knuckles much like Duncan had when he had bidden her farewell. A spark of amusement flickered in his dark eyes, and the way he looked at her sent a shiver racing up her spine. He was effortlessly charming, devastatingly handsome. As soon as he took her hand, Malcolm was at her side, shooting a dark glare at his brother.

"'Tis good to meet ye at last, lassie."

Evie shooed him away. "That's enough of that."

"Aye," Malcolm agreed.

If Chloe didn't know any better, he was jealous. She turned back to her sister.

"It sounds as though you were expecting me." She said it in jest, but the look on their faces told her she had struck on the truth.

Evie cleared her throat, then hooked her arm in hers and led her away from the great hall. "Let's get you to a room so you can rest. I'm sure you're exhausted. I'll explain everything."

Chloe stole a glance over her shoulder and met Malcolm's gaze. He gave her a smile and a nod. She had many questions, questions she hoped Evie would be able to answer.

Evie led her away from the great hall through a doorway and to a stone curved staircase. It was narrow and they had to climb single file up and up and up. At the top, Evie led her down another hallway with several closed doors. She pushed open the last door on the far end.

The room was small with only a bed, a large chest, a couple of chairs in front of the hearth, and a bedside table that held a candelabra. The hearth was cold and dark across from the bed, but Evie set about building a fire as though she'd done it all her life. Chloe watched, fascinated, wondering how she had acquired those skills. They had grown up in Texas where there was no need for a wood burning fireplace except for one or two times in winter. And even then, they had survived by building pillow forts in the living room and bundling up in their favorite flannel.

"You'll want different clothes," Evie said as she placed the logs on the rack. "Roslyn can help with that."

"Who's Roslyn?"

"She's the cook. Well..." Evie paused, and sat back on her heels. She peered up at Chloe. "She's more than a cook. She does a lot of things for the household. She's taken me under her wing and taught me to cook."

"You cook now?"

The only thing Evie knew how to cook was a box of mac and cheese and sometimes she even burned that.

"Not well, but I can knead a mean loaf of bread." She turned back to the fireplace and finally got the fire started. "There, that should warm up the room nicely."

Overwhelmed, Chloe backed her way to the bed and sat. She pressed cold fingers against her temple that was throbbing with a raging headache. Everything ached from her head to her toes and she was cold. She clutched her elbows.

"I don't understand any of this," Chloe said.

"I know but you will." She perched on the bed next to her. "How do you feel? Like hell?"

"Yes," she said.

"And everything hurts?"

Chloe lifted her gaze to meet hers. "Yes."

She nodded understanding. "That's the time traveling. It wrecks you for a few days, but you'll be fine soon enough." Evie reached into her pocket and brought out something clutched in her hand. "Do you have one of these?"

She opened her fingers to show Chloe the piece of stone resting against her scarred palm, the scar that looked remarkably like her own. A strange sensation went over her as she reached into her jeans pocket and pulled it out. She held it up for Evie to see. Evie pressed one edge against her stone. It fit perfectly.

"It's part of the keystone," Evie said, her voice full of wonder.

Chloe's gaze flickered from the stone down to her hand. She opened her fingers and rested the back of her hand against her leg, showing Evie the inflamed imprint. Evie placed her hand next to hers.

"You, too," she said.

"Eve, I don't understand any of this. I looked for you in Edinburgh after you disappeared in the museum. I thought you were kidnapped or worse."

Dead. She didn't want to say it aloud. A shudder went

through her at the thought of losing her sister. Evie was her anchor to the world. When she thought she was gone forever, a well of panic had bubbled through her.

Her sister took a deep breath, expelled it. "I wished there was some way for me to tell you what happened to me, but there wasn't."

Chloe took Evie's hand in hers and held it. "You can tell me now. I'm here."

Evie smiled, her eyes lighting with joy as she nodded. "I'm so glad you are." She squeezed her hand. "Remember the day on the Royal Mile when I left you and Bruce?"

She nodded, fear trickling through her hearing Bruce's name. She thought back on that day and how distracted Evie had seemed and yet how attentive Bruce was. She wondered now if that was all an act. If he had been trying to get close to her—or Evie—to get his hands on the stone.

"I found a little antique store. It seemed to call to me. That's the only way I can explain it."

A gasp escaped her. She remembered the card in her back pocket. Reaching for it, she slipped it out and showed it to Evie.

"Mystic Treasures. It called to me, too. I found this in your luggage."

Evie took the card from her. She traced the gold-embossed letters with her forefinger. "I should have told you about Moira."

She handed the card back to her. Chloe peered down at the glittering letters. It was truly a mystical place.

"She gave you the stone, didn't she?" Chloe asked and she nodded. She understood then why Evie had disappeared. She had fallen through time. It all made sense. "You had it with you at the museum that night."

"I did. When I was in the bathroom, I heard the gunshots. The only thing I escaped with was the stone. I ran up the stairs. I..." Her voice faltered. She paced the short length of the room. "I don't know how to tell you this, Chlo."

"There isn't anything you can't tell me, now, Evie. We're in this together. Whatever *this* is."

She had no real understanding of their current situation. But it was clear Evie was trying to tell her by starting at the beginning.

Evie cut her a glance and nodded, but there was still worry creasing her face. "When I ran up the stairs, a man grabbed me. I managed to kick him and get away. He followed me to the second level. He told me the stone called to him, but I hid behind a statue." She halted her pacing and turned to face her. "Chlo, it was Bruce."

She stared at her in silence, wanting to be shocked but wasn't. She knew before Evie said it. She knew she was telling the truth. Because Bruce had attacked her in her flat.

"He tried to take the stone from you," Chloe said.

"Yes, and I used it. I didn't know what I was doing when I swiped my thumb over it. I had no idea it would send me back in time. I woke up in Callum's bed."

Chloe wiggled her brows. "That must have been fun."

"It wasn't like that." Evie waved away the thought but even so, they shared a giggle.

"Bruce tried to take the stone from me, too," Chloe said, her voice soft. "I thought he was trying to help me find you. Instead, he attacked me. The stone was humming and glowing. I guess in my panic, I activated it."

"Yes," Evie said, a hint of excitement in her voice. "The stone hummed and glowed for me, too. That's how it sent you through time. Here. To me. To us."

A trickle of fear and dread went through her as she looked up at her sister. "It also sent Bruce here."

Evie's face drained of color. "What? How?"

"He grabbed me when it happened. We both landed here together. If it hadn't been for Malcolm..." Her voice trailed off.

If he hadn't been there, the right place at the right time, there was no telling what would have happened to her. She might be dead by now and her piece of the stone would be in Bruce's hands.

She hadn't thought to question why Malcolm was there. Truthfully, it didn't matter.

"Malcolm was there?"

"Yes. You still have a lot to tell me. Like, how you ended up married." She lifted a brow at her sister. "I thought you didn't believe in love at first sight."

But Chloe had. Chloe had believed Bruce was the one and had fallen head over heels in love with him. And yet he had betrayed her.

She flushed again. "Oh, well…I didn't mean to fall in love with Callum. It just happened."

Chloe patted the bed next to her. "Sit and tell me everything. I want to hear all about this man who has captured my sister's heart."

"Geeze, Chlo, it's like you think I'd never fall in love."

"You were busy trying to keep things together for us while I got my degree. My thanks for you doing that was leaving you for a work visa in Scotland."

And how did that turn out? She thought about that a long moment. She was so happy at first, exploring Edinburgh and learning the city. The day Bruce had come into the museum, he had chatted her up. She was enamored with him and enticed by his Scottish brogue. He was witty and charming and gave her butterflies in the pit of her stomach.

"You don't have to thank me for—"

"Yes, I do, Eve. It was because of you I was able to achieve my dreams." She peered down at her red palm in her lap. A lot of good it did her to graduate with honors. If she was stuck in the past, her career was over. She shook herself free of her melancholy and glanced up at Evie. "And if Callum does anything to hurt you, he'll have to answer to me."

They shared another smile and a giggle as Evie sat next to her. She told her how she had landed in this time, how Callum was convinced she belonged to Clan Sinclair and had tried to leave her with them.

"Angus Sinclair?" Chloe interjected.

"Yes."

Nodding, Chloe explained how she had met Angus, his wife, Fiona, and their son. How Malcolm had insisted they spend the night to allow her to recover and how they had traveled to Dundale together.

"I think they're our ancestors."

"I think so, too," Evie said with a nod.

Her sister then told her about Hamish, Callum's father, and how the castle had come under attack. When he was killed, Callum was named laird of Dundale. She told the story with mist in her eyes.

"There's more. It may be difficult for you to understand, but you have to believe what I'm about to tell you is the truth."

She drew her brows together. "That sounds ominous."

Evie kept her gaze down as she fiddled with the edge of her sleeve. "There's a prophecy. Hamish shared it with me before he passed."

She remained still as she peered at her sister's profile. She had more questions now than ever. "A prophecy?"

"Yes, and it's all coming true."

"What is this prophecy?" she asked.

"It started with the Night of Shadows and the Shattering," Evie said. "There were three goddesses representing Past, Present, and Future who protected this keystone that holds all of Time itself. Others tried to steal the keystone and breach the barriers between the mortal realm and the realm of chaos. That became known as the Night of Shadows. So, the three goddesses decided to break the stone into three pieces and hide it to keep it out of their hands. The Shattering.

"*When the stars align and the shadows of chaos eclipse the sun once again, the time will come to unite a warrior's heart and a maiden's grace. Together, they'll reunite the pieces of the keystone and protect it, to safeguard it for time eternal. Three pieces of stone. Two ancient bloodlines. One divine destiny.*"

Evie recited the words as if she had committed them to memory, as if someone had drilled them into her. Then she pulled her piece of the stone out of her pocket.

"I believe my piece of the keystone represents the Present."

"And my piece?"

Evie shook her head. "I don't know yet."

She stared at her for a long, quiet moment as she processed the words, her heart a wild drumbeat.

"Don't you see, Chlo? We were meant to come here just as we were meant to get the pieces of the keystone."

She ran her hand through her tangled hair, the headache continuing to throb at her temples. "You're speaking of fate and destiny, Evie."

Did she believe in fate and destiny? Once, she might have. She wasn't sure if she did now. Everything she knew had changed—the man she thought she loved had betrayed her. The man she thought she wanted to spend the rest of her life with had deceived her. And now, her sister, her best friend, the one she counted on the most, was telling her they were fated to go back in time.

Two ancient bloodlines. One divine destiny.

She thought she understood what that meant—the Sinclairs and the MacLeods were the two ancient bloodlines. And their divine destiny? Protecting all of Time? That seemed farfetched.

"I am," Evie agreed. "I have a piece of the stone and so do you. There is a third piece still missing," she said, giving her a pointed look.

Something about the way she looked at her made her senses tingle. There was a knowing glint in Evie's eyes, as though she tried to tell her something without coming right out and saying it.

She rubbed her temple with her forefinger. "And where will this third piece come from?"

"Moira has to give it to someone to bring to us." Again, it sounded like a hint. "There is only one person who can do that."

Oh, God. Chloe understood then. If Evie was here in the past, and *she* was here in the past, that meant...

"Brianna." She breathed their older sister's name as though it were a curse.

Evie nodded.

"No, Eve. That can't be right." Chloe sprang from the bed and started to pace, clutching her elbows.

The thought of Brianna here, in the past, with them was absurd. Brianna would never go to Scotland, much less time travel. She was a beach bum to the core. She had no thought whatsoever for anyone other than herself.

"I don't believe you."

"Believe it," Evie said. "I can prove it."

Chloe halted and turned to face her, a sudden chill passing through her. Gooseflesh erupted on her arms and skittered down her body.

"Then prove it."

"I will. But first, it's late. You must be exhausted from traveling. And hungry. Plus, you need something to sleep in. I'll fetch you something from the kitchen to snack on and you can borrow a shift."

Chloe stared at the woman across from her as though she had grown a second head. Evie sounded so authoritative, so sure of herself, she hardly recognized her. Truth be told, she *was* exhausted after riding all day with Malcolm. And now that she thought about it, her stomach did rumble with hunger pains.

"Plus, you'll need a change of clothes for this time."

Chloe glanced down at herself. She still wore the cloak as well as her jeans and fuzzy sweater. "My clothes are fine."

She shook her head. "You'll freeze your ass off here in that. You need layers. Trust me on this. I'll be back soon."

Evie headed for the door.

"Evie?"

Her sister turned, her hand on the doorknob. "Yeah?"

"I'm glad we're together again," she said, and meant it.

A smile played upon her lips as she nodded. "Me, too, Chlo.

Me, too."

When Evie left, Chloe stood and removed the borrowed cloak and tossed it on the bed. She peered down at the fire. All of this was too much to take. It was hard to grasp she had time traveled and ended up in what appeared to be the Middle Ages. She understood enough about history to know this time period was not kind and, frankly, she was terrified. Not only for herself but for Evie.

This was a brutal, unforgiving world, especially for women.

Though the way Evie talked about Callum told her she had managed to be okay.

What worried her the most was that Bruce had traveled back in time with her. Where was he now? What was he doing? Did he have plans to find her again? It was apparent to her he was desperate to get his hands on the stone. He knew Evie had a piece and that's why he had chased her through the museum. What was to stop him from coming after them both now?

Fear trickled through her as she leaned on the mantel, peering down into the fire. It was something she couldn't worry about now. She was safe here with Evie and Callum and, yes, even Malcolm. Perhaps even Jamie. She had to trust everything was going to be fine.

The door opened, then, and Evie returned with an older woman carrying a tray with a tea pot, a cup, some bread, and a wheel of cheese.

"Chloe, this is Roslyn."

"I've heard a lot about ye, lass," the woman said, her face crinkling into a bright smile. She placed the tray on a table near the fire. "Pleased to meet ye at last."

She excused herself to return to her final nightly chores, leaving the two of them alone once again.

Evie handed her the thick shift as well as a pair of woolen stockings. "Here. You'll want these, too. There's extra wood and peat for the fire when it starts to die. Toss on the peat and it should keep going."

Chloe didn't know what else to say except thanks.

"I'm down the hall if you need anything," she said. Then she reached for her and pulled her into a fierce hug. When she pulled back, she held her at arm's length. "In the morning, I'll show you that proof. I promise."

"All right," Chloe said.

Evie smiled, her face glowing with joy. "I'm glad you're here."

Then she bid her good night and left her alone. Chloe stood a moment by the fire, numb, staring at the closed door, holding the shift and the stockings, and wondering how she was going to survive in this world.

Thankfully, she had Evie to help her navigate it all. With a sigh, she changed into the shift and the woolen stockings. Evie was right. She was freezing and grateful for the warmth of the stockings. Exhaustion burned through her. She opted to ignore the food and climbed into bed, pulling the blankets to her chin. In a matter of minutes, she was fast asleep.

Chapter Twelve

"Do ye want to explain to me how you came upon the lass?" Callum asked.

Malcolm sat at the long table in the great hall, tracing the scarred wood where Callum's claymore had landed. That was the day he was banished from Dundale for torching the MacDonald village, something he regretted now. His legs, crossed at the ankles, were stretched out in front of him.

Jamie, the youngest, was across from him with his boots propped on the table and a tankard of ale in his hand.

"I told ye," Malcolm said on a sigh.

"Aye, ye did. But no the whole story." Callum stood across from him, his thick forearms folded across his chest.

Since becoming laird, he had been a pain in the arse. Och, aye, his brother was doing what was best for the clan, but did he have to do it with such headstrong authority?

"Ye said ye were with Angus Sinclair," Callum said.

"Aye, I did and I was." Malcolm made no other explanation.

He didn't want to tell his brother he had gone along with Angus to retaliate for the razed village because he didn't want to endure his wrath for the second time.

"And?"

"Och, brother, do ye no see he doesna want to tell ye?" This from Jamie who chuckled as he said it.

Malcolm shot him a look that he hoped conveyed to him to

shut his mouth.

"Ye wanted me to scout the area. That's what I was doing. Angus and his son came along. That's when we saw it. Like a rip in time," Malcolm said, hoping that would give his brother the answer he needed. "The lass fell through it along with the man."

"The man she named Bruce," Callum said.

"Are ye daft? That's what I said."

"Don't be cheeky," Callum chastised. He ran a hand over his chin as he started to pace. "Who is he?"

"I dinnae ken," Malcolm said. "But she came through with the piece of the keystone and he seemed to want it. He tried to get it from her. She said he attacked her."

"Where is he now?"

Malcolm shrugged. "He ran off. Said it wasn't over but by my reckoning, if he tries to harm her, he will have me to deal with."

That stopped Callum's pacing. He gave him a sideways glance. His brows raised as he looked at him, a weak smirk on his face. "Aye, then? Are ye smitten with the lass?"

Malcolm scoffed. The last thing he needed was to be smitten with the lass. Aye, she was lovely with a sharp tongue. Aye, he had enjoyed the feel of her in his arms as they rode to the Sinclair stronghold. That didn't mean he was smitten with her.

Jamie smirked when he remained silent.

"I think that's obvious, isn't it, brother? He wanted to rip my hands off for touching her," Jamie said. He dropped his feet from the table and unfolded his tall frame from his chair. "Malcolm has his eye on her, to be sure."

Malcolm scowled at his brother. "Why don't ye go to bed, ye scallywag."

Jamie held up his hands in surrender. "I ken when I'm no wanted."

He sauntered away toward the curved stairs to head off to bed. When he was gone, Callum eyed him again.

"Did ye ken she was Evie's sister?"

"I didn't at first," he said. "I dinnae tell her the lass was here.

Thought she'd like to find out on her own."

He had to admit, he'd delighted seeing the surprise reunion between the two sisters and how they embraced. There was a real bond between them that was obvious. A bond he had once shared with his brothers.

Since Jamie had spurned the MacDonald lass, their father passed unexpectedly, and Callum learned of his crime when he burned down the village, things were tense between all three of them. They were not as carefree as they were when they were children. They had faced their own troubles when their mother died and then their sister. But nothing compared to the strife that was between them now.

And now with this prophecy hanging over their heads, he wasn't sure if things would ever be back to the way they were.

"It's late. I best be on my way." Malcolm rose from the chair and headed for the door.

"Where do ye think yer going?"

That stopped him. Surprise flickered through him as he turned to face Callum. "I dinnae think ye wanted me here since ye banished me. I made my report and brought the lass back to her sister."

Callum pressed his lips together as he gazed at him, his mind working as he came to a decision. He heaved a heavy sigh. "I dinnae want ye to go. Stay and fight with us."

Malcolm lifted a brow. "Ye say that as if ye expect more fighting to come."

"If the prophecy is any indication, then aye. And now that there are two pieces of the keystone under my roof, they will double their efforts to get them," Callum said.

He understood to whom his brother referred. MacDonald was desperate to get his hands on the keystone to increase his power and rule in the land.

"And if a third piece should arrive…" Callum added, he let his words trail away.

"Ye expect that to happen, then?" he asked.

"Ye ken the prophecy."

He did. The words had pulsed through his mind from the moment he picked up the lass. He couldn't shake the memory of her arms wrapped tightly around his waist, her face buried against his back to shield her from the wind. He had cheered inside when she decided to ride with him because he wanted her close.

The way Bruce glared at her with a fierce determination deep in his eyes was burned into his memory, too. Even in the torchlight of the night, the desperation to get Chloe and the keystone had been written all over his face. He, like Callum, understood things were not over between the MacDonalds. They never would be until the keystone was whole and safe. But when would that be? How would they be able to protect it—and their women—then?

It was up to them, the MacLeods and the Sinclairs, to keep the keystone out of their hands.

Finally, he said, "I do."

"Good."

Callum headed for the stone staircase leading up to the bed chambers. At the bottom, he paused and turned to face Malcolm. A ghost of a smile flickered over his face.

"I'm glad ye are."

It was the closest thing to an apology for banishing him he'd gotten. He'd take it.

THE NEXT MORNING, when Chloe awoke, she was disoriented and confused. She lay in the unfamiliar bed staring up at the ceiling. Her heart kicked into high gear as she tried to recall where she was. Then it all flooded back. The reality of her situation crashed through her mind.

The stone. Bruce. Falling through time. Seeing Evie again. Malcolm.

The way he had planted himself between her and Bruce that night was a memory that wouldn't let go. The strong curve of his shoulders. His rigid back. The way he had pointed his sword at Bruce and threatened him. His voice had been fierce and stern and even thinking of it now sent delicious shivers through her. He had defended her—a stranger—without question.

Chloe had no doubt he would do it once more should Bruce threaten her again.

A knock sounded on her door. She pushed up on her elbows, then rolled out of bed and padded to the doorway. She pulled it open to see Evie on the other side with a bright smile and an armload of clothes.

"Morning!"

Chloe stepped aside to let her in, then closed the door. She couldn't help but notice how cheerful she looked or her rosy cheeks. It was a bit out of character for her stoic, serious sister. She wasn't the carefree type, but maybe being in medieval Scotland married to Callum had changed her disposition.

"You're in a good mood this morning."

Evie dumped the clothes on the unmade bed. "I'm happy you're here. And Callum has decided to let Malcolm stay."

She drew her brows together. "What does that mean?"

"Oh, he banished him, so I guess he's unbanishing him now." She said it in a flippant way as she sorted through the clothes.

"He banished him? Why?"

"Malcolm can be a bit of a hothead," Evie said. "He burned down a village as revenge for Rory MacDonald killing their father."

Shock rolled through her as she thought of Malcolm and his quiet way. He was a man of few words but clearly a man of action. How could he have done such a horrible thing? How could he have killed innocents in retaliation for the death of one man? She had to remind herself she was no longer in her world. She was in the medieval world.

"I do wonder if allowing him to stay has anything to do with you," Evie said, bringing her back to the present.

"With me? Why? Why would he want to stay because of me?"

Evie gave her a knowing grin. "Because...reasons. Now, let's get you dressed so I can show you my prophecy proof."

"That's what we're calling it now? Prophecy proof?"

"Well, that's what it is." Evie turned, holding a woolen gown. "Wait till you see. You won't believe it."

After Evie helped her dress in layers—stockings, shift, woolen gown, and boots, she took her by the hand and led her out of the bedchamber.

"Where are we going?" Chloe asked.

"You'll see."

They went down the curved stone staircase, then crossed the empty great hall to another corridor where she turned a corner and headed to one of the oversized oak doors. She pushed it open and paused in the doorway to wait for her to enter.

She said nothing as Chloe stepped inside and took in her surroundings.

Candelabras burned bright in the room, illuminating it in a soft glow. There was a large bed on one wall with thick curtains. On the other, a cold hearth. In front of that, a chair.

On the walls were large, colorful tapestries. At first glance, they seemed ordinary. But when she peered at them a long moment, she noticed the images moved. She pressed a hand to her throat as a quiet gasp escaped her.

As a historian, she'd seen her share of tapestries. But nothing like this. Nothing with shimmery thread woven through the fibers. They were large enough to cover the walls with six of them around the room.

The first one was of a woman with long silvery hair and bright blue eyes standing on a craggy hill, her fisted hand raised to the night sky. Her hand glowed with streaks of light seeping through her fingers. Two women flanked her—one with black hair, the other with red hair. Lightning flickered all around them.

Below them, an army charged toward them led by a man wielding a shiny great axe.

As she stared at the woman in the center, a sense of familiarity came over her. She was certain that woman was Moira, the shopkeeper from Mystic Treasures. The shopkeeper who had given her the piece of the stone that transported her back in time.

The second tapestry was of a bolt of lightning hitting the ground in front of the three women. The ground was lit up in a bright flash.

The third left her lightheaded when she saw the woman on the ground with the fiery red hair dressed in black. Hair that looked much like her sister's. In the sky, a rip as if she had fallen straight through the hole.

The next tapestry made her weak. Her knees threatened to give out as she peered at the image. The face staring back at her was her own. Behind her, Bruce. As if the tapestry she stared at foretold of her arrival in the past with him hot on her heels. The picture was of when they had plummeted through the portal. The movement of the image was in slow motion, but it was clear to Chloe what she was seeing.

She was looking at her arrival in the past.

The one next to that had a faint image of another woman, but it was a silhouette. She was faceless. The wind blew her hair to one side. She was tall, thin, and curvy.

Chloe understood who this woman was. She was certain it was Brianna.

The final tapestry was nothing more than a damask design in shimmering thread. No image floated on it like the others as though it were blank, waiting for whatever happened next.

She glanced back at Evie who still stood at the door, a calm expression on her face.

"What...what is all this?" Her voice was a weak whisper.

"The prophecy," Evie said, matter-of-factly.

"I don't understand." She shook her head.

Evie moved deeper into the room to join her. She pointed to

the first wall hanging. "This is the Night of Shadows. I told you about that before. The woman…that's Moira."

Chloe wasn't wrong then—it *was* Moira. Hot pinpricks skipped down her spine. "Moira is…"

"A goddess of Time," Evie said. "This one is the Shattering." She pointed to the next one. "When the three goddesses broke the keystone into three pieces. Past, Present, Future. You can see that here."

She pointed to the ground where the stone was broken into the three pieces.

"And the third one?" she asked.

"That's when I arrived here." Evie moved closer and stared at the wall hanging with a mixture of horror and resignation. "Callum said I fell from the sky."

Chloe thought of her own passage through the time portal and how horrible it had made her feel. She stared at her sister with a renewed sense of respect and awe.

"How did you survive?"

She shook her head. "I don't know, but I've decided the stone protected me."

As she mentioned it, she slipped her hand into the pocket of her gown as if to make sure she still possessed it. Chloe did the same and was relieved to feel the jagged piece of stone residing in the depths of her pocket.

"And this, of course, is you and Bruce." Evie stood in front of the wall hanging and peered up at the images. Her gaze was fixed on Bruce. "I had hoped the tapestry was wrong and he didn't follow you."

"But he did," Chloe said, a sudden chill pressing through her. She clutched her elbows. "And he's out there somewhere."

Her sister turned to her, reaching for her. "He can't hurt you here. Callum, Malcolm, and Jamie will make sure of it. They will protect you."

There was a fierceness in Evie as she said it. There was no reason to doubt her sister's word.

She thought of Malcolm, then, and how he had placed his body between her and Bruce with his sword drawn. As if it were the most natural thing to do.

Her gaze drifted from the wall hanging with her and Bruce to the next one with the silhouette of the woman. She and Evie, both, stared at it for a long, quiet moment.

"Do you think that's Brianna?" Chloe asked at last.

"It has to be."

Silence stretched until finally Chloe snickered. "Can you imagine our beach-loving sister *here*? In the Highlands?" She shook her head.

Evie grinned, her face lighting up. "I've thought about this a lot, you know. And I did wonder if she would come." She reached for the tapestry, running her hand down the edge of it. "It's only a silhouette of a woman, but I can't imagine who else it would be."

Chloe considered this for a long moment, too, as she peered at the darkened figure woven through the threads. She thought of their childhood. Brianna was ten years older than they were and had been out of the house by the time they were in middle school, living her own life. Their parents had argued with Bri numerous times before she left. Maybe that was why she had left: She was tired of the arguments.

Their parents had wanted a different life for her. Certainly not one of her wandering through the Caribbean taking photographs and trying to make it as a professional. They had wanted her to go to college; she refused. They had even offered her a free place to live while she went. And yet, she still refused.

Chloe never understood it—why was she so determined to leave? Why did she never come back except for the occasional Christmas holiday? The questions she didn't dare ask gnawed at her. Did she resent her and Evie? Was their closeness too much for her? Was she jealous? The thought stung, but it lingered there, unspoken, like a chasm between them.

Their parents' death shattered everything about their worlds when she and Evie were still in high school. Brianna had had no choice but to return to their hometown as their legal guardian. But even then, Chloe sensed the resentment simmering below the surface. Brianna did what she had to by taking care of them, but it had always felt temporary, like she had one foot out the door. And when the time had come, she was gone again, like they knew she would be.

"Chlo? Are you okay? You looked lost in thought."

She shook herself out of her thoughts and focused on her sister's face, creased with concern. She managed a smile. "I was trying to imagine Brianna here, in the past, with us."

"Do you think it's her?"

"I think if it is, she's going to be pretty angry when she arrives."

✦ ──── • ──── ✦

CHAPTER THIRTEEN

CHLOE FOLLOWED EVIE into the great hall. Her pulse quickened the moment she saw Malcolm. He sat at the long table with a tankard and a trencher of thick porridge in front of him. A stack of what appeared to be small cakes were beside the trencher. His gaze lifted, locking onto hers, and for a breathless moment, the room faded away. It was only Malcolm with his rugged good looks, his quiet charm, and those sea-green eyes that saw far too much. Chloe forced her feet to move to the table, her footsteps and her thudding heart far too loud in the deafening silence.

What was it about him that turned her inside out with a single look?

"I'm going to grab some food for us. I'll be right back."

Evie hustled away before Chloe could object, leaving her alone with the man. Almost as if she'd planned it. Her insides jittered as she perched in the seat as far away from him as possible. A tight knot coiled in the pit of her stomach.

"Did yer sister show ye the tapestries?" he asked.

The question surprised her. She peered at him from across the table. "Yes."

He leaned back in his chair. Their eyes met and for a moment, she thought she could get lost in those sea-green eyes. They were so full of life. He ran his hand over his beard, the coarse hair bristling against his skin. She had never liked men with beards, but there was something intriguing about Malcolm. His long dark hair hung over his shoulders. Another thing. She had never liked a man with hair longer than her own.

"And what did ye think of that?" he asked. He looked genuinely interested.

She tugged her lower lip through her teeth, wondering how to reply. She wasn't sure what she thought about these enchanted tapestries and she had questions about them. Where did they come from? How did they work? Why did they show images of the ancient past as well as their present? It was all a bit of a mystery.

"I'm not sure what to think."

He chuckled.

She said, "What do *you* think about them?"

A ghost of a smile flickered over his partially hidden mouth. "Did yer sister tell ye of the prophecy?"

A question for a question. "She did."

"And do ye no believe it?"

"Evie seems to believe it."

"That's no what I asked ye, lass."

She kept her gaze on him, unwavering. "Do you believe it?"

This time he laughed out loud. "My da told the story from the time I was knee high. He was adamant the day would come when we would have to defend ourselves against the MacDonalds and protect the keystone with our lives." He paused to take a drink of his ale. "It seems that time has arrived."

"And you think our arrival—mine and my sister's—has something to do with this prophecy?"

"Och, I ken it does."

He grinned as he broke one of the small cakes in half. She eyed it as he popped half into his mouth. As if on impulse, he rose from his seat, picked up several of the cakes, and walked down the table to her. He held them out to her.

"What's this?" she asked.

"Oatcakes. Some of the finest around. Roslyn is a fine baker."

She took the stack of oatcakes, their hands brushing. Like before, the touch left an unexpected tingling sensation in his wake. He popped the other half of the oatcake in his mouth and then walked back to his seat.

Chloe broke the dense cake in half and then took a bite. The taste was both savory and sweet with a magical flavor that made her close her eyes as she chewed. He wasn't wrong. Roslyn *was* a fine baker. She had never tasted anything as delectable as that.

When she finished chewing, she opened her eyes and met his gaze. He was smiling.

"So, ye like it then?"

"I do," she said.

Silence drummed through the great hall. She wished Evie would return. She was no good at small talk and had no idea what to say or do. So, she said the first thing that came to mind.

"Evie said Callum banished you but decided to let you stay."

The glower on his face was an indication it was the wrong thing to say. All she had wanted to do was make conversation and instead it appeared she said something she shouldn't have.

"She told ye that, did she?"

"I guess it's a sore spot," she said. "Forget I mentioned it."

"Och, aye, I cannae be doing that, now, can I? Do ye wish to know *why* I was banished from Dundale?" He lifted one dark brow as if in challenge.

She shrugged one shoulder, indifferent, as she tried to play it cool. She already knew the story of why from Evie. Even so, she wanted to hear it from him, in his own words. There was an underlying curiosity about him she couldn't shake.

"Sure."

"I torched one of the MacDonald villages." He said it with such calm it was as though he were speaking of the weather.

She was enough of an historian to understand what that meant. It meant killing innocents and displacing those who had managed to survive.

"You burned people's homes? Why?"

"Vengeance for killing our da." He broke another oatcake in half and ate it, as though this were the most normal conversation to have.

"An eye for an eye, then?" she asked.

He nodded, smiling. As if he were proud of himself.

She remained silent as she considered his answer. Evie had told her the MacDonald laird himself dealt Hamish the death blow. Did Malcolm think killing innocents was the way to get back at the man who had ultimately killed their father? Though, she supposed, that was normal behavior for men of this century.

"Ye seem to disapprove of that," he said.

Chloe was never one to hide her expressions. He must have seen her abhorrence flickering over her face.

"It's not for me to approve or disapprove."

Where the devil was Evie? What was taking her so long to return from the kitchen? She shifted in her seat, uncomfortable under his scrutinizing gaze. She ate another piece of the oatcake as silence descended in the great hall. The pastry turned to ash in her mouth.

She shoved back from the table and stood. "I'm not hungry anymore."

He said nothing as she stalked toward the door to the great hall, pushing it open and slipping into the morning. As soon as she did, she regretted her decision as the morning wind was cold and she didn't have her cloak.

She didn't know where she was going or what she intended to do. She only knew she had to be out of that room with that infuriating man.

Callum was at one of the outer buildings conversing with a tall, dark-haired man. He was deep in conversation with him.

Near him, the stables were a bustle of activity. She saw the stable hands coming and going and assumed they were busy mucking stalls and caring for the horses. She had never been one for horses. Neither she nor Evie had experience with them. Despite living and growing up in Texas, they had never been around them since they lived in the suburbs. She recalled Malcolm telling her his brother's wife—Evie—had become an accomplished rider. She wondered if she, too, would be able to achieve that.

A distinctive clang caught her attention. In another building, sparks flew as the clang sounded again. Excitement pumped through her at the thought of seeing a working forge. She followed the sound until she found her way to the blacksmith. He was busy hammering out what appeared to be a sword. She paused to watch, amazed by his strength.

"If ye wanted a tour, lass, all ye had to do was ask," Malcolm said.

She turned to see him standing behind her. He held her cloak out to her.

"Ye forgot this."

Grateful and glad to stop shivering, she took it from him and wrapped it around her. He, though, wore no cloak. Only his tunic, breeches, plaid, and black boots that looked as though they had seen better days.

"Thanks," she muttered.

Clouds gathered in the sky, making the sun come and go. Some looked gray as though they might bring rain.

"Do ye wish for a tour?" he asked. Hope tinged his words.

She wanted to refuse, especially after learning why he had been banished from Dundale. But something pulled at her to accept his invitation. A gut feeling. Finally, she nodded.

"All right, then. Give me a tour."

He motioned toward the forge and gave her a quirk of a smile. "The smithy."

She couldn't help herself. She laughed. "Yes, I see that."

Malcolm motioned for them to continue walking. Next was the chapel. It was a small stone building sitting off to one side. "There is where ye sister and my brother were handfasted."

She understood, of course, what that meant. They were to be married for a year and a day. The marriage would be final if she produced a child within that time from their union. She wondered what it was like to witness a true, medieval handfasting. Evie hadn't bothered to elaborate on the details of their wedding. She was more interested in telling her about the prophecy and their entwined destinies with the MacLeods.

"Was it a nice ceremony?" she asked. She looked around the small one-room building trying to envision what it was like to witness.

Wooden pews lined up like soldiers. At the front of the room, the alter where the bishop stood to deliver his sermon or where he had bound Callum and Evie together after they exchanged vows.

"I dinnae ken."

She cut him a questioning glance.

"Wee Jamie and I were gathering the men to fight when they were handfasted."

She tipped her head to one side. "To fight?"

"Did yer sister no tell ye?" he asked, surprise flickering over his face.

She shook her head. Yet another thing she had left out. She made a mental note to question her about that later when they were alone. These were things Chloe needed to know. What sort of fighting was there? Why?

"Ah. Well, MacDonald and his men attacked the keep. To take yer sister and the piece of the keystone she possesses. We were outnumbered. The battle was no going well. Callum sent Evie away with the keystone in the hopes she would return to her time." He walked to one of the pews and sat, the wood creaking under his weight.

She sat across from him, intrigued by this story. She held her hands in her lap. "But she didn't return."

"No, she dinnae." There was a light of pride in his eyes as he told her the next part of the story. "She came to the battlefield. In her hand was the keystone. She used it as a weapon to help defeat MacDonald." He paused there, as if remembering the battle.

It must have been horrific. And her sister was in the middle of it all. She tried to imagine it.

"How did she use the keystone as a weapon?"

"Och, lass, ye wouldna believe it. She held it in her hand. It was glowing, sending light shooting out from her fist. It was a strange thing to watch, to be sure. The world around us seemed to slow and then stop. But she…well, she had this strange sort of shimmering light around her, Callum, and Rory MacDonald. I couldna see what happened. But Callum told me later.

"The keystone, he said, gave her the power to show him what would happen if he continued to fight. If she hadna come, he would have died."

Incredible. She stared at him, waiting for him to finish the story. Though she tried to imagine how Evie had felt knowing the man she loved was about to die, she could not.

"What happened then?"

He looked thoughtful as he remembered what had happened during this battle Evie failed to mention.

"MacDonald stabbed Callum in the shoulder. He tried to capture Evie and take the stone from her. But then…" He paused, a ghost of a smile flickering over his lips. "She punched the man right in the chest. Her fist exploded in blinding white light, and it sent him flying backward, soaring through the air until he landed on the ground. He was defeated. Then Rory MacDonald and his men retreated."

Chloe was dumbfounded. She tried hard to imagine her sister punching a man bigger and stronger than her in the chest. She had renewed admiration for her and vowed to ask her about it the next time they talked in private.

"The light…that was this keystone, wasn't it?" Chloe asked.

"Aye, it was. A powerful little object, that."

Her own piece of the keystone was still in her pocket. She resisted the urge to reach for it and pull it out to examine it. How had Evie done it? How did she learn how to harness the power of the stone in such a short amount of time?

"That's some story," she said at last.

"Och, do ye no believe it, then?" he asked. Disappointment flooded his face.

She sucked in a deep breath, expelled it. "It's not that I don't believe it. It's just that I know my sister and she would never harm anything or anyone and she certainly doesn't know how to fight like that."

He stood up quickly, his hands clenched into fists at his sides. "If ye dinnae believe me, then ye should ask her yerself."

"Oh, I plan to."

Malcolm didn't bother to hide his annoyance as he stomped out of the chapel.

CHAPTER FOURTEEN

S HE SIGHED, KNOWING she had to go after him. She shoved off the pew and followed him out into the yard, pulling the cloak tightly around her. He was charging across the green, heading for the stables. She hurried to catch up to him.

"Malcolm, wait."

He spun to face her, his agitation clear. He had a look of expectancy as he peered at her, fire flashing in his eyes. Chloe stopped short, leaving several feet between them. She pulled her cloak tighter around her frame as the wind pounded her. She floundered for a moment for something to say. The last thing she wanted to do was make him angry. He had saved her from Bruce, after all.

"You didn't finish giving me the tour."

His shoulders relaxed and all the fight went out of him. "Do ye wish to resume then?"

She nodded. "I do."

"What would ye like to see next?"

He moved closer to her. She marveled at the heat radiating off his body. Her gaze flickered to the stables where there was a lot of activity. Perhaps if she petted a few horses, it would get her past her innate fear of the large creatures.

"How about the stable?"

He grinned and held his hand out to her. How could she resist? She slipped her hand in his, a zing of elation sweeping through her. She liked her hand in his.

"Do ye like horses, then?" he asked.

The obvious answer to that was *no* but she didn't want to tell him that. She tried to sound neutral when she answered.

"Truthfully, I've never been around them. They scare me a little."

That made him stop walking and turn to face her, surprise evident on his face. "Why?"

"Because they're so big."

He chuckled. "They are gentle animals. They wouldna harm ye."

They resumed walking hand in hand to the stable. Inside, there were several stalls. As they entered, one gray-faced horse popped its head out as if curious to see who arrived.

"That's Mist," he said, nodding to the horse. "Yer sister's horse."

"She has a horse named Mist?"

More surprising things about her sister she didn't know. It seemed rather fanciful for Evie.

They hadn't spent much time together, so it wasn't like Evie had had a chance to catch her up on everything that had happened since her arrival. By her calendar, Evie was missing for a few days. But it appeared to Chloe she had been here, in the past, for weeks. How odd that was.

"Aye."

He tugged her toward the horse, who snorted in greeting. He patted her nose affectionately.

"She's a sweet thing." He said it with a smile in his voice. The horse nuzzled his hand, as if looking for treats, which made him chuckle. "She likes apples."

"Does she?"

He released her hand and moved deeper into the stable, disappearing into one of the stalls. He returned with two red apples and handed her one.

"Go on," he said, nudging her toward the horse.

"I don't know." She hesitated, peering at the apple as if it were a foreign object she didn't want to take.

"Och, she willna hurt ye. See?"

He held the apple in the palm of his hand and stretched it toward the mare. She took it from his hand and chomped on it as if it was the best treat she'd had all day. He extended the second apple to Chloe.

"Give it a try," he said, encouraging her.

Chloe took the apple from him and stepped closer to the horse. The mare snorted in greeting as she extended the fruit toward her. She happily took it from her in one bite. That made Chloe smile and she couldn't resist reaching for the horse to pet her nose. She was soft. Malcolm disappeared for moment and returned with a brush in his hand.

"Here. She likes to be brushed."

"Oh, no, I couldn't—"

But he shoved the brush into her hand and stepped inside the stall. He waved for her to follow. "She willna hurt ye."

Taking a deep breath, she moved into the stall to stand next to him. He reached for her hand, wrapping his long fingers around her wrist and lifting her arm up.

"Like this."

He showed her how to make long, slow strokes with the brush along the mare's neck. His hand was gently wrapped around her wrist in a non-threatening way that made her knees weak and her heart flutter. She relaxed and allowed him to move back and forth in a rhythmic motion that made her drowsy and swoony all at once.

"There. See?"

His voice was soft and soothing in her ear and she realized he stood close. So close to her. She didn't mind. She wanted him close. But at the same time, she wanted her own personal space. It was a strange dichotomy.

If she had learned anything from her experience with Bruce, it was don't get too close too fast. Not that she expected Malcolm to turn on her or betray her, but she had a bit of mistrust. She was acutely aware of the way his breath moved in and out of him. The way heat radiated off his body. The way he stood close to her and made her feel warm and safe.

Her pulse quickened as her eyes met his intense gaze rooting her in place. The rhythmic movement of his hand faltered and stopped, as though he, too, was caught in this fragile, electric moment. Her heart thudded like a drum in her chest as pinpricks of heat flared all over her.

Then her gaze drifted to his lips. The shadow of his beard framed them in a way that sent a forbidden thrill racing through her. What would it feel like to kiss him? To feel the rough scrape of his beard against her skin, the heat of his mouth claiming hers? The thought ignited a fire low in her belly, a warmth that stole her breath.

She tipped her head back, the faintest movement that felt as daring as a leap. Oh, yes, she wanted to kiss him. He leaned in, the air between them crackling with tension, his nearness sending a shiver across her skin. A breath escaped her, unsteady, betraying the longing she was unable to contain. Would he close the distance? Could she bear it if he didn't?

"There you are!"

Evie's voice broke the spell. Malcolm dropped his hand and stepped away from her, out of the stall and into the middle of the stable. Chloe saw her sister hurrying toward them, her cheeks flushed and her eyes bright with concern.

"I've been looking for you. I see you met Mist."

She grinned when she said the horse's name as she paused in front of the stall. She reached up and petted her nose. The mare nuzzled her hand and greeted her with a snort. Chloe let her arm drop to her side, the brush still clutched in her hand.

"Yes," she said at last, her gaze flickering over to him. He had moved to stand across from the stall, leaning on the wall with his arms folded over his chest. "Malcolm was giving me a tour."

"Oh, good!" She turned to her brother-in-law. "Callum is

looking for you. I think he's in the armory."

He nodded. He gave her one last longing glance as he headed out of the stable, leaving the two of them alone.

"Eve, why didn't you tell me about the fight with the Mac-Donalds?" No use waiting for the right moment. Now seemed like the perfect time to bring that up since they were relatively alone.

"Oh. Well." She flushed as she continued to pet the horse. "I don't know. I guess Malcolm told you?"

"He did. And he told me you used the keystone as a weapon."

Her hand stilled on the horse's nose. "He told you that?"

"Yes. You didn't. Why?"

"I was going to. In time." She turned to her, then, meeting her gaze. "We don't know how powerful this keystone truly is, Chlo. I didn't want to frighten you."

"You had lightning coming out of your hands, Eve. How is that not frightening?"

She dragged her lower lip through her teeth. "I know I should have told you. But I didn't know how. Not yet."

"Tell me now. How did you know how to use it?"

"Moira told me."

That made her stop cold. She straightened and stared at her sister with wide eyes. "Moira?"

"Callum sent me to the shore. He wanted me to use the stone to return to the future. But I knew it was wrong. In my gut, I knew it was wrong. I didn't want to go and leave him. I couldn't. I just…couldn't. Moira was there on the shore."

"She visited you?"

"Yes. She told me if I left, it would reset Time and all my memories of this place, of Callum, would be erased. She told me he would die in battle if I left. That's when she showed me how to use the keystone."

The look on her face sent a chill through her. It was clear to Chloe that her sister was irrevocably in love with her husband, which gave a happy squeeze to her heart. And also a bit of jealousy. She wanted a love like that. She wanted to feel like that about someone, too.

"I couldn't let him die," she said, her voice quiet.

"Of course, you couldn't. You love him. And he loves you."

Then, Evie stepped a little closer and dropped her voice. "It's blood magic, Chlo. I'm sure of it."

She stared at her as if she'd grown another head. "Blood magic?"

"Shhh. Keep your voice down. Those that were there that night have accused me of being a witch." She glanced around the stable to see if anyone was listening.

Chloe lifted a brow in amusement. "Are you?"

She gave her a straight face. "You're hilarious."

She shrugged, a grin creasing her lips. "Just asking. So, how does it work?" Chloe asked, genuinely curious.

Evie lifted her palm, the one with the burned image of the stone, and showed it to her. In the center, there was a new silvery scar she never had before. Something had slashed across her palm. She thought she understood what that meant.

"You cut yourself."

"Moira did. She used a dagger to slice open my hand. She told me to keep the keystone in my hand and never release it. The feeling was…" she paused, shook her head, "hard to describe."

Chloe reached for her, taking her scarred hand in hers, and squeezed it. There was a hollow look in her sister's eyes as she remembered. It was haunting.

"Try." She gave her an encouraging smile.

Evie took a deep breath, expelled it. "Remember that time when we were kids and that horrible thunderstorm knocked out the power? It was only out for a couple of hours, but when it came back on there was this surge through all the electronics. It fried the TV and Mom's laptop."

Chloe nodded. She remembered that well. Her parents were upset they had to replace so many electronics. When the power came back on, there was a pop and a flash and then the acrid smell of smoke in the house.

"Are you saying you had a power surge?" she asked.

Evie said, "I think so. It felt like a rush going all the way through me, like a…well…a surge. And suddenly I sensed what Callum was going through. I saw what would happen to him if I didn't go to him, if I didn't try to save him. The strangest thing of all was I projected those scenarios into his mind. I *spoke* into his mind and he heard me."

She shuddered as she told the story as though she had relived the horror of the battle.

"There's something else I should tell you," she said after she paused a moment. She squeezed her hand, holding her tight. "Moira is the Goddess of the Present. One of the Triple Goddesses. When she and her two sisters shattered the stone during the Shattering, they put all their powers into each piece. They scattered the pieces throughout Scotland, only to be found when there was a need again."

Chloe stared at her, her heart ramming hard against her chest. "And you think that time has come?"

"It's the only explanation for it." Evie released her and reached into her pocket, bringing out her stone. She held it up with an expectant look.

Chloe released her hand and did the same. She placed her piece against Evie's and watched as not only the edges lined up perfectly, but also the lines of the triquetra and the circle. It was clear there was a third piece missing.

They both stared at it and then looked at each other.

"Two ancient bloodlines. One divine destiny," Evie whispered, repeating the words of the prophecy.

"If Moira is the Goddess of the Present and gave you her power and her piece of the stone, then what is my piece?"

Evie shook her head. "I don't know but we need to find out."

"How do we do that?" Chloe asked.

She smiled. "I have an idea."

Evie stuck her piece of the stone back into her pocket, then took her by the hand. Chloe fisted hers as she dragged her out of the stable toward the keep. She had a pretty good idea what her sister was up to and she wasn't certain she was all for it.

Once they were in the keep, she took her to the kitchen where it was a bustle of activity. No one seemed to take note of them, as if it were a common occurrence for the lady of the castle to be there. Evie found a kitchen knife, then took her scarred hand in hers.

"Hey, wait," Chloe objected.

"It won't hurt."

Before she objected again, Evie used the tip of the knife to cut her palm. Blood welled along the line through the imprint of the stone. They waited.

"The stone, Chlo," she said with a hint of excitement.

She still clutched the stone in her other hand, so she transferred it to her bleeding one. Evie closed her fingers around the stone.

Nothing happened.

"What now?" Chloe asked.

"We wait."

They stood in the kitchen as maids went about their business. Pots boiled, bread baked, vegetables were chopped. And still nothing happened.

"I don't get it," Evie said, frowning.

Chloe opened her fingers. The stone was slick with blood. At least it was a shallow cut.

"I guess it was worth a shot anyway," she said.

"I guess I was wrong. Come on. Let's get you bandaged up."

CHAPTER FIFTEEN

I T WAS LATER that afternoon, after Evie had bandaged her hand and left to tend to her lady of the keep duties, that Chloe found herself alone wandering the castle. She wasn't sure where she was going, but she ended up at the tapestry room. She was drawn to the enchanted wall hangings though she couldn't say why. It was akin to the feeling she had had when she stepped foot into Mystic Treasures. It was that same pull, that same fascination, that same need.

She pushed open the door, leaving it open, so the light from the hallway illuminated the room, slashing across the floor and up the wall. With slow steps, she approached the strange tapestries. She reached out a hand to touch a textile. It seemed like any other ordinary woven material but there was something about it that was different. Several of the threads shimmered and glowed and morphed as the images moved.

It was both fascinating and horrifying.

The first one hadn't changed much. The one with Moira and the two women. And she understood, then, who they were. The Triple Goddess. If Moira was Present, then it seemed to her the other two represented Past and Future. The question was which part of the keystone was hers? Which goddess did she represent?

The keystone was in her pocket and emitted a little vibration. She pulled it out. The lines were not glowing but there was a definite low hum to the stone. Her brows pulled together as she pondered this, wondering why it now chose to hum. Hoping to ignore it, she stuck it back into her pocket and glanced back up at the tapestry.

As she peered at the first image with the three women on the craggy hill, the dark-haired goddess appeared to turn her head toward her, meeting her gaze.

The startled jolt hit her as she stumbled back a step. The stone hummed louder. The woman, this goddess, continued to peer at her with light-blue, haunting eyes.

Do not fear, lady of Clan Sinclair.

The mellifluous voice fluttered through her mind. Her mouth went dry. Though she knew the words were spoken in her head, she still glanced around to make sure she was alone.

She was.

"Who are you?"

There was nothing more odd than talking to a moving picture on a wall hanging.

I am Bridget, the Goddess of the Past. My sister gave you a piece of the keystone, did she not?

Chloe moved closer to the tapestry to make sure she wasn't imagining things. The image of Bridget was moving and her gaze was fixed on her as though she saw her from her place inside the fabric.

The fabric of Time?

Could it be these magical wall hangings were part of the fabric of Time?

"She did," Chloe answered.

Her cut palm throbbed with a sudden pain she hadn't noticed before. She glanced down at the bandage Evie had tied, wondering if it was too tight. But if it were, then surely it would have throbbed long before now.

Keep it safe. Guard it with your life. There are those who will try to take it from you. Be warned. They will use any means necessary to get it. You are its guardian now. You possess all the power of the stone.

It was as Evie had said—Evie had the power of the Present.

"But what is the power of this stone?"

The power of the Past.

Finally, one question answered. Bridget was the Goddess of the Past, which also solved the mystery of the third stone. That meant Brianna was tied to the power of the Future.

"How do I use it?" she asked.

"Och, lass, are ye talking to yerself?"

And just like that, the spell was broken and the dark-haired goddess named Bridget returned to normal inside the first tapestry.

Malcolm's boots thumped along the stone floor as he joined her in the room, pausing next to her. He peered up at the wall hanging, question furrowing his brow.

"Were ye talking to the tapestry?"

He gave her a glance with a raised eyebrow that told her he might think she was a lunatic.

She laughed it off. "Of course not. That would be ridiculous."

"Aye." But he didn't sound convinced.

Her palm still throbbed where Evie had cut it. She wondered, then, if the blood magic had somehow worked. Was that why she was compelled to come here? Why Bridget spoke to her from her woven prison?

"I was talking to myself," she said, trying to make up an excuse. She waved toward the tapestry with her bandaged hand. "I was trying to understand how these things worked."

He caught her hand in his, staring down at the bandage. "What happened?"

"Oh, it's nothing. Just a shallow cut."

He turned her hand over to look at her palm. Most of the material covered the brand from the keystone in her skin, but it was still visible.

"Ye cut yer hand." He glanced up at her with a knowing look.

"I said it was nothing." She tried to pull her hand free, but he held fast.

His gaze was unwavering.

"Were ye trying to use the keystone?" he asked, his voice low.

The way he said it and looked at her made her feel as though she had been up to no good. Like when their parents had caught them doing something they shouldn't. She shifted from one foot to the other.

"Evie thought…" She took a deep breath, expelled it. "She thought it would help give me the power of the keystone. Like it did when she used it."

He released her hand. "Did it work?"

"No. At least, I don't think it did. Nothing happened when she cut my hand and I held the keystone."

She brought it out of her pocket and showed it to him. She'd cleaned the blood off it, but as she held it up into the slash of light, she saw a dried brown smudge still on it. She cut a glance to the tapestry and wondered if that had anything to do with Bridget talking to her from the wall hanging.

"It's strange that something so small can be so powerful," she muttered.

"Aye," he agreed and reached for her bandaged hand again.

The moment he took her hand in his, something strange happened. A flash of light pounded through her, exploding in her mind. She sucked in a heated breath and tried to jerk away, but he held onto her.

"Lassie?"

His voice sounded far away as the world twisted and turned in on itself, the light from the hallway smearing in front of her. It was as though she transported through some strange portal—not like when she traveled back in time—but different. As though the vision in her mind sprang to life and she found herself standing at the edge of a small village. Several thatched roofs were visible against the night sky. Smoke curled from the chimney of one. Another had yellow light flickering in the window. Most of the small houses were dark and silent, as though the inhabitants had retired for the night. Overhead, stars twinkled in the inky sky. There was no moon.

Sitting atop his destrier was Malcolm. Next to him, his brother, Jamie. They both held torches.

"Get them all out," Malcolm ordered, his voice hard and cold.

Two men galloped past him and Jamie. They pounded on doors, waking up the villagers and pulling men, women, and children from their beds. Sleepy-eyed and horrified, they stumbled into the chilly evening. The wind flickered the torches he and Jamie held.

"Gather them together," Malcolm ordered. "Jamie, help them."

Jamie rode away and barked orders, still holding that torch aloft. Malcolm moved his horse to a slow walk down the center of the village. Houses with thatched roofs lined the dirt road on either side of him. There were a few hundred villagers huddled together at the edge, the sounds of whimpers of children and women echoing through the night.

"Is that all of them?" Malcolm asked.

Jamie said, "Aye."

"Are ye sure, lad? I want no blood on my hands."

"Aye, I'm sure," Jamie replied with a nod.

Malcolm nudged his horse toward one of the small houses, lifting the torch higher in the night sky. "Go to yer laird. Tell him Clan MacLeod sends their regards. Tell him, next time there will be death."

He lit the thatched roof with the torch. It immediately caught, sending flames higher and higher into the sky, illuminating the frightened faces. Jamie used his torch to light the houses on the other side. He moved his horse next to Malcolm's as they watched the village go up in flames.

"What will ye tell Callum?" Jamie asked.

"Nothing," he said, his voice hard and unrelenting. "He will ken what I did soon enough."

"And assume the worst. Ye should tell him ye forced them out before—"

"Let's go."

Then he kicked his horse into a gallop. Jamie and the other two men followed.

And then the vision was over. But it wasn't a vision. It was a memory. *His* memory.

Malcolm released her hand. She stumbled away from him,

her heart fiercely pounding as she tried to catch her breath. She clutched her bandaged hand against her chest in a futile attempt to slow her heart.

"You…" The word came out on a breath as she spoke.

He remained where he was, staring at her with wide-eyed shock. His voice was a whisper. "How did ye do that, lass?"

"Do what?" Her stomach clenched into a tight knot as a sick feeling crept through her.

"How did you show me the night I burned the village?"

Icy pinpricks tickled the back of her neck. "That was true, then?"

He said nothing, his expression impassive and devoid of emotion. The light normally in his eyes faded as he peered at her as though she were an enemy.

She glanced down at the keystone still in her other hand. In her cut palm, blood stained the bandage. The strange vision had happened when he took her hand while she held the keystone—the blood-stained keystone—in her other.

"It was the stone," she said, weakly. The blood drained from her head. Black pinpricks of light danced in her vision. She swallowed hard and shook her head to clear it. "It showed me the past. Your past. When you touched me."

Glowering, he shoved past her and headed for the door. She had the distinct feeling her vision was also in his mind. He relived that moment when he went to the village and burned it.

"No one died," she blurted, her heart racing. "You forced them out before you set it on fire."

That stopped him. He halted in the middle of the doorway, his body nothing more than a shadow against the light.

"But you never told anyone that, did you? You wanted them to believe you had killed innocents. You wanted them to fear you. Why?"

He braced a hand on the door jamb, his back still to her. "I dinnae ken."

That sick feeling was still creeping through her but she forced herself to move. She took several steps toward him, halting within arm's reach.

"I think I do. You wanted vengeance for the death of your father. But you didn't want to inflict more pain than necessary. You wanted to send a message to MacDonald. You wanted him to know your father's death was not without consequence."

The words spilled from her in a rush. Her hands shook as she stared at his back, watching the taut muscles relax as he turned slowly to face her.

"How do ye ken that, lass?" Fear tightened his features, tension creasing the lines of his face.

It was difficult to explain. She glanced down at the keystone still in her hand, understanding dawning. It wanted her to know this about him, to show her who he was, truly. And it wasn't as though it was told to her. It was more of a feeling, a sense of what he'd done and why.

"It was the keystone. It showed me this about you. It has the power of the Past."

She lifted her head, met his glittering gaze where a storm raged in those eyes. A storm of indecision. As though he didn't know whether to trust her or not.

"Malcolm, I understand why you did it."

He startled at the sound of his name on her lips. She stepped closer, daring to close the space between the two of them. Her cut hand throbbed with a fierce, deep pain. She glanced down at it again and saw the bandage soaked through with blood. She swayed, suddenly weak and lightheaded.

He was there in a flash as she started to crumple, taking her in his arms and keeping her upright. She held up her bloodied, bandaged hand.

"I think something happened to me."

It was as though the memory, the power of the keystone, drained her of all energy.

"God's teeth, lassie."

With that, he scooped her into his arms. The moment she was cradled against his warm, strong chest, she lost all consciousness.

✦

CHAPTER SIXTEEN

CHLOE AWOKE TO the pleasant sounds of a fire crackling and warmth surrounding her. Opening her eyes, she saw she was in a large bed with a heavy wood frame and four curtained posts, across from her, the hearth with a blazing fire. She sat up on her elbows and surveyed the room. It was not the room she had spent the previous night in. This room was different.

Next to the bed, a small wooden table where she noticed the keystone rested along with a candelabra. A massive chest was at the foot of the bed. Two chairs and a table were near the hearth. On the other side of the room, a washbasin near the one window which was shuttered against the elements. Under the window, a long cushioned bench. Tapestries—though certainly not the magical ones in the other room—were along the wall. Thick rugs covered the floor. A tall candelabra stood in one corner with six candles, all blazing brightly.

Whose room was she in?

A curious swooping tugged her stomach at the thought she might be in Malcolm's chamber. A heated flush crawled up her neck and took up residence in her cheeks. She lifted her hands to her face only to realize she had a fresh bandage. It was expertly tied as it wrapped around her wounded hand.

The door pushed open. Malcolm entered carrying a tray with two tankards, a pitcher, a wheel of cheese, bread, and dried meat. He placed it on the table between the chairs in front of the fire.

She watched him, curious, as he poured a bit of weak ale into one of the tankards, then took a sip. He turned toward the bed and their eyes met. Her heart leapt into her throat.

What a strange reaction she had to this man she hardly knew.

"Och, yer awake. How do ye feel?"

She felt like death, honestly. Her body ached from head to toe. She had a raging headache. Her stomach growled from not having eaten a full meal. But her hand had stopped throbbing.

"I don't know."

He chuckled, a rumble low and deep in his throat. It was a wonderful sound. He poured the second tankard, then picked it up and walked it to her.

"Here. This will help."

She took the weak ale and sipped it as he moved back to the table.

"Did you bandage my hand?"

"Aye," he said. "Whoever did it the first time did no do a good job."

She flushed, thinking of Evie's hastily tied bandage around her palm. She rushed to get it done before anyone, namely Callum, discovered what they had been up to.

"Well, I guess she was in a hurry," she said.

"I cleaned it. 'Tis a shallow cut, but it was starting to fester a bit. Ye might be glad ye were out when I did that." His mouth turned up into a smile behind his beard.

She shuddered. Yes, she was glad she had been out for that activity. He took a sip of ale, then dropped his tankard to the tray with a thump.

"Ye said something about that wee stone."

"The keystone?"

She glanced over at it. The offending stone rested quietly on the table beside the bed. Not glowing or humming or anything of the sort. It looked like nothing more than a piece of jagged rock.

"You said it has the power of the Past."

He paused, the silence stretching between them. His gaze

flickered to the stone, then back to her again, as if searching how to ask whatever burning question was within him.

"This keystone of yer sister's…what power does it hold?"

"You told me yourself what power it held. You saw it when she came to the battlefield. You said time slowed and light shot out from her hand."

"Aye, I ken that. But…" He gave her a curious glance. "If ye can see the past, then what can she see?"

Ah, she understood then. Evie had told her the keystone showed her Callum would die if she hadn't come to his aid. She saw in that moment how he would die.

"She told me she had to save Callum during the battle because she saw the possible outcomes of the present. All of them showed her he'd be killed."

Malcolm stilled, then, slowly lowered himself into the chair by the fire.

"He never told me," he said, as though he were hurt by the omission.

"That's why she didn't use the keystone to return to her future. Our future."

Chloe pushed aside the blankets and swung her legs down. She was still fully dressed. She walked to the chair and sat across from him, still holding her tankard of ale. She eyed the dried meat, her stomach rumbling.

"And yer piece shows the past," he said.

"Yes."

Though it wasn't a question, she answered as if it were. She reached for a piece of the meat and took a bite. It was a bit chewy and reminded her of jerky.

He seemed a little shaken by the idea she saw his past. It was likely a power he didn't understand or want. Perhaps he was wondering what other past events she would be able to see, what other things he had done. Things he may not be proud of or want her to know.

"I promise I won't do it again," she said in jest.

His face broke into a bright smile. "Good."

"I didn't mean to do it in the first place," she added. "When you came into the room, you asked if I was talking to the tapestry. Well…I was."

His brows rose as he looked at her. She huffed out a breath.

"You must think I'm—"

"Daft? Aye. A wee bit." He picked up the tankard and guzzled the rest of his ale.

She wanted to object and tell him she wasn't daft, but what good would it do? His eyes glinted with humor as he looked at her over the rim of his cup.

"If I dinnae ken any better, I'd say ye'd been in the cups. But…" He paused, then shook his head. "Ye dinnae drink enough ale to be wrecked." Then his mouth quirked into a grin and she realized he was poking fun at her.

"No, I wasn't wrecked." She grinned as she said it, finding the humor in it. "So, do you believe me?"

"I dinnae disbelieve ye," he said. "I've seen the tapestries move myself. Tell me, lass, what ye saw there."

"The dark-haired goddess is named Bridget. She spoke to me. In my mind." Remembering made her shudder. She placed her tankard on the table and reached for the bread, tearing off a piece.

"What did she say?"

"She told me to guard the keystone with my life. That there are those who will try to take it by any means necessary. She said I was the guardian now and…" She paused as she thought of what she'd said to her next. She gulped in a breath. "She said I possess all the power of the stone."

"Like yer sister possesses the power of her stone," he said.

She nodded, her stomach fluttering and twisting into knots. She shoved a hand through her tangled hair. If she possessed this power, and Evie did, then…when Brianna arrived she would possess the power of the future. And what did that mean? Would Brianna, her wayward, free-spirited beachy sister, understand the power?

Hell, neither she nor Evie understood the power of the stones they possessed. How could she expect Brianna to? Now that she thought about this prophecy that was thrust upon her, forever altering her life and her destiny, she was angry. She frowned, her brow furrowing with her displeasure.

"What is it, lass? Ye look a wee bit scunnered."

She shoved up from the chair and spun away, the frustration edging through her. "I don't want this power. I never asked for it."

"Well, ye have it now. There's no going back."

She looked down at her bandaged hand. Evie was right. It *was* blood magic, though it hadn't worked right away. At least, not until she had been drawn to the room with the enchanted tapestries. When the stone had decided to come alive and hum. She didn't recall when it had stopped. Was it after her memory walk inside Malcolm's head? Perhaps that was what had made Bridget come alive. Maybe even have given her the power. She didn't understand how it worked. She would never understand.

But Malcolm was right. She had it and there was no going back.

She heaved a sigh. "What do I do now?"

"Och, lass, I dinnae think there is anything to do but accept it."

She frowned again, thinking of everything she had left in her future. Her job, her flat, her very existence. But thinking of that made her think of Bruce. He was still out there, somewhere. Was he looking for her? Would he find her? Would he come after her again for the stone?

Bridget's words haunted her.

There are those who will try to take it from you. They will use any means necessary to get it.

She sucked in a breath.

"Bruce," she said, his name a whisper on her lips. She turned to face Malcolm who still sat in the chair watching her with interest in his keen eyes. "He's going to come for it, isn't he?"

"He may try," he replied, a fiery light of defiance flickering in his eyes.

She didn't have to explain to him who she meant. He knew. And for that she was grateful.

"But what if he—"

"I will protect ye." He unfolded his tall frame from the chair and moved toward her. "I swear that to ye. I will protect ye with my sword or my own body if necessary."

He said it with such conviction, heat swarmed over her. Though, she decided, it was because he stood so close to her and the fire blazed hot in the hearth. In fact, a cold sweat broke out along her spine as she tilted her head back to look up at him.

He was tall, she realized. She hadn't noticed how tall. And he was broad. Muscular, with large biceps and a wide chest she had been cradled against more than once. A wayward lock of hair fell over his shoulder. She didn't know what possessed her to do it, but she reached up and pushed it away.

He stilled. The only sound in the room was that of her shallow breathing and the crackling fire.

And the drumming of her heart. Could he hear that, too?

"You would protect me like that?"

"Aye."

"Why?"

"Ye ken why."

She shook her head. "No."

"Because ye are under my brother's roof. Ye are part of the family."

"Is that the only reason?"

What was she doing? Why was she asking him this? Of course, it was the only reason. Perhaps the power of the stone had gone to her head and she was—what did he call it?—wrecked. There was no other explanation.

He tipped his head to one side as he peered at her with a look that made her heart ache. "Nay."

He said it so softly, she wasn't sure she heard him.

"No?"

The world seemed to tip on its axis as he brought his hand up and brushed the back of it over her cheek. Then he slipped his hand along the side of her neck.

"Nay," he repeated.

He leaned down, the movement swift enough to dull her senses. Before she processed what was happening, his lips met hers. It stole her breath in the most delightful way imaginable. The coarse hairs of his beard bristled against her skin, a surprising contrast to the softness of his gentle yet demanding mouth. The world fell away and all that mattered was yielding to him in that moment. And in that moment, the flutter of emotion unfurled deep in her chest.

She focused on how his large hand fit against the side of her neck, the way his coarse palm brushed against her skin. Her traitorous mind wondered then how his hands would feel on other parts of her body. How her skin would feel against his. But she shoved those thoughts away. Now was not the time for that. Now would never be the time. He wasn't the one for her.

Was he?

He stepped back to look down at her. A sensuous light flickered through those sea-green eyes. Eyes like summer lightning on a humid spring day before the thunderstorms came.

Oh, God. He *liked* her, didn't he?

But did she like him? Enough to want to kiss him again? She needed to test that theory.

Without thinking and before second-guessing herself, she stood on tiptoe, wrapped her arms around his neck and kissed him again. The boldness of her actions surprised both of them. A rush of heat pounded through her, making her heart thud in loud, untamed beats. For a moment, he froze, taken aback by her audacity. Then his hesitation melted away. His arms slid around her, strong and sure and steady, as he pulled her close into his embrace.

Oh, yes. She liked him enough to do this—more than

enough. And the way he held her told her he might feel the same.

The thought of their mutual kissing enjoyment knocked her off kilter. She didn't need to get caught up in a romance with him. They were from two different worlds. He was a medieval man. She was a modern woman. Eventually, she and Evie would return to their own time.

Well, perhaps not Evie since she was head over heels for Callum. But she would return. She had a career waiting for her in Edinburgh.

She shoved away from him, ripping them apart and turned away, trying to quell the rising desire and need pounding through her. She pressed her fingertips against her still damp, still tingling lips.

"Was that no pleasant for ye?" He sounded wounded.

"Oh, it's not that." She took a deep breath, released it. "It's that I don't think we should be doing that."

"Why not?" he asked, perplexed.

"Because I can't stay here, Malcolm." When he didn't answer, she turned to face him. "Don't you see? I belong in the future. So does Evie, but I doubt I'll ever get her to return."

His face was devoid of emotion as he looked at her. She had seen that look before. It was when he was experiencing a range of emotions and he didn't know how to handle them.

"And," she added, "I don't like kissing men with beards."

She hurried past him, unsure why she had flung that last bit at him. Her emotions ran high and hot. She couldn't deal with that now. He didn't make a move to stop her as she burst out the door, hurrying back to her own room.

Chapter Seventeen

S HE DIDN'T KNOW why she had told him she didn't like kissing men with beards. It was a total lie.

Well, not exactly a lie. More like a reason to shove away those feelings that bubbled up within her when she kissed him. She had never kissed a man with a beard, so she had no reason to say she didn't like it.

She liked kissing Malcolm.

She liked kissing Malcolm *a lot*.

She suspected he liked kissing her back. *A lot*.

Her steps were hurried as she bolted from his room, slamming the door behind her. As she rounded a corner, she halted, pressing her back against the cold stone wall and closing her eyes. Her breath seesawed in and out of her. Her heart raced. Her hands shook. How did she allow herself to get caught up in the moment?

The way his hand had swept over her cheek sent a dizzying feeling through her, making her stomach quiver. It sent her senses soaring in a way she had never experienced before. She had been powerless to resist. Then he had placed his hand on the side of her neck, igniting a flame within her she thought was long dead.

Oh, she had been attracted to Bruce. She had even slept with him. And while their lovemaking had been nice, it was not exactly earth shattering. She decided that was because he was trying to get something out of her. Deep down, he hadn't had feelings for her. Knowing that cut her deeply.

She had no one else to blame but herself. What had been her excuse for allowing herself to fall for him? It was time to get real about that. She had wanted him in her life because she was lonely as she navigated the city in a foreign country, a new job, a new life. She hadn't expected leaving Evie, her best friend and sister, would leave such a gaping hole in her life. She missed her sister with a fierceness she hadn't expected.

Bruce showed up at the right time as though he knew she needed someone in her life. She wanted to believe it was all a coincidence, but now that she'd heard the prophecy, she wasn't sure.

She wasn't sure about anything anymore.

She didn't want to like Malcolm. She didn't want to like kissing him either. But it was hard to deny how he affected her. He swore to her he would protect her with his sword and his body. He said it with such conviction, his eyes blazing, and she believed it.

"Chloe?"

She jumped at the sound of her sister's voice. Her eyes flew open. Evie stood across from her, question on her face.

"Where have you been all day?"

"I, uh…" She blew out a breath. "What time is it?"

"Late. You missed the evening meal. You and Malcolm." She lifted a brow and smirked.

Upon hearing that, her stomach rumbled again. She was starving. She pressed her hand against it hoping to silence it.

"If you'll feed me, I'll tell you everything." She hooked her arm in hers.

"We can grab some leftovers from the kitchen. Roslyn won't mind."

They walked through the hallway, down the curved stairs, and into the great hall, which was empty. She continued on until they made it to the kitchen, which was a bustle of activity. There was so much action, Chloe wasn't sure where to look first.

Maids were busy washing pots and other utensils. Another was busy preparing fish to be smoked or dried. A tall man she didn't know stoked the fire in the massive hearth to keep it going. Roslyn had her hands in a ball of dough as she kneaded it. She paused her kneading, reaching for a kitchen towel to wipe her hands when she saw Evie enter.

"My lady, did ye need something?"

It was hard for Chloe to get used to hearing her sister called *my lady*.

"Any leftover pottage? My sister was indisposed and missed the evening meal," she said.

Roslyn gave her a grin as she bustled around the kitchen. She ladled a large portion of stew into a bread bowl, stuck a spoon in it, then carried it over to her.

"Here ye are, lass," she said as she handed it to her.

The bread was still warm from the stew as she took it from her with a nod. "Thanks."

Evie waved her to follow. "Come on."

Back in the great hall, Evie perched on one of the seats at the long table. Thankfully, they were alone. No one else was about. Chloe sat next to her. Smelling the delicious stew made her mouth water. She dug in, taking her first bite of the steaming stew. It was thick and hearty and delicious. Evie waited with her hands folded in her lap.

"Well?" she prompted when she her patience ran out.

Chloe took another bite, thankful her stomach was no longer rumbling. "I had a strange experience in the tapestry room."

"What happened? Did they change again?" Excitement mixed with a hint of fear was in her voice.

"No. Well, sort of. The keystone—"

She sucked in a breath and dropped her spoon as the realization pounded through her. She'd left the stone in Malcolm's room. In her haste to flee, she had forgotten it. Well, she would be damned if she was going back to get it now. In the morning, she'd find her way to his room and retrieve it. Hopefully while he was out so she didn't have to face him again.

"What about it?" Evie asked.

She held up her bandaged hand. "When you cut my hand, we thought nothing happened. We thought wrong. After you bandaged me up, I noticed the stone started to hum and I felt this incredible pull to go to the tapestry room."

She told her about Bridget speaking to her in her mind, warning her to guard the stone with her life, that there were those who wanted it for themselves and they would stop at nothing to get it.

"I think it was the magic in the stone," she said.

Evie stared at her with wide, round eyes. "You heard her voice in your head?"

She nodded. "And that's not all. Malcolm found me in there. The stone was humming still. I was holding it. I noticed there was a bloodstain on it. He took my hand and when he touched me…" She paused, wondering if her sister would believe the weirdness of what she was about to say.

But she had a knowing look on her face. "You saw something, didn't you?"

"Yes. I saw his past. When he burned the village."

Evie's face drained of color as she stared at her, unblinking. "You saw this?"

"He made everyone leave their houses. He told them to tell their laird the MacLeods send their regards. Then he and his brother torched it."

Evie said nothing as she leaned back into the chair, her face devoid of color. "No one died?"

"No."

A breath shuddered out between her lips. "All this time, he led us to believe he had killed innocents. Why? Why would he do that?"

"He wanted to send a message to MacDonald."

"But why would he never tell Callum the truth?"

"Pride. And he wanted to seem as though he were a fierce warrior," Chloe said. It was what she sensed from him when she saw the memory. "It was strange, watching that happen. As though I were standing there with him. As if it were in real time."

"You have the power of the Past," Evie said on a breath. "That means, Bri—"

"Has the power of the Future."

"What does this mean?" Evie asked.

"I don't know. I don't know what purpose it serves for me to see the past," she said.

"Perhaps there is something more you have to learn yet. Something you have to see about the stone," Evie suggested. "Maybe something in the past."

Chloe was shaking her head as she said it. "I don't want to learn anything else about the past or the keystone."

"Why not?"

Chloe took another bite and eyed her over the near empty bread bowl. "The power of the stone is all-consuming, Eve. Didn't you feel it when you used it? And that reminds me. Malcolm told me about your power. Why didn't you? You left that part out."

She flushed. "Oh, well. I was throwing a lot at you at the time. I didn't want to overwhelm you."

"I'm overwhelmed," she said tersely. "The prophecy, the keystone, being here. You."

"Me? Why do I overwhelm you?" She sounded utterly shocked.

"You're married. No, *correction*, you're handfasted. A year and a day. I wasn't there for you. I thought we agreed we would be in each other's weddings?"

Chloe hadn't realized how much it hurt to learn her sister had married the man of her dreams without her. They were thirteen when they had made that pact and Chloe had experienced her first heartbreak. Evie, in an effort to console her sister, promised her she would marry one day, and she could be her maid of honor.

"I-I don't know what to say, Chlo. I'm sorry. Everything happened so fast and, well, you were in the future. I didn't know if I would ever see you again and I—" She paused as she choked on a sob.

It killed Chloe to see her eyes fill with tears. Guilt swarmed through her. She hadn't meant to upset her. She heaved a sigh and reached for her hand, squeezing it in hers.

"It's all right. And don't be sorry. You're right. I was in the future, hundreds of years away from you."

She released her hand and sat back, peering down into the empty bread bowl. She broke off a piece of the rich, dense bread and popped it in her mouth.

"After that happened with the stone," Chloe said, picking up her story again, "I felt odd. Lightheaded. Weak. My hand started to bleed through the bandage."

"That's the power in you. It drains you," she said.

"If Malcolm hadn't been there, I'd probably still be passed out on the floor. He caught me. I woke up in his bed with a fresh bandage on my hand." She held it up so her sister could see.

"I should have done a better job of bandaging you."

Chloe said nothing at that as she placed her hand back into her lap. She stared at the half-eaten bread bowl. The words erupted from her before she could stop them.

"He kissed me."

Evie sucked in a breath of surprise. "He did?"

She cut her a glance. "Don't get excited. That's all that happened."

But Evie's grin was so bright, her face glowed. Chloe frowned.

"Why does that make you happy?"

She shrugged. "I don't know. I want you to be happy. And Malcolm is…" She clamped her mouth shut.

"More handsome than Bruce? Stronger? Better? With eyes like the sea after a storm…" Her words trailed off.

She flushed when she saw Evie looking at her with a knowing

grin. Chloe's frown deepened.

"You were right about Bruce, Eve," she said. "I should have listened to you."

"For once, that's something I don't like being right about."

"He's going to come after me, isn't he?" Chloe fiddled with the wooden spoon.

"Let's hope not. And let's not speak of that anymore. I have news."

Chloe's head snapped up to her. Her cheeks were rosy, a dreamy look on her face.

"What is it?"

Evie, still beaming, said, "I'm pregnant."

She wanted to be shocked about that but she wasn't. Her sister practically beamed when she talked about Callum. It was clear Evie was happy and madly in love with her laird.

There was a small pang of jealousy that went through her. She wanted to have that kind of happiness with someone—she thought that someone was Bruce—and now she wasn't so sure. She wanted to fall madly in love, too.

She shoved aside the jealousy as she grinned. "I knew it."

"Oh, sure. How did you know?

Chloe rolled her eyes. "Sis, you're glowing."

"Oh. Well…" She cast her eyes downward and blushed. "Maybe I am."

"You are," she insisted. "How am I supposed to throw you a baby shower in the fourteenth century?"

Evie giggled. "You don't."

Then something else occurred to her. "What about medical care? This is practically the dark ages."

"There's a midwife," Evie said, as though it were the most normal thing in the world. "It's not like I have any other choice."

"I know, but I worry."

"You always did worry about me, but you don't have to."

"Yes, I do. I will always worry about you because you worked yourself to the bone putting me through college. I wish there was some way to repay you for that." She fiddled with a torn piece of the bread bowl.

"You being here is all the payment I need. Come on. Let's get you to bed. You look exhausted."

She pushed up from the table and stood, her chair raking back. Chloe did the same. Together, they left the great hall and headed up the stairs. She still got a bit turned around in the keep, but she was starting to get the hang of the place. The bedchambers for the family were in the east tower on the second floor. The west tower hosted the tapestry room.

At her door, they bid each other good night. Chloe pushed inside her room and found all the candles blazing. Someone had set a fire in the hearth for her, warming the room. She was glad because she certainly didn't know how to do that. She kicked off her shoes and stripped down to her shift, falling into the covers. She was too tired and drowsy to change.

The last thought she had was how she was going to get that stone back from Malcolm without him knowing.

THE WOMAN HAD darted from his room as if her skirts were on fire. No lass had ever been so quick to get away from him, especially after sharing a kiss such as that. He growled and fought the urge to kick the table with the food, pitcher, and tankard on it.

"I don't like kissing men with beards," he repeated, his voice high as he tried to mimic her. "Well, lass, ye sure have a funny way of showing it."

He was certain she'd liked it. He was *more than certain* he'd liked it. In fact, he wanted to do it again. As she had stood there, looking up at him with those big green eyes, he had a hard time resisting her. And her mouth...her perfect heart-shaped mouth seemed to beckon him.

He blew out a heated breath as he turned and kicked out his foot. The toe of his boot struck the leg of the chair and it toppled over with a muffled thud against the thick carpet.

The lass was infuriating.

He glanced at the rumpled bed where she had slept away most of the day.

When she had passed out in his arms once again—she seemed to do that a lot—the only place he could think to take her was his bedchamber. When he had stomped through the great hall, no one was about. Not even Jamie who tended to lurk about looking for trouble, drinking ale, and pestering Roslyn for more oatcakes.

He'd kicked the door shut with the heel of his boot and placed her on the bed. Her head had lolled to one side as she slept, her face in beautiful repose. She had long lashes that curled upward and the most perfect, smooth ivory skin. He had resisted touching her face.

He had left her for only a moment to collect clean bandages and a dram of whiskey. She'd never made a move as he unwrapped her hand and revealed the shallow cut along the burned image of the stone in her palm. The slice had been red and angry with the first sign of streaks pulsing outward from it. Perhaps she had used a dirty knife when she cut her hand, but why she would cut her hand in the first place, he didn't know.

Using the dram of whiskey, he had dribbled it over the cut. He'd paused to see if she had any reaction but she didn't. Then he'd dabbed the blood with a clean bandage until it had finally stopped bleeding and rewrapped it, tying it loosely. He'd placed her hand on her chest, pulled the covers over her fully clothed body, and stepped away.

Only when he had realized the hour was late did he leave to find food. He had sweet-talked Roslyn into giving him a tray for the lass. When he'd returned, she was sitting up in the bed, looking confused.

There was something about her rumpled look, the way her tangled, messy hair framed her face, and the way she blinked her big, green owlish eyes that had sent him over the edge. In that one moment, he knew had to find a way to have her.

He did not regret kissing her. Not one bit.

Now, he stood in the center of his bedchamber peering at the empty bed after her sudden departure. What was he going to do about her now? He simply could not allow her to fling those words at him and then leave. He was convinced she enjoyed the kiss, too.

And he was going to prove it.

But how?

Then he found his answer.

She had left the keystone on the table beside the bed. When she passed out, he had pocketed it to keep it safe. After he'd bandaged her hand, he had placed it on the table for her. He didn't want her to think he intended to keep it from her. She was the one with the power, after all, not him.

He ran his hand over his beard, his skin whispering against the coarse hair.

Perhaps the lassie was on to something. The hair on his chin had become thick and unruly over the last few months. He hadn't properly groomed himself like he should have and his beard was getting a bit out of hand. After all, he didn't want to look as though he didn't care.

He made the decision. He would shave it off and in the morn, he'd find the bonnie lass and return the keystone to her.

And perhaps, if he were lucky, he'd get to kiss her again.

CHAPTER EIGHTEEN

At the first sign of dawn, Chloe bounced from the bed, shoving away the blankets. She regretted leaving a mess of clothes in her wake when she readied for bed. It took her way too much time to gather everything together and dress herself.

It wasn't easy, either. She was used to Evie helping her. But this morning, she didn't want to wait around for her sister to show up and help her.

She pulled the overdress on over her head and fumbled with the laces, finally tying them with her arms at awkward angles. She stuck her feet in her shoes and hurried toward the door.

She cracked it open to peer out into the hallway. Everything was still and silent.

Good. Then everyone was still asleep.

Her heart throbbed against her ribcage as she pulled the door closed with a soft snick. She stood there a long moment, her back against the aged wood, as she took a deep breath to gather her courage.

This was either going to be the best idea she ever had or the worst.

She hoped for the best.

Creeping down the hall, her slippers silent on the stone flooring, she made her way to the stairway. She recalled Malcolm's room was around a corner. At the end of the hallway, she turned left. With her hands clenched into fists at her sides, and her cut hand throbbing, she paused as she peered down the corridor.

There were several closed doors ahead of her. Which one was Malcolm's room? She didn't want to guess wrong and enter someone else's room. Indecision flashed through her. This was a bad idea. She turned to head back to her own room when she heard the scrape of a door opening.

She halted and pressed her back against the cool stone wall as she waited, holding her beath, to see who it was. A moment later, the youngest brother, Jamie, exited his room. He stomped down the hall, his boots echoing around him, and then stopped short when he saw her. His brows lifted in mild surprise and he grinned at her.

"Och, ye must be looking for my brother, aye?"

She chewed the inside of her lower lip, trying to decide how to respond. If she said yes, then what would Jamie think? If she said no, would he think she was lying? Thankfully, she didn't have to respond.

"His room is the third door." He thumbed over his shoulder, then gave her a wink and continued strolling on his merry way.

Chloe waited until he was out of sight. "This is stupid," she muttered under her breath.

Her hands shook as a mixture of anxiety and hope balled in the pit of her stomach. Anxiety for what she was about to do. Hope that the keystone would still be there on the bedside table. Without letting herself think, she took a step. And another. And another.

"This is so stupid," she whispered.

Yet, she continued on to that third door. When she arrived, she paused outside it, staring at the solid wood and the iron hinges. She wasn't going to knock to announce her arrival. She was going to enter and hope he wasn't there. If he wasn't, she'd snatch the keystone and scurry out. If he was…well, she wasn't sure what she was going to do.

After taking another cleansing breath—with all these deep breaths, she should be calm by now—she placed her hand on the solid wood in the middle of the door and gave a little push. When it opened a crack, she halted. Before she lost her nerve, she pushed it enough to slip inside. The hinges belched a creak.

She swore under her breath as she gently pushed the door closed.

The lump in the bed was unmistakable. He shifted slightly. She dared not move or breathe. With every part of her shaking, she waited for several rapid heartbeats until she heard the deep, heavy breathing of his sleep.

Her mouth had gone dry. She couldn't lose her nerve now.

She took a step toward the bed, keeping an eye on him as she advanced to the bedside table. The keystone was where she had left it, inches from his head. Now was her chance to swipe the stone and get out before he awoke.

Her gaze landed on it as she reached out a hand for it.

Strong arms wrapped around her waist and pulled her away. She yelped surprise as she landed on her back on the feather mattress. His big body pressed against hers, pinning her there. Heat radiated outward from him and she realized, with some trepidation and a hint of excitement, he was bare chested. She looked up into a face that was familiar and not.

That mischievous glint sparkled in his sea-green eyes as he gazed down at her, his lips curving into a lazy, sensuous grin. But it wasn't the smile that threw her—it was the smoothness of his face. Clean-shaven. Her fingers itched with the urge to reach out and touch his skin, to feel the unfamiliar softness under her fingertips.

"Well, lass, care to tell me what yer doing here?"

"I—"

Words froze in her throat. She had no idea what excuse to give him. Instead, she stared at him, utterly dumbstruck.

God, he was gorgeous. All sharp lines and rugged angles in his weathered face. High cheekbones swept upward, his square chin strong and unyielding. But it was his eyes…those eyes. The moment they locked with hers, it felt like being pulled into a vast ocean with no life preserver. She was drowning, and he didn't even know it.

"You shaved."

They were the only words that managed to come out. His features softened. The roguish mirth melting into a deep desire that pierced her resistance.

"Aye."

"Why?"

He lifted a dark brow. "Do ye not know?"

A hot tingling took up residence in the pit of her stomach. An intense fiery sensation flared through her in such an overwhelming way, she wasn't sure how to handle it. Her heart jolted. Her pulse pounded. Her senses vibrated. She was certain, since he was against her, he was aware of every pulse, every beat, every breath shuddering out of her.

She was also certain she felt his heart beating a quick cadence against hers.

"You did that for me?" Her voice was weak as she asked.

That sexy grin returned. A smoldering flame sparked deep in the ocean of his eyes. She should be alarmed. She should push him away. She should demand he release her.

But she didn't. She couldn't. She didn't have the strength.

He radiated a vitality and a dizzying desire she was unable to resist.

Chloe lifted her good hand to his face. Her fingertips grazed his smooth cheek. That did not assuage the burning craving. If anything, it fueled the fire even more. When her fingers landed on his face, he closed his eyes and turned into her hand. He planted a soft kiss in her palm.

As soon as his lips brushed her hand, there was a maddening eruption of need pounding through her, fanning the flames of her desire. It wrapped around her, cocooning her and making her body ache for his touch. A curious swooping pulled at her innards.

She flattened her palm against his cheek, her hand sliding

along the smooth edge of his jaw, tracing the outline of his strength to the indention of his chin. Her body shuddered against his. A little mewl escaped her. She was unable to stop the sound even if she had wanted. The spark had ignited. The embers sizzled.

Now, what was she going to do about it?

She had two choices—nothing or… something. And that something called to her, stirring a curiosity she couldn't ignore. The thought of wanting someone so fully, so intensely, sent a thrill through her. It tugged at her, daring her to give in.

Thinking of releasing her inhibitions sent a molten wave of hunger moving through her. In all her years, she had never allowed it to overtake her. But what if? What if she did with Malcolm?

"God's teeth, woman."

He practically growled the words. Before she had a chance to respond, he lowered his head. The moment his lips met hers, everything inside her unraveled. The fiery chasm opened, consuming her. She was lost to him. Completely and utterly lost to him.

His kiss was gentle at first, but she wanted more. Needed more. She slid her hand through the length of his hair, letting her fingers tangle in the length. Her back arched toward him in a desperate attempt to get closer to him. The rasp of material between them chafed her. She wanted to claw away her dress to bare herself to him. To let him touch her.

He rumbled a response, his chest vibrating against her, his mouth still plundering hers. Finally, she managed to wrap her arms around him, her hands landing on his smooth back, making their way down the length. At his waist, she paused and realized with some surprise, he was naked.

A warm chuckle escaped him. He lifted his head to gaze down at her.

"Och, lass, ye tempt me."

In his throat, she saw the rapid beat of his pulse. It was an indication he wanted her as much as she wanted him.

"Well, you know what they say about temptation, don't you?"

He looked intrigued. "And what is that?"

"The only way to get rid of it is to yield to it."

For once, the Oscar Wilde quote served her well. Thinking it was one thing. Saying it aloud was another and yet, she found she was unable to stop the words from bubbling through her. He stilled against her as indecision flashed across his face. He, like her, was trying to decide if they moved forward.

After all, he was already naked.

Though his lower half was still under the blankets, she was aware of his arousal pressing against her thigh.

That slow, lazy, sexy grin reappeared on his mouth, now damp from kissing her. When he made no move, she took matters into her own hands.

Feeling bold, she lifted her head to nuzzle his neck. His skin was warm and soft with the hint of the lilac soap he used to shave. She liked the way he felt next to her. She liked the way he smelled. She liked he shaved his beard *for her*. It was endearing.

In a brazen moment, without thinking, she tasted him. Then she raked her teeth across his skin and nipped. Just enough to get his attention.

She got his attention.

The rumble through his chest was all the response she needed.

His hand fumbled with her skirt, trying to pull it up, but her legs were tangled underneath him. He'd pinned her to the bed. Now, she wanted to wiggle free. She wanted to feel his hot hands on her, touching her, caressing her. She wanted to know what it was like to part her legs and let him slide into her.

In a desperate attempt to move things along at a quicker pace, she nudged his hand away and fisted her skirt, trying to pull it upward. Since she was laying on it, the material was stuck underneath her. She huffed her frustration, which made him chuckle.

He slid his arms around her and rolled. She yipped her surprise as he settled her on top of him. She braced her hands on his strong, muscled chest with that sprinkling of hair. He felt good under her hands, under her body. Glancing down, she saw the blankets were bunched around his waist, but even so, she got a hint of what was underneath. Narrow hips tapered downward, making her imagination run away with her.

Malcolm fisted her skirt in his hands, pushing away the material to reveal her expanse of thigh.

"I cannae say I expected to have ye in my bed so early this morn," he said with a lopsided grin.

"It wasn't the plan."

She tried to remain calm and keep her voice steady as his hands brushed across the tops of her legs. She was acutely aware of his arousal now as it pressed against the apex of her thighs. For the moment, she regretted continuing to wear her modern lingerie. Evie told her she had ditched them several weeks ago when she decided to stay in the past. But Chloe was unable to part with them yet.

"And what was yer plan when ye snuck into my room?"

He continued to caress her with gentle touches. Her heart flipped as her eyes fluttered closed. Did he have any idea what he was doing to her? Yes, he probably did and that's why he continued to do it.

"The keystone," she said, her voice a breathy whisper.

What the devil was wrong with her? She wasn't the type of girl to get lost in her own emotions. She was cool, controlled, confident. She never let herself get so carried away. But there was something about the way he touched her, the way his deep, sexy voice rumbled through his chest under her hands, and the way he kissed her. Oh, yes, definitely the way he kissed her.

His hands moved under her skirt to cup her bottom and then he paused.

"What's this?"

Her eyes flew open as she gazed down at him, realizing he wouldn't understand why she had cloth covering her bottom. He looked genuinely intrigued.

"It's, um…" She bit her lip, unsure how to explain. "Maybe I'll show you."

A dark brow lifted, amusement flickering over his features.

As much as she hated to, she pushed off him and stepped off the bed. First, she kicked off her shoes. He sat up on an elbow and watched as she pulled off the wool overgown and dropped it to the floor. Then the shift, revealing her boring taupe colored bra and panties. She was never one for satin and lace, after all, because she was a practical girl.

He eyed her with some curiosity before he pushed to the side of the bed, the blankets still bunched around his waist, which gave her some relief. She wasn't sure she was ready to see him in all his naked glory.

"What are ye wearing?" He hesitated, as if he wanted to reach for her but was unsure.

She stepped closer, the chill in the room skittering up her exposed arms and legs, leaving gooseflesh in its wake.

"In my time, this is what ladies wear." She motioned up and down her body.

His appreciative gaze flickered over her cloth-covered breasts then downward, pausing for a long moment before lifting back up to her face. Another step closer and she was inches from him. His body heat was so intense, it radiated from him, warming her.

Shouldn't she feel timid and shy? That was how she always was when she was about to be intimate with someone new. She had allowed Bruce to take the lead, to undress her, to set the pace of their lovemaking.

But now, as she stood before Malcolm, she wanted him to see her. She reached behind her and unclasped her bra, letting the material slide down her arms. She dropped it on the floor at the edge of the bed.

He said nothing as he looked at her, not moving, an unreadable expression on his face.

"Should I go then?" She started to reach for her discarded bra.

He reached for her, taking hold of her wrist. "Dinnae think of leaving me now."

"You wish me to stay then?"

Her words were surprising. She didn't recognize this wanton woman she had become.

He tugged her closer, his other hand sliding around her waist. His heated breath breezed over the skin between her breasts.

"Och, aye. I wish ye to stay for as long as ye want."

His mouth landed on one dusty peak. She sucked in a breath, her body rigid as his mouth did wonderful, lovely things to her. Chloe slid her arms around him, her hands tangling in the length of his hair. She arched her back into his tender kisses, enjoying every moment.

When she thought she might unravel at the seams, a knock sounded on the chamber door.

He released her, but she held him in place.

"Don't stop. Maybe they'll go away," she whispered.

But another knock sounded on the door. He growled, deep and low in his throat, and nudged her to the side. As he stood, and the blankets fell away from his hips, it took every ounce of strength to keep her eyes on his face.

"We're not finished yet." He cocked a grin, then kissed her cheek. He gave a nod to the bed. "Wait for me, aye?"

Then he stomped to the door, naked as the day he was born, and jerked it open and barked, "What?"

She was grateful he managed to shield her from view as she quickly climbed into the bed and pulled the blankets to her chin. As he barked at whoever was on the other side, she quickly shimmied out of her panties and tossed them aside. Whatever was happening between them, she didn't want it to end. Not yet. She wanted him.

It was all so unlike her.

He shut the door with a snap and then padded back to the bed, sliding in between the sheets next to her.

"Now," he said, in a low purr, "where were we?"

CHAPTER NINETEEN

H E WASN'T SURE why she had decided to sneak into his room that morning after dawn, but he was glad she did. When he heard the door open and her light footsteps, he feigned sleep to see what she would do next. He assumed she was there to take back the keystone. He had intended to return it to her when he roused that morning. But then, she appeared at his bedside as though she had stepped out of his dreams.

After that kiss, he had dreamed of her most of the night. Wanting her was all he'd thought about.

When she reached for the keystone, he could not resist snatching her into his arms and pushing her down onto the bed. He expected her to object, to demand he let her go.

But she didn't.

Instead, she looked up at him with those big, emerald eyes full of wonder and surprise. She was in awe of the fact he had shaved his beard for her. And when she touched his freshly shaved face, he lost his head.

He hadn't intended to bed her. At least, not yet. But there she was within his reach, pliant in his arms. Willing. Receptive. And wanting.

He wanted her, too.

He wanted her from the moment she had fallen through the portal and he saved her from the brutal attack of the man who had fallen through with her. The moment he had scooped her into his arms and took her from the village. The moment he had held her against his chest as they rode to the Sinclair keep.

He had never expected her to be in his bed now. She was standoffish and had seemed uninterested. But when she had told him she didn't like kissing men with beards, he was determined to make her like kissing him, period.

Apparently, his smooth cheeks and chin won her over.

"Who was at the door?" she asked.

"It doensa matter."

He reached for her and realized with some surprise, she had shed the material that covered her sex. She scooted closer to him, tucking her head under his chin and doing that thing she did before where she nuzzled his neck.

"You're nice and warm."

Curses, he should have started the fire when he was still out of the bed. But now, with her moving against him, he was reluctant to get up to do that. Especially when her hand trailed up his chest, and she then gave him a gentle shove.

He fell to his back. Delight flickered through him when she moved back into the position she was in before they were interrupted. She settled her hips over his, his hardened length between them.

"I think this is where we were before we were interrupted." She gave him a lazy grin.

Did she know what she was doing to him?

She lifted her hips and then positioned herself over him. His hands dug into her hips, holding her steady before she moved again. Question flickered through her eyes as she glanced down at him.

"Did I do something wrong?"

"Och, nay, lass, but are ye sure about this?"

She dragged her lower lip through her teeth. "Yes. Am I moving too fast for you?" A twinkle of mirth appeared in her eyes.

He chuckled.

"I'll take that as a no."

She slid her body down onto him. He pushed inside her, filling her up. A gasp escaped her as she sat straight, her back arched. She tipped her head back, the ends of her long auburn hair brushing his legs.

The moment their bodies connected, the moment he was with her, was the moment he knew he was lost to her forever.

His hands landed on her hips but he allowed her to set the pace. Their bodies fell into a perfect rhythm, as though they were made for each other. As though they were meant to be together. Mayhap they were. Mayhap the prophecy pushed them together, intertwining their destinies as it did with Evie and Callum.

Chloe leaned forward then, placing her hands on his chest as she continued to move against him. Her eyes were closed, her face flushed, her expression one of unadulterated pleasure. Her breasts brushed his chest, heightening every awareness in him, making his senses ignite with blistering fire. She was everything he imagined and more.

She cried out with pleasure as she came against him. He was moments away from climax but managed to maintain control. When her body slowed against him, he sat up, gathered her to him and flipped her to her back, pulling out at the same time as his own climax came.

Malcolm settled next to her, holding her close. She rested her head on his chest, her skin dewy and flushed. Silence stretched between them. The room was still, quiet, and he again regretted not building the fire to warm the chamber.

"What happens now?" she asked, sounding timid.

He wanted to stay there forever, to hold her close to him. To do it all over again and then when night came, keep her close as she slept. But he knew that was not possible.

Dougal had arrived at the door with a message telling him Callum was looking for him. But he was too far gone with thoughts of Chloe. He refused to leave her, naked and ready in his bed. She had come to him. He was not going to let that opportunity pass him by.

He took in a deep breath, expelled it.

"Malcolm?"

"Aye, lass, I have duties to tend."

She propped her chin on her hand and looked up at him, those big green eyes full of question and longing. "And I've kept you from them? Someone was at the door to fetch you. Am I right?"

"Aye."

She rolled away from him, the simple movement leaving him feeling alone, cold, and mourning her absence. Before he could reach for her, to stop her, to pull her back down into his arms, she was out of the bed, gathering her clothing.

"I should go. Evie is probably looking for me."

He sat up on one elbow, watching her as she started to dress. "Ye dinnae have to leave."

"Yes, I do."

"Chloe."

At the sound of her name, she stopped gathering her clothes to look at him. Her eyes were wide with question as she held her clothes to her chest, covering her best assets.

"I mean it. Ye dinnae have to leave if ye dinnae want to."

"You mean stay here?" She pointed to the floor to indicate staying in his bed chamber.

"Aye."

The thought of her being here when he returned warmed him and stirred deep desire within.

"Wait for me here," he added.

Color rose in her cheeks as she cast her eyes down. "I don't know."

He moved off the bed, reaching for her, taking her bandaged hand in his. "Stay. Wait for me."

When she still refused to look at him, he took her chin in his other hand and tipped her head back. Their eyes met and that sensuous fire he felt earlier sparked once again between them. God's teeth, he didn't want to admit he was falling in love with her, but he was falling in love with her.

"I—"

"I'll be back when I can," he assured.

"And then what?" she demanded, sounding agitated. "I don't belong here, Malcolm. This isn't my world, my time. Evie doesn't belong here, either, but I suppose she'll never leave now that she's pregnant."

He froze as he stared down at her, the shock rolling through him. "The lass is with child?"

Her eyes flew wide. "Oh, crap, you didn't know?"

"Nay," he said slowly.

He was going to be an uncle. The thought sent a tingling of joy skipping through him.

Chloe tried to tug out of his grasp, but he held firm. "Let me go, Malcolm."

He pulled her to him, clutching her in his arms. She struggled only a bit as the clothes she held tumbled to the floor. Her breasts pressed against his bare chest. It was the best feeling in the world. He pushed her auburn hair off her shoulder, holding her close. She stopped struggling, her body going limp as she allowed him to hold her.

"What are ye afraid of, lass?"

"Everything," she whispered. "Being here. You. That cursed keystone." Her breath hitched as a sob clotted her throat. "Bruce."

He squeezed her. "I willna let him hurt ye. Ye have my word on that. As for the keystone…well, I gather there is naught to be done about that."

She tilted her head back to look up at him. "And what about you?"

He softened at that, holding her tight. "I willna hurt ye, either. Ye have my word on that."

Chloe placed her head on his chest again, wrapping her arms around him. They stood like that for a long moment, in the peace of the morning, holding each other.

"I don't believe in destinies or prophecies," she muttered. "I believe in facts and choosing your own fate."

"Aye," he said slowly. "I believe that, too. But I've seen things to prove the prophecy is real and all our destinies are tangled together. Yours. Mine. Your sister's. My brother's."

She shivered in his arms. "And Jamie?"

"Aye, Jamie, too." He pushed back, then, holding her at arm's length. "But we dinnae have to think about that now, lass. We never have to speak of it again if you dinnae wish to." He brushed her cheek with the back of his hand. "Will ye stay here and wait for me?"

Indecision flashed through her eyes for a moment. Then she nodded. "Yes. I'll stay."

"Good. Now, as much as I hate to see that bonnie body of yer's covered, we must dress. I have to find my brother. And keep that cursed keystone safe and on yer person."

Chloe glared at it as it rested on the bedside table. "It is a cursed thing. Isn't it?"

Still keeping one arm around his waist, she leaned out and reached for it. The moment she picked up the stone, her body went rigid. She sucked in a sharp breath, her back went ramrod straight. Then her knees gave out and she crumpled. He held on to her as she fell, keeping her from hitting the stone floor.

"Lass? Are ye all right? Can ye hear me?"

But her eyes were closed, her body quaking, and she definitely did not hear him.

THE VISION STARTED the moment she touched the keystone. It was as if the world fell away and she was there, standing at the base of the craggy hill with the icy wind ripping through her hair. The scene was familiar to her—she'd seen it in the enchanted tapestry. But this one was different. There was no lightning flashing, no battle raging, no Triple Goddess or keystone in the center of it all. Chloe was seeing the events through someone else's eyes—not her own.

Alexander MacLeod assembled all his men on the field at the base of the crag. He sat atop his destrier and peered across the vast field at the man who had betrayed him. He should have known forging a truce—fragile that it was—with Brodie MacDonald was a mistake. But Alexander felt as though he had no choice. It was the only way to protect their lands from the northern invaders.

When he discovered—by way of Padrig Sinclair—the man secretly plotted against him, he had to act. MacDonald was driven by greed and great ambition and intended to destroy all the northern clan leaders to take control of their lands.

His land. His and Padrig's land.

He would never stand for this. Nor would Padrig.

Across the field, their enemy outnumbered the Sinclairs and the MacLeods three to one. He and Padrig did not expect to win this battle, but they had to try. Each refused to allow their enemy to take what was theirs by birthright.

Behind them, their army was at the ready. Despite the insurmountable odds, they stood their ground with their round shields and their spears or swords in hand. Pride spread through Alexander's chest, knowing his men had come to fight, determined to keep their own lands out of the hands of the MacDonalds.

At the head of the opposing army, Brodie held aloft his great axe at the ready, and he nudged his destrier into a trot toward the middle of the field. The blade appeared to be glowing, which did nothing to temper the fear skipping through Alexander. He had to set aside that fear. Alexander and Padrig exchanged a glance.

"Mayhap he wishes to negotiate," Padrig said.

"I dinnae believe he came all this way with his army to negotiate, my friend. However, there is only one way to find out."

The two of them rode to the middle of the field to meet him and halted there. Alexander stared at the square face of Brodie MacDonald. His dark, beady eyes stared back. He continued to hold aloft that glowing great axe with a look of smug defiance.

Silence stretched between them, thick and heavy in the air.

"There's no need for a battle," Brodie said. "I am a man of mercy. Get off yer horses and surrender and we can avoid the bloodshed."

"Ye wish us to surrender to ye?" Alexander shook his head. "Ye want it to be that easy, aye? Ye want us to hand over our lands as if we were handing over nothing more than a piece of bread. I willna submit to ye."

"Nor I," Padrig agreed.

Brodie's eyes flickered between the two men, then paused on Padrig. "So, ye've thrown in with the likes of this one, aye? Ye disappoint me, Padrig."

"After ye betrayed me and my clan, after framing me for deaths that werena my fault, after terrorizing my people...aye. I've thrown in with the likes of Alexander MacLeod. A good, decent, honorable man unlike ye. I cannae trust ye, nor will I ever trust ye again."

"Very well, Padrig, if that's yer decision, so be it. Ye are out-marched. Ye have no heavy calvary. How do ye think to defeat me?" He shook his head. "I will destroy ye both. Ye have no chance of beating me or my men." He clutched his great axe tighter, his knuckles leeching of color. "As I said, I am man of mercy. I will give ye both one last chance to leave the field. And if ye dinnae leave, then ye give me no choice."

"Ye are no more a man of mercy than I am a man of the cloth." Alexander drew his claymore. The blade sang with a shing as he unsheathed it. "I willna surrender."

"Nor will I." Padrig also drew his sword.

A glower crossed MacDonald's face as his gaze flickered from one to the other. He turned his destrier and trotted back to his line of men. Alexander cut a glance to Padrig.

"I dinnae think he'd back down," Alexander said.

"Nor I," he agreed. "If he wins, then he controls all the lands on the northern part of the isle. Including yer own keep."

Alexander's jaw tightened as he stared down at the man on the other end of the field with the great axe. He still held it aloft as it continued to glow.

"He willna win," Alexander said, sounding sure of himself. "We cannae allow him to win."

There was a spark of determination in his wild, blue eyes.

As swiftly as the vision began, it ended. It faded from her mind. When she came back to herself, she felt the keystone biting into her palm, her fingers clutched tight around it. Malcolm cradled her against his chest, holding her tightly. Dimly, she realized she was in his lap as he sat on the floor holding her.

"Lass?"

She blinked up at him, her head pounding with a raging headache. "What happened?"

"I dinnae ken. Yer legs gave out."

"And you caught me again." The words came out on a breath. She seemed to end up in his arms a lot. Not that she minded.

"I'll always catch ye when ye fall. What happened?"

Her limbs ached. She had no energy to push out of his arms, nor did she want to. She remained where she was, gazing up at him. His face had a worried expression, his eyes glinting with a bit of anxiety.

"When I picked up the keystone, I had a…a vision."

"Like before?"

"Yes. But different. This time, I was looking through some-one else's eyes. Someone named Alexander."

His eyes widened a bit. "MacLeod?"

"Yes."

"My ancestor." He said with a sort of reverence she had never heard before. "What was this vision?"

"There were two other men. One named Padrig. One named Brodie. The man named Brodie had a great axe. It was—" She halted, unsure of her next words because it sounded crazy to her own ears. "The great axe was glowing."

"Is this the same great axe in the tapestry?"

"I think so."

He made a low noise deep in his throat. "That is Brodie MacDonald. Our clans have been sworn enemies for hundreds of years."

"Alexander said something about being betrayed. I didn't

understand, but I had the sense the feeling of betrayal was strong."

It was more than that, though. Chloe downplayed it because she didn't want to alarm him to how much she *felt* while being in that vision. She sensed the sting of perfidy running deep within Alexandar when Brodie broke their truce—a truce to keep their lands safe from the northern invaders. She assumed he referred to the Vikings who had raided the shores of England and Scotland for hundreds of years.

"Aye, there was that. The MacDonald turned the Sinclairs against us. Padrig was the clan leader of the Sinclairs, as Alexander was the clan leader of the MacLeods. That was over five hundred years ago, though."

Confusion skipped through her. How could she have seen something from so long ago? Why? What did it mean?

"Was there a battle?" she asked.

"Och, aye. A bloody one at that. And if what yer telling me is true, then this battle is the one that happened around the same time as the Shattering."

That got her attention. She managed to sit up, pushing out of his arms and blinking owlish eyes at him.

"The same Shattering that's depicted in the tapestries?"

"Aye, the verra one."

She pressed cold, shaking fingertips to her lips. She was convinced the vision meant something. She had to find Evie and tell her everything. Maybe she would have answers as to why she had had the vision. Unlikely, but she needed her sister.

Flushing hot, she realized she was still naked. And so was he.

Quickly, she gathered up her clothes and started to dress. She placed the keystone on the edge of the bed to pull her shift on over her head, keeping an eye on the offending stone the entire time.

"I've kept you long enough from your duties. I'm sorry about that."

"I'm not."

She glanced at him to see a smirk on his face. He had already donned his tunic. He tugged on his plaid, securing it around his waist, and then pulled the remaining material up and over his shoulder.

"If yer hungry, see Roslyn in the kitchen." He kissed her cheek. "I hope yer here when I return."

"I'd like to be."

With one last longing look, he left her alone in the chamber. She glanced down at her hand with the bandage. It no longer tingled or seemed to bother her. She unwound the gauzy material to check the wound.

There was nothing left of the cut except a pink silvery line where it had healed.

CHAPTER TWENTY

B RUCE MACDONALD SAT at the great hall table with a tankard of ale in his hand listening to the arguments of the men around him. One of them was his ancestor, Rory MacDonald, known as Rory the Fierce. They were arguing about how to best their archenemy and get their hands on the pieces of the keystone. They'd been searching for it for over five hundred years, ever since that fateful night when the Triple Goddess destroyed it, then hid it across the far reaches of Scotland, only to be found when it was time for the Final Convergence.

That time was nearly upon them.

There was still one piece missing from the keystone. One vital piece that, when the stone finally came together, would allow the bearer to become powerful and control all of Time.

Unfortunately, Bruce was unable to secure the pieces in his own time and now he was stuck in the past with his warmongering clan.

He'd walked for miles over the course of several days. He had had no food and only found water from nearby streams. He had spent the nights sleeping on the ground or in a farmer's barn, making sure to be gone at the first light of day. When he had arrived at the keep, he was bone weary, dirty, hungry, and not in the best of moods.

But heading to MacDonald's stronghold was the only idea he had had after landing in the fourteenth century. They took him in, albeit reluctantly.

It had taken some convincing that he was from the future. When he told them of the Night of Shadows and the Shattering, they started to believe. When he told them he knew what power the ancient great axe held, they were convinced. When he told them he knew where to find two of the pieces of the keystone, they allowed him to live. Rory's son, Rufus, was the one who accepted him fully, proclaiming the Descendance Prophecy had finally come to fruition. It stated a man from the future, a descendent, would arrive to help them in their quest to find and acquire all three pieces of the ancient keystone.

These medieval warriors believed Bruce was the one.

He accepted that because he wanted revenge on the man who stood between him and Chloe. Most of all, he wanted that keystone. He understood the power it held, even if it wasn't fully intact. He suspected Chloe's sister was also here in the past with her piece. He also suspected Chloe was hiding in Dundale Castle with the MacLeod brothers and her sister.

If he got his hands on the two pieces, he could put them together. Granted, the magic within the stone wouldn't work fully without the third piece, but at least his ancestors would see the true beginning of its power.

"We cannae march upon Dundale. MacLeod will be expecting that," one of the men shouted.

"Our forces are weakened. We havna the numbers we did," another added.

"Aye, we dinnae, but we have something else. We have him." Rory pointed to Bruce.

It was unsettling, seeing the piercing gaze of the man who would murder innocents in their beds and raze villages.

All turned to him, staring at him and waiting for him to say something. While he listened to the men argue over who was going to do what and when, he formulated a plan while drinking their watered-down ale. He was remembering his history. He had a passing interest in great tales of medieval kings and knew a thing or two about them.

"Och, how can he help us?" one of his men asked.

Bruce may not be a military man or a strategist, but he could fake it. "I have an idea. And I think it will work."

When he paused too long, Rory barked, "Out with it then."

"You can use that great axe of yours to split the fabric of Time. Then we march the army through the portal to Dundale," he began.

Rory huffed. "We cannae attack that castle. MacLeod has it well-fortified."

"We aren't going to attack," Bruce said, his voice calm and sure. "We're going to be a distraction. You only need half your army for that."

The laird's gaze narrowed. "Aye? Go on."

"Surely you have mercenaries you can hire for a fair sum," Bruce said, clutching his tankard tighter. Gambling. He was gambling with his life and others.

"Aye," he agreed slowly. "And?"

"Dundale sits on a loch. The back of the castle faces that loch. Send the mercenaries to swim through the loch, then use siege ladders or ropes or whatever means you have necessary to scale the castle walls. With the men busy at the front trying to defend their walls, it is a prime opportunity to find and take the women," Bruce said. Then, he added, "And the pieces of the keystone you seek."

"How do ye ken it will work?" His eyes narrowed with suspicion.

"I don't. You'll have to trust me." And, he prayed it *would* work.

Silence descended on the great hall as they all gaped at him, likely thinking he was some sort of mastermind. He hoped they accepted that ruse because he didn't want to lose his head over something that might not work.

Finally, Rory nodded. "Rufus, hire the mercenaries. Pay them whatever they want."

"Aye, Da. It will be done."

As Bruce sipped his watered-down ale, the men went back to planning their ruse. All he had to do was keep his head on his shoulders and in the good graces of these barbarians. When they had captured Evie and Chloe and the two pieces of the keystone, then he'd return to the future. Then he'd be the powerful one.

CHAPTER TWENTY-ONE

MALCOLM MADE HIS way out of the keep and into the yard where Callum was overseeing the fortification of the outer walls. He caught sight of Malcolm and waved him over.

"There ye are. I sent for ye over an hour ago." Agitation creased his brother's face. But that was quickly replaced by surprise. "Ye shaved?"

Malcolm pressed his lips together. "Aye, but now is no the time to discuss that."

"Where were ye?" Callum asked.

"I was indisposed at the time."

Callum said nothing. Merely raised a dark brow as if he understood what being indisposed meant.

"Will ye speak with me in private? I have news," Malcolm said.

"Aye. Walk with me. I was about to ride out to check on the harvest." He motioned toward the stables.

"That can wait. This cannae."

Intrigued, Callum gave him his full attention. "Aye? What's so urgent, then, brother?"

"The lass, Chloe…she has developed powers like yer wife." He dropped his voice low to ensure Callum was the only one who heard.

"From the keystone?" he asked.

"Aye. The keystone. Did ye ken yer wife sliced her hand open to see if Chloe would have the same power as she?"

"Nay, I dinnae ken that."

They arrived at the stables, then, where several stable hands were mucking stalls. Callum headed to his horse but paused outside the stall. The horse gave him a hello nudge and he patted his nose. Malcolm followed, pausing there with him.

"Did it work?" Callum asked.

"It seems it did. She can see into the past, Callum. She saw the beginning of the battle the night before the Shattering," Malcolm said.

"How?"

"I cannae say, but when she reached for the keystone, she went rigid. If I hadna caught her, she would have hit the floor. It was a peculiar thing to watch, too. Her body was stiff. Her eyes were rolled back into her head. She turned cold, her lips turning blue. She was only that way a few moments before she finally came awake and told me about Alexander MacLeod and Padrig Sinclair." He paused there to let that sink in.

Concern creased Callum's face. "The battle before the Shattering. That means Brodie MacDonald was there, too."

"Aye with his great axe. A great axe, she said, that glowed."

Callum stared at him in stony, shocked silence. "That wasna in the tapestry images."

"No, it wasna. But what if it is now?"

There was only one way to find out. They both knew it. They had to check the tapestry room to see if it was true.

The tapestries were strange, enchanted things. It seemed their morphing images changed at will. Perhaps it was a way for the Triple Goddess to send them messages about what they needed to know. It showed the past, the present, even the future. There were still a few that appeared to be nothing more than woven textiles, but would they remain that way? It was hard to say. One had filled in. One with Chloe and the man she called Bruce.

Malcolm was aware Bruce was still out there. Plotting his revenge, no doubt. It was only a matter of time before he would come for Chloe. He understood, as Callum did, the calamity of the situation. That the MacDonalds wanted the pieces of the keystone with a fiery desperation. But what would they do to get it? That was the question.

"We should look at the tapestries," Malcolm said when Callum remained quiet.

A strange look passed over his brother's face when he said it. As though Callum wasn't interested in the tapestries. Or mayhap he didn't believe in them even when he'd seen them with his own eyes.

"Ye dinnae think we should?" he asked.

"I dinnae ken. The tapestries are a strange thing. They cannae be explained."

"Ye saw them with yer own eyes when Evie arrived. Ye saw the moving pictures. Nay, they cannae be explained. But do they have to be?"

He was aware his brother believed in things that made sense. Logical things. Moving pictures were not logical to him, yet he seemed to have accepted them with Evie's help.

Their da, Hamish, had believed in the prophecy. He'd regaled them with stories of the Shattering, the Night of Shadows, and the Triple Goddess for years. None of them had expected the prophecy to come to fruition. But it had. And they were living it now.

"We should at least check," Malcolm urged. "If the great axe is glowing, then…"

"Then what? Why did we no see the glowing great axe before?" Callum demanded.

"I dinnae ken, brother, but as ye said, they are strange things that cannae be explained. Mayhap only the Triple Goddess can explain them."

He watched Callum intently, who continued to pet the horse's nose absently. Finally, his brother nodded.

"All right, then. Let's go see for ourselves."

CHLOE STUMBLED OUT of Macolm's bedchamber, the keystone secure in her pocket. She needed to find Evie. But where would she be this time of morning? She headed down the hallway, thinking to find her sister in her own bedchamber. It was still early. Maybe she wasn't up yet.

As she rounded the corner, she saw Evie exiting her room. Her face was pale. Chloe hurried to her side.

"Evie, you don't look well. Are you sure you should be up?"

"I have things to do." She sounded weak as she pressed her hand against her stomach.

Chloe understood. "Morning sickness?"

She nodded.

"Let's get you something to eat. Maybe that will help."

Chloe took her by the elbow and led her away from the bed-chamber, down the curved staircase—which was so narrow they had to go single file. At the bottom, they headed across the great hall and into the kitchen, which was a flurry of activity. Roslyn was nowhere in sight.

On one of the counters, there was a stack of oatcakes. Chloe headed for them. No one seemed to notice their presence, so she grabbed the stack and turned back to her sister, handing her one of the cakes.

"Here, try this."

"It should help," Evie said and gave a weak smile. "And some herbal tea."

"I don't think you'll find any herbal tea packets around here." Chloe munched on one of the oatcakes.

Evie grinned. "I'll show you how to make it."

She gave her a nod to follow and headed for the open door at the back of the kitchen. She snatched up a basket on her way out. Chloe followed, curious to see how her sister had discovered how to make herbal tea in the fourteenth century. As they exited into the fragrant garden, Evie handed off her half-eaten oatcake, then knelt in front of what looked like tall weeds.

"How did you learn this?" Chloe asked, watching in fascination as her sister went about clipping the weeds.

"I figured it out myself. When I was desperate for something other than weak ale and watered-down wine." She held up one of the clippings with a bright smile. "Smell."

Chloe did as she was asked and leaned over to sniff. "It smells like mint."

Nodding, she placed the long stem into her basket. She continued around the garden plucking more stems and flowers and placing them into the basket.

"Roslyn grows all her own herbs," Evie said. She placed a few more plants in her basket. "Come on. I'll show you how to make the tea now."

She headed back inside. Chloe trailed after her, her curiosity piqued. Evie placed her basket on the nearby counter. She removed the stems one by one, chopped them or crushed them, and then placed them in the folds of what looked like cheesecloth. Then she placed it in a cup and poured boiling water over it. After a quick stir, she lifted the cup, steam rising from the liquid, and brought it to her.

"Taste it," she said.

Chloe did and was surprised at how much it tasted like herbal tea. "I'm impressed, Eve."

Grinning, she sipped the tea. As she swallowed, she closed her eyes and sighed, as if it had calmed her stomach instantly. "That's what I needed."

"You mean, what the baby needed."

Her eyes flew open. "Shh. Not everyone knows yet."

"Hopefully, Callum does."

She flushed and nodded, took another sip.

And now Malcolm because Chloe had blabbed by accident. She decided to keep that to herself.

"Eve, I need to talk to you about something." She glanced

around the busy kitchen. There were too many ears to overhear what she wanted to tell her.

"That sounds serious. Let's go to my chamber. We'll have some privacy there."

Evie led her out of the kitchen back to the stairs where they headed up. She entered a room that hosted a large four poster bed with curtains, with an oversized chest at the foot of it, a wardrobe, a small dressing table with a mirror, a writing desk. Tapestries—certainly not magical ones—hung along the walls to insulate the room. The hearth was devoid of a fire. Evie took the chair from the dressing table and pulled it close to the writing desk, then motioned for Chloe to sit.

She still held the half-eaten oatcake and handed it to Evie, who took it with a smile.

"Something is weighing on you," Evie said.

"How did you know?"

"We're twins." She flashed a smile and took another bite of the oatcake.

"Yesterday, I left the keystone in Malcolm's bedchamber." Evie gave her a hopeful look as she said it, but she ignored it and continued. "This morning, I decided to retrieve it from him and..."

She sat up straighter, hope creasing her face. "And?"

Chloe didn't want to tell her sister anything about their time together. They weren't teenagers anymore, after all. And besides, what if this thing with Malcolm didn't work out? She had let her emotions overcome her. She had a lot to think about.

Instead, she reached into her pocket and pulled it out. "I got it back. When I touched it, though, I had another vision."

"Of the past?" That got her attention.

"Yes. This time, I was looking through the eyes of one of their ancestors."

She told her about the vision of Alexander, Padrig, and Brodie. Their armies were on the field at the foot of a crag, ready to do battle.

"But the strangest thing of all was the great axe Brodie Mac-Donald held was glowing."

Evie gasped. "What do you mean, glowing?"

"It was glowing the entire time he held it. Malcolm said I saw the battle before the Shattering."

"In the tapestry, the great axe is not glowing," Evie said.

She shrugged. "I know what I saw. It was glowing. Like a pulsing white light."

Evie chewed on her lower lip.

"What does it mean?" Chloe asked.

"I don't know. Maybe it's a message."

"What kind of message? A message from the past?"

"No. A message from the Triple Goddess. You said Bridget spoke to you in your mind. What if she's trying to tell you something more? Something important?"

"Why is the glowing great axe important?"

"Because I think it might be magic."

Chloe scoffed. "Do you believe that?"

"After what I've seen, yes. And you should, too. You're here in the past, after all." Evie frowned, clearly disappointed she didn't have the same feelings.

She shoved up from the chair, placing the keystone back in her pocket and started to pace. "It all seems so unreal."

"It is real, though, Chlo."

She turned to look at her sister, who sat clutching the cup between her hands.

"Do you believe in this prophecy, or are you going along with it?" Chloe demanded.

Evie's eyebrows lifted, disbelief flashing across her face. "Don't you believe it? You've seen the tapestries."

She ignored her question and pressed on. "Do you expect me to believe our lives are intertwined with these medieval Highlanders?"

She nodded emphatically. "Yes."

"I don't believe in fate and destiny," she said.

"I didn't believe in love at first. Until I met Callum," Evie said, her voice soft and unyielding. "I saw what would happen to him if I didn't intervene during that battle. I knew he'd die. Moira helped me see that. Moira gave you a piece of the keystone, just as she will give the final piece to Brianna. What more proof do you need?"

She didn't need proof. It was her own stubbornness that kept her from wanting to believe, to accept the truth in front of her. To accept that she and Malcolm were destined to be together. Did she have feelings for him? She didn't know. All she did know was that she liked being with him, in his bed. She liked that he had asked her to be there when he returned. Part of her wanted to wait for him, in his chamber, in his bed. The other part of her, the rational part, told her it was crazy to continue down that path.

What future did they have together?

She had a future waiting for her in Edinburgh in her own century.

The thump of the cup on the table got her attention. Evie stood and stepped toward her, taking her hands in hers. As she did, she glanced down at her hand and halted. She turned over the palm that was cut and stared down at the faint line that had healed far too quickly. The branding from the keystone was faded, but still there. Evie traced the pink scar.

"Your hand healed."

She nodded. Her sister's warm gaze met hers.

"And you don't think that's a sign?"

"I think it's strange," Chloe said.

Evie squeezed her hands, then. "I can't make you believe in prophesies or destinies. I want you to, of course, but it's up to you to decide."

She released her and headed for the chamber door.

"Where are you going?" Chloe asked.

"To see if the great axe is glowing in the tapestry." She pulled open the door and disappeared into the hallway.

Huffing out a breath, Chloe followed.

CHAPTER TWENTY-TWO

EVIE HURRIED DOWN the hallway and the winding stone stairs, Chloe on her heels. They crossed the great hall and headed to what they were now referring to as the tapestry room. When they rounded the corner, they saw the door already stood open.

Her sister halted and gave a questioning glance back to her. Chloe shrugged but when she heard Malcolm's distinct voice, she knew who was inside.

He and Callum stood in front of the tapestries. Malcolm had his hands propped up on his hips while Callum stood with his feet shoulder width apart and his arms folded over his chest. They were both looking at the tapestry with the battle of the night of the Shattering.

The picture in the cloth depicted Moira and her two sisters standing high atop the crag with lightning around them. Moira held something in her fist, which glowed—the keystone—below them, the encroaching army led by Brodie MacDonald holding aloft his great axe.

It was the same great axe she had seen in the vision.

The same great axe that had glowed.

It was glowing in the tapestry.

Evie sucked in a sharp breath the moment she saw it. The men turned to her, not at all surprised to see her or Chloe there in the room.

"It's true, then," Evie said.

"Aye," Callum said.

Chloe made her way toward the tapestry to get a closer look. She paused next to Malcolm, aware of the heat radiating off his body. Was he always so hot?

"This is what ye saw, lass?" he asked.

She nodded as she stared at the now glowing great axe. "It wasn't doing that before, was it?"

"No," Evie replied. "It wasn't."

"Is it some kind of message?" Chloe asked, something she'd wondered since she first had the vision.

"It could be. Maybe the Triple Goddess is trying to tell us something," Evie replied.

"But what?" Callum asked. "Why show it now and not before?"

"I think it *is* a message," Chloe said. "I think Bridget is trying to tell us something about the great axe." She turned to face the others. "Why else would it be glowing?"

"There's only one, well, three people who know the answer." Evie's gaze was on the Triple Goddess.

"They can't exactly speak to us, Eve," Chloe said.

But that was wrong. Bridget spoke to her in her head when she stood in this room alone. She was the one who had told her to guard the keystone with her life, that she possessed all the power of the stone.

"But," Chloe added, "maybe there is a way to find out."

"What do you mean?" Evie asked.

She reached into her pocket, brushing the surface of the stone with her fingertips. The two times she had had the most powerful visions of the past, she had held the stone in her hand. She pulled it out of her pocket and clutched it in her fist, thinking about how it felt when she had the visions. But this time, nothing happened.

She wasn't sure how to make it work again.

"You're trying to have another vision," her sister said, moving closer to her. "Do you think you should?"

"I think I have to try. We have to know why it's glowing, if it's truly a message. And if it *is* a message, what it means."

She cut a glance to Malcolm. His face was creased with concern.

"Are ye sure that's a wise idea, lass? I saw the last two," Malcolm said. "Ye dinnae fare so well during them."

Something clicked inside her. *He saw the last two.* Yes. He was with her both times. The first time he was holding her hand. The second time she was wrapped in his arms.

She glanced down at the keystone resting in her scarred hand. Then she held her other hand out to him.

"Take my hand, Malcolm."

He hesitated as he glanced from her open hand to her face, question flickering in his sea-green eyes.

"Why?" he asked.

"The last two times we were touching while I held the stone. I think that's the key. I think we have to be touching each other while I hold the keystone to make it work. Because I'm the link to the past and…" she halted and swallowed hard, "you're the link to me."

Destinies intertwined. It was true, then. As much as she didn't want to admit it, their fates were tied together.

"Chlo, are you sure about this?" Evie asked, concern edging her tone.

"No," she said, honestly. "But I have to try. We have to know."

She met Malcolm's gaze as he reached for her. He grasped her hand as she closed her fingers around the stone.

And then it happened again.

The vision burst through her mind with forceful clarity. And there she was in the midst of the battle between three clans— Sinclair and MacLeod against MacDonald.

Brodie MacDonald held the glowing great axe as he cut down man after man. The smell of death and rot and blood permeated the air with a pungent odor. Dead littered the ground. Men screamed in agony. Swords clashed against swords. Alexander MacLeod was losing. Most of his men were dead. Padrig Sinclair was nowhere in sight.

On the crag, the Triple Goddess stood together. Moira in the center. Bridget to the left of her. The third sister, Athea, to the right.

Past, present, future standing together as Brodie MacDonald fought his way toward them.

Moira held the keystone aloft and whispered an incantation to the wind. The stone began to glow.

"Get that stone, lads!" Brodie shouted.

"You cannot think to defeat us, MacDonald," Moira said, her voice even and calm. "I will destroy you."

But Brodie MacDonald seemed not to care. He lifted his great axe higher in the sky. The words he uttered were lost to the wind. The great axe exploded into life with a bright, white light pulsing upward into the night sky, illuminating everything around him. Then he pointed it at the Triple Goddess.

Bridget and Athea went into action. The two moved to stand in front of Moira, clasping hands and using their bodies as a shield to protect her. The shot of power from the great axe went around them and then dissipated out of sight.

But only for a moment.

The space between Brodie and the Triple Goddess appeared to have ripped, pulling apart at the seams between them. Time and space ripped apart as the two women stood in front of Moira to weather the storm that came from the rift. Brodie pulled back the layers of time, causing a temporal disturbance.

Bridget's voice boomed loud over the din of battle.

"Tell them, Chloe. Tell them what you saw here today."

The vision ended. But there was more to that night than anyone knew. Bridget continued to speak in her mind, telling her everything that had happened that night with sharp, quick words that pounded through her. Words she didn't have time to comprehend. She sucked in a sharp breath, her lungs burning. Her head throbbed with stabbing pain. She groaned.

"Lass?"

Malcolm. His strong arms were around her, holding her, cradling her against his chest. She still clutched the keystone in her hand. With her free one, she reached up to place her palm against his cheek.

"I know what happened the night of the Shattering. I saw it."

Chloe was dimly aware that Evie was asking her more questions, but she felt as though she were in a tunnel. Far, far away from her and everyone. Even Malcolm. Her head hurt. She couldn't think. Her eyes flickered closed. She allowed the darkness to overcome her.

CHAPTER TWENTY-THREE

THE KEYSTONE DROPPED from her hand. Malcolm snatched it up, pocketing it into his sporran. Then he swept her into his arms and rose from the floor, holding her slight weight against his chest. There was some commotion between Evie and Callum, but he ignored it.

"She's out. I'm taking her to my chamber."

He stomped by them without waiting for a response from either Evie or his brother. When she first came out of the vision, her body quaked against him in a violent shiver. Even now as he carried her through the great hall and up the stone stairs, her body was cold.

"Malcolm, wait!" Evie called out, but he ignored her.

He didn't want to turn back. His first priority was to get Chloe warm. The only way he knew to do that was to put her in his bed.

He kicked open the door, crossed the room in two long strides, and lowered her down to the soft mattress. She didn't even stir when he pulled off her shoes, then covered her with the heavy blankets. Then he quickly built a fire in the hearth. A faint moan from the bed got his attention.

He hurried over to her, sitting on the side of the bed. Her eyes fluttered open, fixing on his. First confusion, then worry as she tried to sit up.

"Rest, lass."

"The keystone—"

"I have it. It's safe."

Relieved, she melted back into the pillows and closed her eyes. "I know what happened, Malcolm. The night of the Shattering. I know why his great axe was glowing."

He stiffened, a coldness settling over him. He brushed a lock of her auburn hair off her forehead.

"Ye dinnae have to tell me now."

"I do," she insisted. "His great axe can open a time portal."

He stilled. "How?"

"I don't know. I only know he tried to open one the night of the Shattering. It's a portal to the Realm of Chaos, causing a temporal rift. That's why the Triple Goddess broke the keystone into three pieces. They used the power to mend the rift and close the portal. Or they tried to. The rift was only stitched back together."

He didn't understand what a temporal rift was or where the Realm of Chaos was located. But he did understand it didn't sound good. Her voice was weak. She sounded exhausted.

"Rest now."

She rose up, gripping his wrist with cold fingers. "They had to stop him. Don't you see? If they hadn't, then all would be lost. The MacDonald clan would control Time. The lightning in the tapestry was from his weapon, not from Moira as we thought. I have to tell Evie."

Fear embedded deep into her eyes. Fear at what she'd witnessed. He understood then. If Brodie MacDonald had used the power of the great axe over five hundred years ago, what, then, would stop Rory MacDonald from using it in this time?

She tried to get out of the bed, but he pushed her back down.

"Ye need rest. Yer too weak to move."

He started to rise and leave the bed when she reached out for him, grasping him by the hand and squeezing tight.

"Don't leave me, Malcolm."

It gave him pause. He lowered back down to the edge of the

bed. She blinked up at him with her big green eyes fringed in dark lashes and some long-burning question buried deep inside them. Her thumb traced over the back of his hand.

"Do you believe in prophecy?" she asked, her voice quiet in the silence of the room. "I need to know."

He could tell it was a question that haunted her. A question she needed him to answer, to put her mind at ease.

"Och, lass, ye sound like Callum. He dinnae believe, either, until yer sister arrived. Do ye no believe?"

She released his hand and turned away. "I don't know what to believe."

He took a deep breath, loosed it. "I grew up hearing stories from my da about the keystone, the night of the Shattering and that we were destined to be the protectors of this stone. He liked to tell it after he'd been deep in his cups."

He chuckled, recalling the many times his da had told the tale in a drunken stupor. As a young boy, he had been enamored with the stories. He had envisioned himself as a knight protecting the keystone. He'd never envisioned the keystone would be brought to him by a bonnie lass such as Chloe.

She rolled to her side, then, and propped up on one elbow, gazed up at him. "What about destiny? Do you believe in that?"

He thought he understood then where this was all coming from. Mayhap she wanted some reassurance that everything happening was for a reason. That she was destined to hold the keystone and he was destined to protect her with his life.

"I dinnae. No at first. But then, yer sister arrived by falling from the sky. I wouldna have believed it myself if I hadna seen it in the tapestry. But there she was within the fibers of the wall hanging. And then when ye appeared...well, I dinnae need another sign."

"But—"

"Rest," he said again, interrupting her.

He rose from the bed and sat in the chair by the hearth to stare into the fire.

CHLOE REMAINED WHERE she was as he walked to the chair, lowering himself down in it with a heavy sigh. Firelight flickered over his face as he folded his massive forearms over his chest. His handsome face was pensive. She admitted she liked him without the beard.

It was hard to squelch the déjà vu erupting through her. The strange dream she had had of the man—which she had not thought of since it happened—flooded back to her. He'd had chiseled features like Malcolm. He'd had incredible sea-green eyes like Malcolm. He had held his arms out to her in invitation. She'd slid into his arms and allowed him to wrap her in his warmth.

Och, lass, I cannae resist ye.

It was *him*. Malcolm was the man in her dream.

The jolt zapped through her, electrifying her memories and her senses. She sat up, the blankets falling away as she swung her legs over the side of the bed. His gaze flickered back to her, his expression softening as he looked at her. When he did, a vaguely sensuous light passed between them, calling her, beckoning her. Indecision flashed through his incredible sea-green eyes and then, he held his arms out to her in invitation.

She was unable to resist. She pushed off the bed and went to him, sliding into his arms as he wrapped them around her, surrounding her in his warmth. He nuzzled her neck.

"Och, lass, I cannae resist ye," he said. It was the same thing he'd said in her dream.

It was all coming true.

His sweet words rumbled through his broad chest. His breath was warm against her skin, sending tingles through her entire body. She tilted her head back.

"I can't resist you either," she whispered. "You *do* catch me every time I fall."

And she was falling hard.

His lips met hers in a tantalizing kiss. It took her breath away. Her arms slipped around his neck, her eyes closed, and in that moment, nothing in the world mattered other than Malcolm kissing her.

She allowed herself to believe in destinies and prophecies, in the idea they were meant for each other. Because no one else had made her feel safe like Malcolm did. It was more than comfortable safety—it was euphoric. As if the stars aligned just for her. As if the universe brought her this man who was meant to love her.

And while she wanted to believe in love at first sight—it had not worked out for her—she was a level-headed, down-to-earth, logical, intelligent woman.

A level-headed, down-to-earth, logical, intelligent woman who was smitten with a sexy Highland warrior who had taken her breath away the moment they met. Here, in his arms, she allowed herself to *feel*. There were no destinies or prophecies. She was a woman kissing a man who kissed her back with the same fervor. A man who, as she perched on his lap, clearly wanted her for who and what she was. There was no deception. There were no lies.

There was only truth and honesty.

She did not deny she wanted him, too. Nor would she deny that for herself anymore. When she broke the kiss, as he gazed down at her with fire in his eyes, she knew exactly what she wanted.

"Malcolm?"

"Aye, lass?"

Oh, how she liked when he called her that. It was a leap of faith, telling him what she wanted. She wasn't the kind of girl to do that. But here, now, in his arms, she took a deep breath and said what she wanted.

"Take me to bed."

A sexy grin pulled at the corners of his mouth. "Aye, lass."

He picked her up, carried her to the bed, and then she knew she would be lost to him for the rest of the day. Gently, he placed her on the bed. She sat on the edge, and held her arms out to him, inviting him to stand in front of her. When he did, she slipped her hands under his thick tunic, up and over the hardened muscles of his chest, over the sprinkling of coarse hair that sent a tingling sensation through her.

Chloe tipped her head back to look up at him. When their eyes met, she was acutely aware of the deep desire and need sparking in his eyes. It sent her senses reeling. At that moment, she decided there was no other man for her. No other man who made her feel so alive. No other man who caught her when she fell.

His hands slipped into the length of her hair—she had refused to braid it like her sister, preferring it long and loose. He seemed to like that as much as she liked him running his fingers through the long locks. She closed her eyes, enjoying the feel of him, and leaned into his hands.

"Och, lass, ye dinnae ken what that does to me."

The sound of his voice was low against her hands as it rumbled through his broad chest.

"Tell me." Her voice was a roughened whisper. "What does it do to you?"

"I'd rather show ye."

She rose, pushing her hands under his tunic to his shoulders. "I'd rather you show me, too."

When she nudged the material further, he complied, helping her remove it. He dropped it to the floor at their feet.

As she kissed him again, she realized with some deep satisfaction, his face was covered in stubble. It was rough against her face and, she realized, she wanted to feel it chafing her skin. The moment the thought sprang to her mind, she shivered as a little mewl escaped her.

"Do ye like the way I kiss ye, then?" he whispered against her mouth.

"I thought that was obvious." She raked her knuckles over the coarse hair on his chin. "Are you growing it back?"

He lifted a brow in question. "Do ye no want me to?"

"I kind of like this in-between state." She gave him what she hoped was a lazy, sexy grin.

"Then it stays for as long as ye like."

"Good."

She wanted to say, *now let's get on with it so I can feel that stubble on other intimate places,* but she refrained. It seemed too brazen even for her.

Instead, she quickly stripped down to her shift while he shucked his boots, kicking them aside. Then she got busy removing her woolen stockings. She understood the need for all the layers, but it was doing nothing but causing a delay in what she wanted most.

Moments later, they were both undressed and slipping under the thick blankets together, bare skin sliding against bare skin. For a man of the Middle Ages, his was smooth. His hands, though were rough and calloused. Especially his sword hand, which landed on the flat plane of her abdomen.

Chloe stretched out, opening her thighs to him and arching her back. His hand slid between her legs, moving inside her. Her eyes fluttered closed the moment he touched her. She rocked against him, long and slow, enjoying every touch, every breath that whispered over her skin, every kiss he placed along the long column of her throat.

Her hand fumbled between them until she found his hardened length and wrapped her hand around him. They moved together, coaxing each other higher and higher. The force built deep inside her, pounding through her. She arched her back, letting him move deeper. Her pleasure came in a pounding, wild beat, shuddering through her until she cried out.

Malcolm moved on top of her, pulling her to him with his strong hands and then slid inside her before her climax subsided. She cried out as he moved against her, bringing her to the edge once again.

She wrapped her arms around him, pulling him down to her.

Their mouths fused in a heated kiss. In a perfect moment, they came together. When it was all over, he collapsed to the bed, pulling her to him and cradling her against him.

She rested her head on his shoulder, her hand flat on his chest to feel the rapid beat of his heart. Her own heart matched his, beat for beat. They had come together in a way she had never expected to come together with anyone. He loved her like no other. He looked at her as though she were the most beautiful woman in the world. He treated her as though she were precious, to be cherished and loved all the rest of her days.

And when she thought this, she realized the truth. She would never be able to return home. She understood, then, how her sister felt about Callum. She also understood the power of the prophecy and that their destinies, no matter how she wanted to deny it, were intertwined with each other.

Her life would never be the same.

THE KEYSTONE UNDER Evie's pillow hummed so loudly it woke her from a deep sleep. Her heart pounded a wild, erratic beat as she sat up to reach under the pillow for the stone.

"What is it, lass?" Callum's sleep-filled voice asked next to her.

But as he said it, and her hand closed around the stone, the vision pounded through her mind with a furious energy she had never felt before. She'd seen the outcomes of Callum's death when he fought the battle against Rory. She knew if she didn't intervene then, he would die.

Now, she saw the potential outcome of what was to come in the present. The glowing great axe. The MacDonald using the power of that great axe. The army transporting themselves to Dundale without marching for days. The castle under siege. The battering ram pounding the gate. The army pouring inside to find her and Chloe.

She sucked in a breath as the vision ended as quickly as it had started. Callum was sitting up straight, reaching for her. Her gaze found her husband's, glittering with concern.

"They are coming," she whispered.

CHAPTER TWENTY-FOUR

THEY HAD SPENT the rest of the day in bed together. It was a luxury Chloe had never afforded herself—to spend a day in bed with a sexy Highlander seemed indulgent. One she would have never allowed her past, career-driven self.

A sensual, tender indulgence. As she lay in his arms, remembering everything they did with each other, her cheeks warmed. And yet, she found she was unable to sate her desire for him.

She decided she was under a spell from the keystone and that was the reason for her wanton actions, even though she knew, deep down, the truth was she had allowed herself to fall in love with Malcolm.

Night had fallen. It pressed against the window, plunging the bedchamber in flickering shadows from the candles he had lit and the fire he stoked. The yellow-orange glow gave the room a warm, quixotic radiance. For a moment, she allowed herself to believe they were the only two people in the entire keep. No one and nothing else mattered. There were no prophesies or destinies or black-hearted men out there wanting to steal the keystone away from her—or worse. It was just her and Malcolm. He dozed next to her. She listened to his rhythmic deep breathing, memorizing everything about him, loving everything there was about him.

A knock sounded on the door. It startled her out of her dreamy trance, making her heart thunder in her chest. She sat up, clutching the blankets to her chest, wondering if she'd imagined it.

But no. The knock sounded again. This time louder. She nudged him since he seemed not to have heard.

"Malcolm, there's someone at the door."

As another, more urgent knock landed on the door, he grumbled under his breath as he pushed from the bed. He grabbed his tartan to wrap around his waist as he padded across the room to answer it.

Chloe shrank back into the shadowy alcove of the bed, clutching the blanket in her fists, and holding her breath. She was unable to see who was on the other side, but it was a low man's voice. Callum, perhaps. They exchanged quiet words.

Malcolm cast a worried glance back to her, which made her heart thunder louder. Something was wrong. It sent icy pinpricks through her as she waited.

"A moment," Malcolm said.

"We dinnae have a moment."

"I need a moment, brother."

He slammed the door without waiting for a reply and turned to her. There was a fierce look on his face. One that was a mixture of terror and worry. She didn't like it one bit.

"What's happened?" A knot of fear coiled in her chest.

"Evie had a vision."

By the sound of that, it wasn't good. "A vision of the present?"

He nodded, his face solemn, but he didn't answer.

Chloe scooted to the edge of the bed, the blankets bunching up around her waist as her legs dangled off the edge. "Tell me."

"Yer sister saw Rory MacDonald using the power of the great axe to come here. To invade. She thinks ye are both in danger."

A coldness settled over her as pinpricks of fear trickled up her spine. "How does he know how to use it?"

"I dinnae ken."

It was a question to which Chloe thought she might have the

answer, one she needn't have asked aloud. Maybe when Bruce arrived, he had brought with him some ancient knowledge about the history of his clan. Maybe he had shared that knowledge with Rory and now they were on the move. She had no proof of this, of course, but she remembered with clarity the look of stern determination in Bruce's eyes when he'd promised things were not over between them.

"Callum wants ye both to get to safety." He paused then, swiping his hand across his stubbled chin. "I want that, too."

"What does that mean—get us to safety?" A sudden quake overtook her as she feared his answer.

"There's a secret way out that—"

"No," she said at once.

Instantly, she thought of Evie's story when Callum had tried to send her away before the battle. The battle that would have taken his life if she had not stayed and used the power of the keystone.

Malcolm crossed the room in two long strides. He reached for her, releasing the material of his tartan. It pooled around his feet and he stood before her in all his glorious flesh. His hands landed on her shoulders as he gripped her tight, so tight. She saw the apprehension and the trepidation deep in his eyes.

"Ye must go with yer sister. Both of ye with yer keystones."

"That's why he's coming, isn't it? He wants us and the stones."

"It seems the only explanation for his arrival under the cover of darkness."

"But Evie is pregnant."

"Aye. All the more reason to send her away. To protect both her and the bairn." He paused then, reaching up to trace the edge of her jaw with the pad of his thumb. "And ye. I cannae allow anything to happen to ye, either. Understand?"

It was such an affectionate touch, it nearly made her unravel at the seams.

"And here." He bent to reach for his sporran. Reaching inside, he brought out the piece of her keystone, then pressed it into her scarred hand. "Take this. Keep it with ye. Keep it safe."

"I will, but, Malcolm—"

Before she finished her sentence, a low rumble rocked the walls of the castle. The sound lingered far too long for it to be anything but what they feared. She stared at him as it sounded again.

"What was that?"

Malcom's face turned grim. "He's here."

MALCOLM DRESSED, GAVE her a passionate kiss, and then left as Evie arrived. There was fear shining in her eyes as she urged her to hurry. Chloe knew Callum must have sent her.

"We have to go now," Evie said.

Thankfully, Chloe had managed to pull on her shift before her sister arrived.

But as she reached for her overdress, dizziness swept through her, making her head throb. She paused to put a hand up to rub her temple and steady herself. She chalked it up to remnants of her visions and too many hours in bed. But then, she had enjoyed every hour she was under the sheets with Malcolm.

"Chloe!"

"Stop shouting," she grumbled.

She pulled the dress on over her head, then stuck the piece of her keystone in her pocket. Evie buzzed around the room gathering the rest of her clothes.

"Shoes. Cloak. Now."

The urgency in her sister's voice made her head snap up and focus on her. Her face was lined with worry as she stood by the bed trying to hand her the cloak.

Evie pressed on. "The castle is about to be under siege. We're going to the Sinclair stronghold, but we have to go *now*."

Chloe stuck her feet in her shoes and snatched the cloak from Evie, who was already wearing hers. She hurried toward the door.

"Malcolm said there was a secret gate. Is that how we get out?"

"Yes."

She pulled open the door and peered into the hallway. When it was clear, she ran out, her feet silent on the stone flooring. Chloe followed, pulling the cloak tight around her thin frame. Down the stone steps, Evie crossed the great hall and headed for the kitchen.

With her body sore and craving rest, Chloe had no choice but to follow.

"Dougal and Jamie are waiting at the edge of the loch with horses," Evie said over her shoulder as they entered the kitchen.

It was deserted and utterly devoid of activity. It was an eerie sight.

"Where are the other women?"

"In hiding." Evie burst out the back door and into the gardens. "They'll be safe."

Her sister stopped and spun toward her, as if remembering some crucial bit of information.

"Your piece of the stone. Do you have it?"

She stuck her hand into the pocket of her dress to make sure it was still there. "Yes."

"Good."

They exited the gardens and hurried across the lawn toward the back of the castle where the gate loomed in the stone curtain wall. It stood open, as if someone had already left through it. Beyond the gate was the rocky landscape, the light of the pale moon glimmering along the water, making it shimmer.

Once they were on the rocky shoreline, they picked their way down the edge of the loch, the water lapping against the rocks. Chloe peered ahead, her heart a rapid beat in her chest as she followed her sure-footed sister. Ahead was nothing but trees standing as dark sentries against the gloom of the night.

The surface of the glistening loch broke, and the figure of a man emerged, walking up the shoreline as if he were merely taking an early morning dip. At first, Chloe was confused by this, and her foggy mind did not understand. Until she saw another man. And another.

"Evie!"

Her sister halted her steps and turned around to quiet her when she saw the men approaching. Evie sucked in a sharp breath, her gaze flickering to her full of panic and fear.

"Run," she said, low and urgent through her teeth.

Without waiting for a reply, Evie ran toward the copse of trees, holding her gown up off the ground and hopping over large rocks as she went. Chloe ran after her as worry gnawed at her. There were so many things wrong here. Her pregnant sister fleeing the castle, men darting out of the dark waters of the loch, and now two men on horses bursting out of the trees riding at breakneck speed toward them brandishing their swords.

Her heart climbed to her throat as she watched, horrorstruck, hoping they didn't trample right over her sister.

But they didn't. Evie seemed unconcerned with their approach and never slowed her run. The men rode past her. Chloe realized with some relief it was Dougal, though she had not been properly introduced, and the younger brother, Jamie.

When he was past Evie, Jamie leapt off the horse and took on the men who had come from the loch. Dougal rode through them, cutting down man after man. It seemed they continued to materialize from the water. Swords clashed between them. The smell of blood filled the air. Evie turned to her, waving her to hurry but then her eyes went wide and round and a strangled sob escaped her.

Strong arms wrapped around her upper torso, keeping her from moving. Hot, rancid breath grazed her ear and she realized she was in the arms of the enemy.

"Get the other one!" the man holding her shouted.

"Run, Evie!"

He tightened his grip on her. "Another outburst and ye will regret that."

The point of something sharp pricked her kidneys. Evie tried to run while Dougal and Jamie fought. Dougal was knocked off his horse, scrambling for his sword. Jamie was there in an instant, but then the opponent slashed him on the upper arm. Blood spread on his tunic. Despite that, he continued to fight. He cut down the man he fought but another took his place. Dougal managed to recover his sword and continued the fight.

Meanwhile, Evie was captured by one of the others who managed to slip by Jamie. He picked her up and tossed her over his shoulder as if she were nothing more than a sack of potatoes.

The man holding her shoved her at one of his henchmen, who snatched her by the arm and dragged her in the same direction as the man carrying Evie.

A man stood at the edge of the trees. A man with familiar steel-blue eyes. A man she thought she once loved.

Bruce.

Chapter Twenty-Five

Malcolm hated the thought of Chloe leaving his protection, but he and Callum had decided it was best for them to get as far away from the fighting as possible. They both knew Rory MacDonald was after them and the keystone. If they weren't in residence, then he couldn't capture them if anything went terribly wrong.

He and Malcolm quickly organized the rest of the castle for battle. They emptied the armory and lined up the few archers they had along the ramparts, readying for the worst.

Torchlight glinted off spears, swords, and many other sharp things as the army approached. At the head of it, Rory MacDonald clutched his great axe. Next to him, his son. Both of them rode on their destriers, dressed and ready for battle.

Thankfully, the weapon was not glowing this time.

MacDonald's army outnumbered them. If he decided to lay siege to the castle, they would have a difficult time defending it. If he decided to starve them out, that could take months. His brother had prepared for this moment all season. He'd made sure the larder was stocked, and they had plenty of livestock.

But what of the women? Malcolm worried, as Callum did, that they would not make it away from the castle. Dougal and Jamie planned to escort them to the Sinclair stronghold. It gave him some peace of mind to know his younger brother and the steward were with them. They were the only two men he and his brother trusted to see to their safety. Should anything happen, they'd protect them with their swords and their lives. They would remain there, in the safety of their ancestral home, until he and Callum rode for them.

Standing on the ramparts next to his brother, Malcolm clutched his claymore in his sweaty palm, watching the horde approach. At the head of the army, a group of men pushed a battering ram. Not exactly the best news.

"What's yer plan, brother?" Malcolm asked.

"We fight them," he said, his face impassive, his voice grim. His gaze was fixed on the distant army. "They'll attack the gate first."

"We're outnumbered."

"Aye," his brother agreed. "We will use the archers to take out as many as we can before they attack."

"And that battering ram?" Malcolm asked, eyeing the large equipment headed right for them.

"I have an idea for that as well."

The army stopped their forward march out of reach of the castle walls. Rory MacDonald and his son sat on their destriers at the head of it. They were flanked by their men, each holding torches. The orange-red light flickered over their battered breastplates, showing every nick and scar along the steel. Neither Rory nor his son wore helms, as though they did not expect to fight.

"Open yer gates and we will no attack," Rory called.

Malcolm cut a glance to his brother. His face remained impassive, his jaw hard and clenched. The muscles ticked along the edge.

"And why should I open my gates to the likes of ye?" Callum called back.

"Because ye dinnae wish to die this night, MacLeod," he fired back.

In the distance, there was a commotion. Malcolm heard it and tipped his head, straining his ears to listen. He narrowed his eyes, as if that would give him a better view in the darkness. He saw nothing. He thought for sure he had heard panicked voices on the wind.

Movement distracted Rory. He turned his head and peered into the distance. A fierce grin split his face.

"Yer in luck this night, then, MacLeod. We willna attack."

Alarm pounded through Malcolm. Why would Rory Mac-Donald come all this way with his army if he didn't intend to attack? It didn't make sense.

Then a man rode through the ranks, moving toward the front. As he neared, Malcolm recognized the man's face as the light from the torch flickered over it. He would know those piercing blue eyes anywhere. It was the same man who had followed Chloe through time. The same man who had tried to take the keystone from her.

Bruce MacDonald. The man from the future. The man who had vowed things were not over between him and Chloe.

"Is it done then?" Rory asked.

"It is," Bruce said with a nod.

Wild, hot terror pumped through Malcolm then as he realized the army before them was nothing more than a decoy.

Rory's glittering gaze flickered back up to Callum and Malcolm standing high on the ramparts. A smile—a dreadful, sickly smile—parted his lips.

"Ye left me no other choice, MacLeod," he said.

"What do ye mean?" Alarm tinged Callum's voice. His fist clenched at his side while he continued to grip the claymore in his other.

"We have what we came for," Rory replied. "All this..." He waved his hand to encompass the army behind. "'Twas nothing more than a show of force and a distraction."

Next to him, Callum stiffened. Malcolm's stomach plummeted to the soles of his boots.

"By God's blood, ye filthy jackal, what have ye done?" The words burst out of Malcolm before he was able to stop them.

But neither Rory nor Bruce answered.

The distant thunder of hooves neared. Moments later, two men galloped around the edge of the castle walls, heading right for Rory, Bruce, and his son, Rufus. Riding with the men, their hands bound and their mouths gagged, were Evie and Chloe.

In a fit of fury, Callum pointed his sword at Rory. "Ye will pay dearly for this treachery, MacDonald!"

He merely grinned, lifted his great axe into the air. It exploded into a bright, white light, ripping the space in front of them. And then, Rory, Bruce, Rufus, and the two men holding their women captive rode through. Chloe's gaze lifted to his moments before she disappeared. Her emerald eyes were full of dread. And then she was gone.

The moment they disappeared, Callum emitted a frustrated war cry that sent chills through Malcolm, making the hair on the back of his neck stand on end. He had never heard anything like that from his brother.

Malcolm's stomach was tied in knots. He had failed in his promise to protect her with his sword and his body. Now, she and her sister were in the hands of their enemy.

MacDonald's army retreated, thundering away from the castle, leaving them standing there on the ramparts to watch their forms disappear into the dead of night, heading back to MacDonald land.

No one moved. No one said anything. No one dared breathe. The archers stationed on the ramparts remained until their laird ordered them otherwise.

Jamie and Dougal had failed to protect the women. Which meant they were incapacitated or—worse—dead.

Rory had their women and the two pieces of the keystone.

In a strangely calm fashion, Callum sheathed his claymore. His gaze still remained on the horizon, watching the retreating army growing smaller as more distance was put between them and Dundale Castle.

"That bloody knave has *my wife* and I will see him dead for it."

Callum said this so calmly, it sent a twinge of fear through Malcolm. He didn't dare point out that he had the woman he loved, too.

It had never occurred to him until that moment that he was in love with Chloe.

Now, he had to get her and her sister back.

His brother turned from the ramparts and stalked down the rough-hewn steps to the ground. With his shoulders pulled back and his back taut with tension, he was a man on a mission. As he marched across the bailey to the stable, Malcolm knew what he intended to do. He sheathed his sword and followed.

"Callum, wait."

He spun toward him, fury creasing his normally calm features. This was a man on the edge. A man ready to rip his enemy to shreds and not even think twice about it.

"I'm going after them."

"We need a plan first. We need to find Dougal and Jamie."

As if remembering their younger brother and the steward, the rage was wiped from his features as he glanced toward the gate that remained closed. He realized, as Malcolm did, that something must have happened to the two of them.

"Open the gate!"

A shout rose up from one of his men still on the wall. Callum shoved by him and ran toward the gate. Malcolm followed. The portcullis started its slow ascent. When it was open enough, two men hobbled inside the gate. Jamie held his arm against his side, his tunic damp with blood. Dougal limped beside him, favoring one of his legs. As soon as they were inside, they lowered the gate.

"What happened?" Callum demanded, halting in front of them.

"Ambush," Jamie said. "Mercenaries."

"There were too many of them," Dougal added. "I'm sorry, Callum. We failed."

Regret and torment gleamed in both men's eyes.

Callum clenched his jaw again, tight. "We dinnae expect

mercenaries."

"Welsh ones," Jamie added, then spit to show his distaste for them. "We can go after them, brother."

"Aye, we can and we will. But for now, ye need yer arm stitched," Callum said eyeing the cut down his left arm. "Malcolm, fetch Roslyn. Have her meet us in the great hall. And then we will decide how we get the women back."

THEY RODE HARD throughout the night. Chloe tried to keep her panic down, but it was difficult when she was terrified of what was to come. Bruce made sure to ride next to her, keeping a watchful eye on her. On the other side, Evie and her captor.

All Chloe thought about was Malcolm would come for her. Callum would come for Evie. They would be saved from these brutal barbarians. Chloe knew enough about medieval history and how they treated women to start formulating her own plan of escape. She didn't know how yet.

Horses' hooves thundered over the wooden drawbridge as they headed through the portcullis and into the bailey of the castle of Clan MacDonald. She realized the army hadn't returned with them. Only Rory, Bruce, and a few others. As they came to a halt, she glanced at Evie. Their eyes met. Chloe saw the fear behind her sister's eyes. She wanted to give her reassurance that everything was going to be all right. She tried to convey that with her eyes, but even she wasn't sure everything would be all right.

After dismounting, they were taken through the bailey, into the keep, and through the corridors. It was a maze with lots of twists and turns, ensuring they would never find their way out should they escape. They were being taken to the dungeon. They would be imprisoned until Bruce pried the keystones from them, until he used some force of will to compel them to turn over the pieces.

She wasn't sure how cruel he was, deep down, but she saw the hatred and the brutal determination behind his eyes.

One of the men shoved open the cell door. Bruce pushed them both inside. Then the door slammed shut, enclosing them in gloomy darkness.

It was hard to tell how big the room they were in was. The musty, damp smell, though, permeated her nose and clung to her clothes.

The men hadn't even bothered to remove their gags or untie their wrists. It was so dark, it was hard to see anything but she heard her sister whimper and knew she was nearby. Chloe edged closer to her, nudging her. Evie leaned into her.

Chloe worked on the knots binding her wrists. Her skin burned as she jerked on the roughened rope. A moment later, with her wrists slick with sweat, she slipped one of her hands out. She shoved off the rope and removed the gag.

"Evie?" she whispered.

Her sister made a strangled noise behind the gag. Chloe waved her arms in the dark until she bumped into her.

"Give me your hands."

When she did, she went to work on the knots, bending back and breaking fingernails. But she succeeded in releasing her. As soon as she did, Evie ripped off the gag and wrapped her arms around her, hugging her tight.

"What are we going to do?" she whispered against her hair.

"We're not going to panic," Chloe said. "We're going to figure a way out of here."

"How?"

"I don't know yet," she replied.

"Callum and Malcolm will come for us," Evie said, sounding sure.

"Of course, they will," she agreed. "But in the meantime, we're not going to sit here like helpless women and wait for..." She let her words trail off.

"I remember my history, sis," Evie said, a hint of fear in her voice.

"Well, they have to keep us alive. The keystones won't work without us."

Without their blood magic, she thought, but she didn't say it. They'd keep them alive, certainly, but they could do other horrible things. She reached into her pocket, her fingers grazing the cold stone that was there.

"Mine is humming," Evie said. Apparently, she'd had the same thought as her.

"Mine isn't," Chloe said. "What do you think it means?"

"I have the power of the present," she said. "Maybe it means I'll have another vision."

On impulse, Chloe brought her stone out of her pocket. To her surprise, the lines were glowing. When Evie saw it, she gasped. Chloe brought it closer to her face. In the faint light, she and Evie exchanged a glance, both of them confused and unsure what it meant. Without a word, Chloe lifted her piece up, the jagged edge pointing toward her sister. Evie lifted her stone and pressed it against the jagged edge. They snapped together as if they were puzzle pieces coming together.

They both started to hum and glow.

"What now?" Chloe asked.

Evie shook her head. "I have no idea."

Outside the cell, they heard men's voices. Chloe pulled hers away and stuck it back in her pocket. Evie did the same.

The door scraped open. Bruce walked in first, holding a torch. He placed it in a bracket beside the door. Several other men followed him in, each carrying a torch.

Bruce stood before her, eyeing her with those sharp, hateful eyes. Eyes that had once gazed at her longingly. Now, she knew that was nothing but a lie. He was dressed in clothes from the time. His dark hair was uncombed. Once she'd thought he was handsome. Now, she despised everything about him.

"Hello, Chloe. I see you managed to get out of your bonds. Resourceful, aren't you?" His gaze flickered to her raw wrists.

Her mouth filled with saliva. She spit at him. It landed on his face. He instantly backhanded her. Evie cried out as Chloe went down, her cheek stinging. Her sister bent to help her back to her feet. Chloe pressed a hand against her cheek as Bruce wiped her spittle away.

"Bitch," he said. "Do that again and you're dead."

"Kill me and you will have all of the MacLeod clan after you," she shot back.

Evie's grip tightened on her arms as she continued to hold her. "What do you want with us?"

Bruce's glittering blue eyes flickered to hers. "Don't you know? I thought that was obvious."

Chloe was certain she heard the faint hum of Evie's keystone in her pocket. She was also certain her own keystone continued to glow.

"We will never hand over the stones." Evie lifted her chin a little higher in defiance.

"You will. But I'll give you a little time to think about giving me the stones voluntarily before I take them by force."

Chloe wanted to bite off another acid retort, but Evie squeezed her arm again in warning. She clenched her jaw tight to keep silent. Bruce cut her another scathing glance before turning back toward the open door. The men filed out, the door slammed closed, leaving them alone once more.

"Chlo, I think I know what we have to do." Evie's eyes were still pinned on the closed door, watching and waiting for their captors to return.

"What?"

She turned, locking eyes with her, and there was something sharp and glittering deep within, hinting at hidden knowledge. Or perhaps it was merely her best guess. Chloe's stomach clenched as she braced herself for whatever her sister was about to propose.

"We have to use the stones together."

She drew her brows together as her chest tightened and her palms grew damp. She had a feeling she wasn't going to like this.

"How?"

Evie took a deep breath, expelled it, determined apprehension swarming in her eyes.

"Blood magic."

✦

CHAPTER TWENTY-SIX

"WHAT DO YOU mean by that?" Chloe clutched her elbows and shivered.

She'd thought it already, but now she wasn't so sure. How would they even invoke the blood magic? Was there a ritual? Was it simply slice the palm, squeeze the stone, and hope for the best?

Judging by what had happened to her when she had a vision, she wasn't sure she wanted to do that here in this dank place. She wasn't even sure what happened to Evie when she had a vision. Did she have the same reaction? Did she faint from the sheer exhaustion of seeing the different scenarios of the present?

Evie told her about helping Callum during the fight with Rory, but she never elaborated on how she felt in the aftermath.

And then, when Evie sliced open her palm, nothing happened right away. She shuddered to think what would happen should they try again with two pieces put together. What power would that give them both? And what would that power do to each of them and Evie's unborn child?

"We put the stones together and then slice our—"

"No," Chloe said sharply. She clenched her jaw until it ached.

Torchlight flickered over her sister's face as she looked at her, the orange and reddish light playing across her confused features.

"But—"

"No, Eve."

"Why not?"

"You don't know what that power will do to you. To me."

"I'll be fine," she said with a wave of her hand as if to dismiss the thought.

"You don't know that. You *can't* know that."

Evie's eyes sparkled with purpose as she gazed at her in the torchlight. "I have to believe I will. *We* will. I have to believe the Triple Goddess would not give us this power if it harmed us."

Chloe huffed out a breath, exasperated. "How are we going to slice open our hands anyway?"

She looked around their baren cell. There was a chamber pot in one corner and a three-legged stool in another.

"I'll find a jagged stone or something." She ran her hands over the stone walls, looking for a loose stone with a sharp edge.

At the thought of slicing open her hand with a random jagged rock, a wave of disgust went through her followed by a surge of stubbornness. "I don't want to do that."

She paused her search and turned to face her. "It may be our only way out of here."

"We will wait for the guys," Chloe said, her voice determined and hard.

"But what if they don't come?"

"Seriously? Do you believe they won't?" Chloe looked at her as though she may have lost her mind.

"Well, no, but what if—"

"Stop with the what ifs, Eve. *If* they don't come, then we decide our next steps." Clutching her elbows, she paced the short length of the cell. "Besides, I have faith in Malcolm and Callum. They'll come for us."

Evie was silent as she watched her pace back and forth. She chewed on her lower lip. "Fine. We'll do it your way and wait. But I'm still going to look for something to use."

Her sister went back to her desperate, intense search for some tool to enact the blood magic residing within them in conjunction with the keystone. A hard flash of resolve glinted in her eyes. Her hands shook, but there was a fierce determination burning within her. Chloe understood then—it was Evie's deep-rooted desire to protect them both at any cost, driven by their unbreakable bond forged through their hardened years of sacrifices and struggles.

She admired that about her sister. She had always been the one to take care of things while Chloe was busy studying into the long hours of the night, paving the way toward her future. A future, she realized, that didn't include Evie.

Guilt swamped her.

"Eve?" Chloe said, her voice timid in the shadowy darkness, echoing through the cavernous room.

She halted her search and turned to look at her. "Yeah?"

"We're going to be okay, you know. We're going to get out of this. You should rest before you wear yourself out." Then she lowered her voice to a whisper. "Think of the baby."

Air whooshed out of her lungs as her shoulders slumped in defeat. Her chin quivered as though she were about to break. Chloe rushed to her, wrapping her arms around her, hugging her tightly.

"You *know* I'm a sympathy crier, sis," she said against her hair.

Evie giggled, which was nothing more than a cover for the emotion shuddering through her slender frame. Chloe hugged her harder, squeezed her, then pulled back.

"You've always been the strong one," Chloe said. "You've always been the one to take care of us, even after Brianna left. And here you are, pregnant and looking for a way out."

She gave her a weak smile, tears pooling in her deep brown eyes. "It's what I do, you know. Take care of you. It's what I've always done."

"Well, now you have to take care of yourself. Have faith. They'll come for us. And they'll make him pay."

Evie wrapped her arm around her waist and clung to her. They walked to one side of the cell—the side farthest away from the chamber pot and the three-legged stool. Together, they lowered down to the ground, resting against the cold stone wall, clinging to each other. They were each other's salvation.

Chloe forced herself to tamp down the rising tide of worry, but her mind kept slipping into a shadowed spiral. She remained silent, swallowing the words before they surfaced. Bruce would return. She knew this as sure as the silence grew thick. She didn't need Evie sharing in her dread.

Resolve settled over her. It was her turn to take charge and find a way out of this for the both of them. She turned her hand over with the scarred palm facing upward. The imprint of the stone was still there. The scar from the slice had turned from pink to a muted silver.

Maybe her sister was onto something with this blood magic thing. But, then again, maybe there was another way out of this.

As they clung to each other, Chloe shoved aside the worry, the overwhelming trepidation, and focused. She was a historian, after all. She needed to use that knowledge to work for her, not against her.

As they huddled in the shadowy darkness, Chloe vowed to find a way to beat Bruce at his own game. And she was going to do it alone.

"He'll have them locked in the dungeon," Callum said.

He leaned on the great hall table staring down at the crudely drawn map of the MacDonald keep. It would take days to ride there to rescue them and both he and Malcolm knew that. Impatience vibrated off his eldest brother.

"I dinnae ken the layout of the MacDonald keep."

And that frustrated him, too. Malcolm stood next to him, peering down at the drawing, wondering how they would be able to get the women back without assistance. They were a small band of warriors.

"We need help," Malcolm said.

Jamie sat in a chair opposite them, his arm stitched and freshly bandaged. Roslyn ushered Dougal out of the great hall to tend to his wounds elsewhere. But Jamie remained to help plan their next move.

"Och, and what will ye have us do, then, brother?" Jamie asked. "Who will help us?"

"The Sinclairs," he suggested.

"They've helped us enough," Callum said. "We cannae ask them again or they'll think us weak."

"Then what?" Malcolm asked. "What can we do? Storm the castle ourselves?"

Jamie snickered. He knew Malcolm's suggestion was flippant. But Callum straightened, folding his thick forearms over his chest and eyeing his brother.

"Aye, laddie. That's what we'll do."

"Are ye out of yer mind?" Malcolm snapped. "It was nothing but a jest."

"But 'tis something MacDonald willna expect, aye?" Callum said.

"Ye might be onto something there, brother," Jamie added, sounding intrigued.

"Ye both are mad." Malcolm said and huffed. "How can the three of us invade the MacDonald keep?"

"We will go to their stronghold. Jamie, take our fastest horse and ride out to observe their guard rotation. Look for unguarded exits, a breech in the wall, sewer grates, anything that can aid us in getting inside the keep undetected," Callum said.

A wide grin spread on his face. "Aye, brother, I can do that."

"Good. Then, the two of us will ride out to meet ye. Our meeting point will be in the nearby village at the inn."

"And what are the two of us going to be doing while Jamie is gathering this information? I dinnae like the idea of the lassies in the hands of MacDonald for so long."

"I dinnae either, but we dinnae have much of a choice. We will sharpen our swords and gather provisions. Enough for us and the lassies for our return trip. They'll need horses, too."

"Chloe cannae ride," Malcolm interjected, thinking of his past experience with her.

"Och, then one horse for Evie. Chloe can ride with ye. Once we meet up with ye, Jamie, ye'll give us whatever ye found. Ye have the gift of stealth, so I will be counting on ye to gather as much information as ye can," Callum said.

Jamie nodded.

"Once we ken what we're up against," Callum continued, "I will create a diversion to draw the guards away. Malcolm, I want ye to be the one to take out any who spot us right away."

He folded his arms over his chest. "And while ye are distracting the guards and I'm killing them, what is Jamie doing?"

"I'll be finding the dungeon and rescuing the bonnie lassies," he said with a grin.

Malcolm glanced from his younger brother to his older one. "Did ye tell him this before?"

Callum shook his head. "No, but sending in wee Jamie is the last thing MacDonald will expect. So, aye, he'll go in after them."

"And what if something goes wrong?" Malcolm wanted to know.

He wasn't sure he liked this plan but it was the only one they had. If it worked, Evie and Chloe would be safe in Jamie's hands.

"Did ye forget the lassies still have control of their pieces of the keystone?" Callum asked.

"I did no forget such a thing," Malcolm replied.

"If anything goes wrong..." Callum paused, took a deep breath, and pinpointed Jamie with his glittering blue eyes. "I want ye to tell them to use the power of the stones."

Malcolm stared at him for a long moment. Jamie seemed unconcerned about the power of the stones, but he had seen what it did to Chloe with his own eyes. It drained her to the point of unconsciousness more than once. What would happen, then, if she and Evie were to use the power of the stones together? It could bloody well kill her.

"Och, brother, ye *are* mad. Ye dinnae ken what yer asking."

"I do." Callum turned his gaze to him and locked eyes. "I saw what it did to Chloe. I ken what it does to my own wife when she uses the power of the stone."

"What does it do?" Jamie asked, genuinely interested.

He hadn't been around any of the times Chloe had used the power of the past. When Evie had saved them at the previous battle with MacDonald, they were at a distance and unable to see what had happened to her. All Malcolm knew was what Callum had told him.

"It drains their energy," Malcolm said. "Are ye sure that's safe for—"

"It might be the only way," Callum said, cutting him off.

His gaze bored into him and in that one look Malcolm saw the fear and the worry gnawing at him. It was a risk, he knew, as did Callum. A risk he was willing to take if it meant life or death. But the question was, would Evie comply with his request?

"It would be better if we had Angus Sinclair with us," Malcolm said, trying one last time to get his brother to agree.

But Callum shook his head. "No. We cannae ask him. The three of us do this alone." He looked at Jamie and asked, "Do ye agree?"

"Aye, I do," Jamie said, sounding strong and sure.

Callum glanced his way, then. Malcolm clenched his jaw so tight his back teeth ached. Finally, he nodded, though it was against his better judgment.

"Aye, I agree."

"We havena any time to spare. Can ye ride out tonight, Jamie?"

Jamie was already on his feet striding to the great hall door, as if he hadn't survived a battle of his own with Welsh mercenaries. That was Jamie. He was resilient and strong.

"I will ready my horse and be gone within the hour."

As Malcolm watched him walk away, a sense of dread washed over him. He hoped this was the right plan just as he hoped, for Rory MacDonald's sake, the lassies were alive and unharmed when they found them.

CHAPTER TWENTY-SEVEN

CHLOE HAD LOST track of all time. It seemed an eternity had passed being locked up in the dimly lit dungeon. How long had it been? An hour? Two? A day? Her stomach rumbled with hunger. They'd settled on the cold stone floor. Chloe wrapped her arm around Evie. She'd dropped her head on her shoulder and was softly snoring.

Chloe was no closer to figuring out a way out of there than she was when they had first arrived. She thought of the stone in her pocket. She pulled it out with her free hand and stared down at it, resting it against her scarred palm. The lines were faintly glowing.

Evie's hand rested in her lap with her fingers relaxed. Her palm was scarred, too. Like hers. Idly, she wondered if—when—Brianna arrived if she would have the same scarring on her palm. Chloe was certain her older sister's arrival was inevitable.

She peered around the small, dank cell. On the far wall, the three-legged stool. Next to it, the chamber pot. The torch still blazed in the bracket by the door. How long did they expect them to rot in his hellhole?

Forever, likely. Bruce didn't care what happened to her. He only wanted the keystone.

There was a faint humming coming from Evie's pocket. Her stone.

Footsteps were forthcoming. She clutched the stone in her fist and nudged her sister.

"Wake up, Eve. Someone's coming."

Evie startled awake instantly. Together, they got to their feet.

"They're coming for the stones," she whispered. "Aren't they?"

Chloe nodded. It was the only possible reason. She bit her lower lip, refusing to voice the terrible thoughts floating through her mind. She didn't want to worry her sister even more than she already was.

The door scraped open, and Bruce stepped inside. He stood in the doorway, the light at his back, making him nothing more than a tall, menacing, faceless figure outlined there. Chloe remained where she was, clutching the stone in her hand and trying to ignore the faint hum of Evie's stone. She pushed her sister behind her. Evie didn't even protest as she allowed Chloe to be the buffer between the two of them.

"Have you come to your senses yet?" Bruce asked. His gaze flickered from her face down to her clenched fist. "Will you willingly give up the keystone?"

"Why do you want it so badly?" she countered, lifting her chin a little higher. "What can you possibly do with a chunk of worthless rock?"

Behind her, she sensed Evie stiffen. If her sister knew her— and she did—she'd realize she was stalling for time and trying to needle information out of him at the same time.

A slow, annoyed smile played upon his lips. "Do ye think it's worthless?"

"Isn't it?" She tried to sound as defiant as possible.

"It brought ye here, didn't it? It brought us both here."

A fact she didn't want to remember. He'd physically attacked her, clawed at her hand trying to get the stone from her. It was only when she had landed here, in the past, that she was safe from him. Thanks to Malcolm. He was her warrior who liked to seem more dangerous than he truly was.

"You didn't answer my question," Chloe snapped, shoving

aside the thoughts.

"Why I want it is no concern of yers."

"They *will* come for us," she said, then, thinking of Malcolm and Callum.

"Oh, I certainly hope they do." His smile was terrible. He held out his hand. "Give it to me and no harm will come to ye or yer sister."

Chloe remained still. "No."

"Ye give me no choice then."

He snapped his fingers. Two men entered the dungeon and headed right for Evie. They took her by the arms as she protested the entire time.

"Leave her alone, Bruce! Let her go."

"She has one of the stones. Search her," Bruce said to his two henchmen, ignoring her.

"With pleasure," one said, an oily smile on his face.

"Stop!" Evie snapped. "You can have it."

"No, Eve!" Chloe gasped.

Her gaze flickered to hers and she saw something in Evie's eyes she hadn't seen before. Defeat. Evie wrenched her arm free from one of the men and stuck her hand in her pocket, intending to hand over her piece of the keystone.

"It's easier this way," Evie said quietly.

Chloe was shaking her head.

"See, there? Yer sister has come to her senses." Bruce held his hand out to Evie. She dropped her piece of the keystone—which was still humming—into his palm. Then he turned to her. "Now, hand over yers."

Blood magic. Use the stone. The words whispered through her mind in a familiar voice. If she didn't know any better, it sounded like Bridget.

For a moment, indecision paralyzed her. Hand over the stone and let Bruce win. Or use the stone and defeat him. But how?

Blood magic, the voice said again.

Even her sister believed blood magic was the only way to

defeat Bruce and the MacDonalds and get out of the dungeon.

I'll find a jagged stone or something.

That's what Evie had said to her. But didn't they have their own jagged stones? Even now, as she clenched her hand tighter, she felt the prick of the edges of the stone. Perhaps they would be sharp enough to slice open her hand. Not a deep cut. Just enough to make her bleed.

"Give it to me, Chloe!" he demanded, his voice harsh and cold.

As she stared at Bruce, all the anger and the pain of betrayal hit her full force. She despised his face and everything about him. He was nothing more than a liar. He'd used her. And the worst part was she'd thought she was in love with him.

She should have been more like Evie. She should have listened to her gut instincts, but she hadn't. She'd allowed herself to get carried away with her emotions and fall for the handsome Scot.

"Did our time together mean nothing to you?" she fired back, allowing herself to feel that torrid anger. "Were you using me to get what you wanted?"

His expression hardened as though he didn't want to think about their time together in the future. He dropped his hand and clenched his jaw, the muscles working along the edge.

"Ye try my patience, lass. Don't make me take it from ye by force," he said.

"You told me you loved me," she continued, thinking of all those moments they had together. "You said you wanted to spend the rest of your life with me. It was all a lie, wasn't it?"

"I—"

"All you want is this jagged piece of stone." She opened her palm and glanced down at it to see the lines were not only glowing, but pulsating. "You were the one who chased Evie up those stairs in the museum that night. You were the one who attacked her. Because you knew what she had."

"Chlo?" Evie's timid voice whispered through the darkness

behind her. "What are you doing?"

"Aye, what *are* ye doing, lass?" Bruce said, his Scottish brogue coming out thicker. "Give me the bloody stone and let's be done with this walk down memory lane."

"I will do no such thing."

Then she moved lightning fast. She swiped the jagged edge of the stone down her palm, splitting the skin. Blood oozed. Then she clutched the stone in her palm and dropped to her knees. Immediately, the stone started to glow, the light seeping through her fingers.

A feral, raw power pulsed in a wild beat, shooting through her. Warmth spread through her as though she had taken a shot of whiskey. It pounded through her, making her ears throb and her eyesight swim. Bruce shouted something.

Use the magic, the voice said. Bridget's voice.

Chloe lifted her fisted hand and pounded it against the stone. The floor and walls shook, vibrating outward from her hand as though she were the epicenter of an earthquake. Shouts. Evie's scream. Chloe pounded her first against the floor again and again and again.

The next thing she knew, she was on her back looking up into Evie's worried face. She was speaking to her, but her voice was muffled. It was as though something had burst her eardrums, and she was in a deep, dark tunnel. She shook her head and tried to speak but couldn't.

She forced a yawn and popped her ears. Everything was back to normal.

"—hear me?" Evie sounded frantic when she said it. Her face was pinched with worry.

Finally, Chloe nodded.

"You scared the life out of me!"

Evie grasped her by the arm and helped her up. She shook her head to clear it and looked around the cell. The door was closed and they were alone once again. She uncurled her hands to see blood smeared along the glowing lines of the keystone.

"Where?" she croaked but her throat was raw, and it hurt to talk.

"They left. You scared them pretty good." Evie chuckled, then she turned serious. "How did you…"

"I heard Bridget in my head," she said then, her voice stronger than before. "She told me to use the blood magic."

"You sliced your hand with the stone," she said, her voice full of awe. "Why didn't I think of that?"

"I don't remember much after that."

"When you hit the ground, your hand glowed bright white," Evie said. "You pounded the floor. The walls and ground shook so violently, the men scurried from the cell as though the devil himself chased them. One called you a witch."

A natural response to seeing something so unusual. Magic did not exist here. Or shouldn't. But the little piece of stone in her hand was evidence.

"Bruce will be back. Chlo, he has my stone."

Chloe frowned. She had forgotten Bruce forced Evie to hand over her piece of the keystone. Now they had to figure out a way to get it back. As she glanced around the dungeon, she saw hairline cracks in the stone walls.

"We need to bandage your hand," Evie said.

The sound of ripping caught her attention. She turned to see her sister ripping a strip of cloth from her shift.

"You don't want an infection."

She made a motion for her hand. Chloe obliged. Evie plucked the keystone out of her hand and dropped it in her pocket, then used the strip of cloth to wrap around her cut. She tied it off.

"I think there's a way out of here." She eyed the cracks in the wall.

"How? They'll never let us go after that show of magic. Bruce will want to keep you under lock and key until he can make you use that keystone for him."

"I'll never do that." The fierce words exploded through her.

Feeling stronger, she stomped over to the three-legged stool and picked it up. She wasn't sure it would work, but she was willing to try. She swung the stool as hard as she could at the wall. A loud crack sounded. One of the legs broke off.

"What are you doing?" Evie asked.

"Finding a way out."

Chloe swung the stool again. This time when she hit the wall, the mortar crumbled a little, and pieces of stone rained down. She looked at Evie, triumph pounding through her. It was going to work. Evie glanced around the dungeon looking for something to use.

"Not the chamber pot!" Chloe said. "That's gross."

She flung the stool at the wall over and over. Until there were more shards of mortar and stone raining down. Until there was a larger crack. Until the wall gave way and there was a small opening.

Cool, dank air whooshed through it. Evie gasped. Chloe moved closer to peer through the crack. There was a chamber beyond.

No. Not a chamber. A passageway. Odd place for a passageway.

She glanced down at her bandaged hand. Blood seeped through the material.

"I know what I have to do," she whispered. "Give me the stone, Evie."

"What? No. Why?"

She spun to face her sister. "Give it to me and I'll show you."

As Evie pulled the stone from her pocket, Chloe untied the knot. Her hand still oozed.

She wasn't sure if she could recreate the magic, but she was going to try. The lines were still glowing. Her blood was still smeared across it. She clenched it tightly in her hand, closed her eyes and let the magic of the stone push through her. It shot up her arm, to her shoulder, across her chest and down her other arm. Then flooded the rest of her body.

Evie sucked in a breath.

When Chloe opened her eyes, her hand was glowing like before. With all the force she had, she punched the wall at the crack.

A low rumbling, followed by a vibration, and the wall crumbled and gave way, revealing a doorway and a secret passage.

"Oh, my God, Chloe!"

She wobbled on her feet, weakened from the magic. Evie was at her side in an instant, taking the stone from her hand, and pocketing it once more. Chloe suspected since the blood on her palm merely oozed, the power wasn't as strong as before. Evie wrapped an arm around her shoulders.

"Can you walk?" she asked.

"Yes. Now, let's find your keystone."

"Wait." Evie clutched her arm. "Shouldn't we have some sort of a plan before we go in there?"

Chloe worried her lower lip. "The plan is to get your keystone and get out of the castle."

"Oh, easy, huh? How are we going to find it? Once we do, how do we get out?"

All valid questions. Ones for which she did not have an answer.

"One step at a time," she said. "We'll find Bruce. He won't let it out of his sight."

Evie peered into the darkness of the passageway, apprehension in her gaze as the cool breeze ruffled the sprigs of hair around the side of her head. Her braid hung over one shoulder, the plaits loosened. Fatigue lined her face. There were dark circles under her eyes.

It was a lot to ask of her, Chloe knew. But she was certain it was the only way. They could wait for Malcolm and Callum but that could be days. She didn't want to wait any longer. They were no ordinary medieval women, after all.

Bruce had left behind the torch. It still rested in its bracket by the cell door, flickering with its yellow-orange light. She hurried over to it and lifted it out, carrying it back to the opening.

"Hold my hand," Chloe said. "It will be like when we were kids doing something we knew Mom and Dad wouldn't like." She flashed a smile to reassure her sister.

"But we don't even know where this goes."

"No, we don't," she agreed. "We'll find out together. If it leads nowhere, we'll come back."

After a long moment of silent indecision, Evie grasped her by the hand. Together, they stepped through the door and entered the passageway.

CHAPTER TWENTY-EIGHT

A S SOON AS they had provisions and horses gathered, Malcolm and Callum rode into the night, pounding the ground at a full gallop to get to the meeting point in the village. Malcolm hoped Jamie had all the information needed to get into the MacDonald keep and get the lassies back. But there was a foreboding feeling deep in his gut that was telling him something was wrong.

After nearly two days of hard riding, they arrived at the rendezvous point in the village as the sun was coming up over the horizon, turning the inky sky into shades of indigo and crimson. The blustery wind had never stopped during their frantic journey and, even with his tartan wrapped tight around him, Malcolm was chilled to the bone.

The village itself was starting to come to life slowly.

A misty fog lingered above the fields. Farmers were already hard at work tending to their crops and livestock. The early morning sun cast long shadows along the thatched roofs of the cottages and buildings. White and gray smoke curled in lazy tendrils from the chimneys. The earthy smell of bread baking permeated the air. In the village itself, the market vendors were out early to set up their stalls of food and cloth. Their low chatter between each other was a quiet hum.

The inn was at the end of the street. A tavern connected to it, but since it was still early, it wasn't open for business yet. There was a fair amount of activity at the inn. When they entered, they headed to the common room, where a servant was stoking the fire. The aroma of fresh bread filled the air, making Malcolm's stomach rumble. Though they had their own provisions for the ride to the village, they had rationed them to make sure they'd have enough for the lassies on the return trip.

Callum selected a table in the far corner where they both sat and observed the door. A servant bustled over to take their order.

"What can I get ye?" he asked.

"Bread and ale," Callum said.

As the servant left, Malcolm took in their surroundings. There were several tables around the room, most of them empty save for a few of the early-rising guests. A rough looking man sat alone in the opposite corner. His dark gaze flickered over them before he looked away and hunched over his bowl of porridge.

Two more men entered the inn and headed for the common room. Malcolm met their gazes. They peered at him, then his brother, before taking a table between them and the hunched man in the other corner.

Unease shifted through him. "I dinnae like this."

"Nor I," Callum replied, keeping his voice low. "Jamie should be along soon."

"And if he isna?" Malcolm asked.

"We will deal with that when the time comes," he replied.

The servant returned with a large loaf of dark brown bread and two tankards of watered-down ale. He placed them on the table without a word and then headed off to tend to the other customers.

The two newcomers made Malcolm uneasy. He kept his eye on them as Callum tore off a hunk of the bread.

Impatience bubbled through his veins as he eyed the few who were inside the inn's common room. Callum shoved the bread toward him.

"Eat something," he suggested.

But his stomach was twisted into a knot as he thought of Evie and Chloe held captive in the MacDonald dungeon. A few more people trickled inside, taking seats around the room. A sense of unease passed through him.

"How long do we wait?" Malcolm asked.

"As long as we need to."

Callum seemed far more calm than he. How, he didn't know. Malcolm drummed his fingers on the wood table.

The two men who came in together rose, standing a moment at their table. The taller of the two cast a suspicious glance at Malcolm and Callum. Then the two walked toward them. Callum reached for the hilt of his sword, wrapping his fingers around it in anticipation of a fight. Malcolm sat straighter and did the same. They came to a halt in front of their table.

"Can I help ye?" Callum asked, his eyes wary.

"We ken who ye are," the tall one said. "We ken who yer looking for. Ye will no find him here."

Remaining calm and cool, Callum said, "I dinnae ken who ye mean."

A smile crept along the man's face. "Och, aye, ye do, MacLeod. Yer brother was captured and is being held in the keep."

"Lies," Malcolm spat.

The man's gaze landed on him then. "'Tis no a lie. I tell ye true." Then he looked back to Callum. "If ye wish to save him, there is a way it can be done."

Callum relaxed his grip on the hilt of his claymore but kept it there in case he needed to use it. "Who are ye to help us, then? MacDonald's own men wouldna give us this information."

The tall man gave a questioning glance to his companion, who have a quick nod. Then the tall man motioned to the chairs opposite Malcolm and Callum.

"May we sit?" he asked.

Malcolm stared at his brother. They exchanged a silent communication until finally Callum nodded.

"Aye."

Each man pulled out a chair and sat. The tall one rested folded hands on the table. He leaned toward them.

"My name is William. This is my brother, John."

John gave a nod of greeting as William continued, dropping his voice low.

"We have no love for our laird. He taxes us, takes our crops and livestock when he wants, and doesna offer us protection in return. I offer ye this bit of information in return for yers."

"My protection?" Callum asked.

"Aye," William said.

Malcolm and Callum exchanged a glance. He shook his head to indicate he didn't trust these two. He saw the contemplation flickering over Callum's face as he glanced back at the two brothers.

"Tell me," Callum said. "And ye have it."

"There's a rocky creek leading into a cave on the north side of the castle. That, in turn, will take ye up a path where there's a postern gate. It's no guarded. Ye can enter the keep there. The dungeon is on the south side. That's where ye'll find yer brother."

And Chloe and Evie, Malcolm thought, but kept that to himself. Willam seemed not to know about the two lassies and he wanted to keep it that way.

Callum dropped two silver coins on the table and pushed them at the two brothers. "Ye have my thanks, lads. Go to Dundale. Tell Dougal I sent ye. If ye betray me or my clan, then the both of ye will be put to death."

William swiped the silver pieces off the table and closed them in his fist. "I wouldna expect anything other than that."

The two of them rose and walked away. Malcolm kept his gaze on their backs as they exited the inn.

"Do ye trust them?" he asked.

"No," Callum answered honestly. His clenched fist rested on the top of the table, his knuckles leeched of color. Impatience and determination emanated off him in waves. "If he leads us into a trap, then he dies when I return to Dundale."

His brother sounded confident he would, in fact, be returning to Dundale.

Malcolm nodded. "Aye, then. Let's hope there is no trap waiting for us."

IT WAS A long, dark, cold walk through the passageway from the dungeon. At times, the cobblestones were slick. Other times, there was no air within the confining passage. They went up an incline, then back down. There were twists and turns leading them through the bowels of the keep. To where, neither of them knew.

Evie kept her hand tight on Chloe's as they walked. Chloe kept the torch held aloft in front of them to light their way, but it wasn't much light to hold back the shadows. They hadn't spoken since leaving the dungeon cell. Chloe knew when their absence was found, the alarm would be sounded and it would be difficult to escape unnoticed.

Once step at a time, she reminded herself.

At one point, the path started to ascend, which gave Chloe hope that they were headed to higher ground. Perhaps even closer to the main floor where they'd find the great hall and, hopefully, Bruce.

Next to her, Evie emitted a faint whimper.

"Are you all right?" Chloe asked.

"I need to stop a minute," she said.

They halted where they were. Evie released her hand and leaned against the wall, blowing out a breath. Her head thumped back against the stone as she closed her eyes.

"I'm tired," she said.

"I know. But we have to keep going," Chloe replied.

She lifted her head and opened her eyes to look at her. "We've been walking a long time and we've seen no hint of a way out."

"We have to keep going," Chloe insisted.

She waved the torch toward the passageway. The flame flickered against the sudden movement.

"I can't walk another step," she whined.

"You have to. I can't leave you here. And we're not going back. We have to get your piece of the keystone."

"But how?" Evie asked, her voice tinged with a bit of hopelessness.

"I don't know yet, but we'll figure out something."

The worry on her sister's face made Chloe step closer to her. She reached for her, placing a hand on her arm in reassurance.

"You're stronger than you think, Eve."

She scoffed. "I'm not."

"Yes, you are. I watched you run up those stairs in the museum that night. I watched you kick Bruce in the face."

A small smile flickered over her face. "I did do that."

"You did. We've never talked about that night," Chloe said. "I was terrified something horrid had happened to you. I had no idea where you were. When the police came afterward, they brought me your shoes and handbag. They swore to me you were nowhere to be found."

Her face contorted in pain. "I'm sorry, Chlo. I never intended to use the keystone to go back in time."

She grinned. "I know that now. I retraced your steps that day we spent on the Royal Mile with Bruce. That's how I ended up at the antique store."

"Mystic Treasures," she said with a nod. "And you saw Moira there."

"I did. And she gave me the piece of keystone I have now." She patted her pocket to reassure herself it was still there. The weight of it was slight but the object was still there.

They lapsed into silence as Evie continued to rest against the wall.

"What do you suppose Brianna is doing right now?" Evie asked.

Chloe snorted. "Probably lounging on a beach somewhere in the Caribbean, sipping a drink with a little umbrella."

"Probably. But I do wonder how she's going to end up in Edinburgh at Mystic Treasures when she hasn't spoken to us in years."

It was something that had crossed Chloe's mind as well. She and Brianna didn't get along so well. The grudge Chloe held wasn't small—her sister's behavior after their parents had died etched a bitterness too deep to ignore. Brianna had been interested in doing what she had to do to make sure she and Evie graduated high school. Once they'd turned eighteen, she washed her hands of them. She'd headed back to her sunny beaches and her mojitos as if they'd never existed.

It cut Chloe to the bone.

Evie, though, was more forgiving. She liked to give Brianna the benefit of the doubt. Chance after chance. Brianna, though, did nothing but disappoint them both time and time again.

"You know she's not interested in what we're doing," Chloe said. "I can't see her stepping foot in Edinburgh. Not after spending most of her adult life as a beach bum."

"But we know there are three pieces to the keystone. Three pieces that represent Present, Past, and Future. Brianna is the future. She *has* to come, doesn't she?"

Hope lit her sister's face, spilling into her voice. Chloe had her doubts about their older sister appearing in the past, but the last thing she wanted was to crush that spark.

"Maybe Moira will find a way to bring her to us," she suggested. Then she changed the subject. "Are you ready to keep going?"

Evie pushed off the wall and nodded. "No, but I don't think we have much of a choice."

She laced her arm with Chloe's. Together, they started through the inky shadows once more. They walked and walked and walked. Eventually, the narrow corridor widened, giving her hope. At last, they saw what appeared to be a door carved into the wall. Halting, Chloe stared at it for a long moment, then glanced at her sister.

"A way out?" she whispered.

"There's only one way to find out," Chloe replied.

She handed the torch off to Evie. Then she pressed both hands against the door. There was no knob. It looked as though it were merely an indention within the wall. Taking a deep breath, she gave it a weak push. It didn't budge. She tried again, pulling instead of pushing, and it cracked open.

A whoosh of cool air seeped through the crack. She peered through it but saw nothing. Or, rather, it appeared to be a tapestry. The hidden door was behind a wall hanging. Men's voices floated to her. At first, she was unable to make out what they were saying.

"I say we kill him," said one man, his voice rough and gravelly.

"Och, we cannae do that, laddie," replied another man. "If we do that, the whole MacLeod army will be upon us."

Chloe sucked in a sharp breath. *MacLeod.* Who was on the other side of that tapestry? Was it Malcolm? Had he been captured?

"What is it?" Evie whispered.

Chloe shook her head to indicate she didn't know.

"Ransom him."

That was Bruce's voice. She was sure of it. The sound of his voice raised all the hackles on the back of her neck.

The first man snorted derision.

The second man said, "Ransom him, eh? MacLeod kens we have his brother and their women. He'll want them all back. Nay. We willna ransom any of them."

"Then what, Da?" the other man asked.

A cold, shivering fear went through her. She turned to Evie.

"I need to see who's in the room," she said.

Evie shook her head. "No way. That's too dangerous."

Chloe reached for her, grasping her free hand and squeezing

it. "They captured one of them."

Evie stared at her, hard, for a long, quiet moment. "One of them?"

"Malcolm or Callum. I don't know which. I need to find out."

Her sister took a deep breath, expelled it, and then nodded agreement.

Chloe turned back to the door. She nudged it open enough to squeeze through without disturbing the tapestry. With her hand shaking and her breath quaking, she reached for the edge, pulling it back a scant inch to see into the room.

The man called Rory MacDonald stood in the center with his arms folded over his chest. Bruce was seated, his feet propped up on a nearby table. The third man she was unable to see.

But there, in a chair, with his hands bound behind him, was not Malcolm or Callum.

It was Jamie.

CHAPTER TWENTY-NINE

CHLOE JERKED BACK from the tapestry and stepped away, turning back toward Evie. Her eyes were wide, her heart was pounding. Her sister knew instantly something was wrong.

"What is it?"

"They have Jamie," she said. "They want to ransom him."

Evie cursed under her breath. Then, "What are we going to do?"

"I don't know," Chloe said.

They needed a plan. She was too weak to try to use the blood magic again and Bruce had Evie's piece of the keystone.

"Let's keep going," Evie suggested as she glanced down the corridor. "Maybe there's another door."

Meaning, maybe there would be another way out. Chloe nodded. She took the torch back from Evie. Together, they headed down the passageway once more. It wasn't long before they came upon another door. They exchanged silent communication. Evie gave her a nod as if to say go ahead and open it.

Chloe handed off the torch once more. She placed her hands on the door and took a deep breath, glancing at her sister for reassurance. Upon her nod, Chloe then pulled open the door. It creaked, but hopefully not enough to alert anyone who may be on the other side. Light slashed through the open door, pushing back the shadows. She peered inside.

It was an empty room. It looked to be someone's bedchamber. There was a large four poster bed with curtains, a wardrobe, and a chest. At least, that's all she could see. She pulled open the door wider.

"Let's go," she said, her voice strong and sure.

"Are you sure about this?" Evie asked. Though she sounded nervous, she followed her sister through the door anyway.

"It's our only chance."

"What do I do with the torch?" Evie stood inside the doorway still holding the flame.

Chloe stepped back through to glance up and down the walls. "Here's a bracket."

Evie handed off the torch. She placed it in the backet, the flame flickering in the drafty, empty corridor. Then she closed the secret door.

"Come on."

She waved at her to follow. They hurried across the bed-chamber to the door. When they reached it, Evie pressed her back against the wall while Chloe cracked the door enough to see into the hallway.

"Looks clear."

"This is insanity," Evie said, her voice shaking. "What if we're caught?"

She turned back to her sister. "Do you want to stay here and wait for Callum and Malcolm?"

"Well…"

"I don't want to risk that," Chloe said.

Evie pressed her hand against her abdomen. "But—"

"I know you're scared. I am, too. I don't want to wait around for them."

"How do you plan to get my keystone back from Bruce?" she demanded. Her worry and fear were replaced by irritation.

Chloe pressed her lips together, unable to answer her questions. She hadn't thought that far in advance and didn't know the answers to her questions. But she was still determined to go through with this to get out of the keep.

"You don't know, do you?" Ire flashed in her eyes.

"I don't, but—"

"Is something burning?" Evie asked, then sniffed the air.

Chloe smelled it, too, then. She glanced around the room. At the secret door, grayish-white smoke seeped around the edges.

"Oh, crap," she muttered.

She hurried back across the room and pushed open the door. Smoke poured inside. Coughing and covering her mouth with her hand she peered around the edge of the doorway. The rafters—dry and aged from being in the darkened passageway—had caught fire from the flickering torch. And the fire was spreading.

"It's on fire!" Evie gasped.

"We have to get out of here now."

Chloe spun back to Evie, leaving the door open. She grabbed her by the hand and dashed to the chamber door, yanking it open. They rushed into the hallway, heedless of any guards or others that might be roaming the area. A man stomped up the stairway and appeared at the other end of the hall. Evie sucked in a sharp breath as they came to a screeching halt.

"Fire!" Chloe shouted. "There's a fire in the bedchamber!" She pointed behind her.

The man spotted them then, halted, surprise evident on his face. Chloe glanced behind her to see smoke rolling out of the room's open door. She grabbed Evie by the hand and rushed by him, leaving him gaping at the smoke. Down the curved stairs they went. At the foot of the stairs, she paused to get her bearings.

Men's voices echoed through the keep, men who were coming closer to them. A door to their right beckoned. Chloe pulled her sister along and burst through the door, banging it open. They ended up in the cool night, the breeze fluttering over Chloe's damp, clammy skin. Behind her, Evie's breathing heavy from the exertion.

"I have to rest," she said.

"No time to rest," Chloe said. "We have to keep moving."

She whimpered. Still clutching her hand, Chloe headed across the darkened bailey. The open portcullis gate was in sight. They were going to make it. They were going to get out through the gatehouse.

But then a sharp, biting pain erupted through her shoulder. She lost her footing, her knees buckling. She managed to release Evie's hand before she went down. She landed hard on the ground, banging her elbows as she broke her fall.

"Chloe!"

As she glanced over her shoulder, she saw the arrow sticking out of it. Then Evie's startled cry ripped through the night air. Bruce held a knife to her throat with an oily smile on his face.

"Well, well. Isn't this convenient?"

Chloe managed to climb back to her feet. She tried to ignore the pain lancing through her. "Let her go, Bruce."

"I will if you give me yer keystone."

She clenched her hands into tight fists, her crudely bandaged hand throbbing. She met Evie's gaze and in them she saw defiance.

"And then what? You'll let us go?" she demanded. "I think we both know the answer to that."

"Yer right. We need ye and yer blood to make the stones work. How about I spill yer sister's blood right here, right now and use her stone against *ye*?"

Chloe clenched her jaw so tightly, the muscles ached. "You wouldn't dare."

"Wouldn't I?" He pressed the blade closer to Evie's throat.

Hesitation flickered through her. She wasn't all too sure Bruce wouldn't slice Evie's throat. He wasn't the man she thought she knew. She reached into her pocket and pulled out her piece of the keystone. Thankfully, it was no longer glowing. As she looked back at Evie, her eyes glistened with tears.

"All right. You win." She stretched her hand out to him. "Release her and you can have it."

She had no weapon. She had no way to stop him once she handed over her piece of the keystone. But she wanted Evie safe. As soon as he released her and she handed off the keystone, she and Evie would make a dash for the open gate.

Jamie would be on his own. Something told her, though, he would be able to find his own way out and to safety.

Bruce removed the knife from Evie's throat, leaving behind a well of blood. He shoved her out of his way and stalked toward Chloe, holding the knife down to his side. Chloe kept her gaze on his face, his glittering blue eyes, and something inside her cracked. She hated him at the moment. She hated what he did to her, what he continued to do to her. She hated that he threatened her sister, her best friend, the only other person in the world who understood her. She hated that he tried to take Evie away from her. And she wanted him to pay for that.

The keystone rested in her palm as she held it out to him. He paused within a few inches of her outstretched hand, smiling triumphantly.

"I'm glad to see you came to yer senses."

He plucked the keystone from her hand. Then he reached into his pocket and brought out Evie's piece. He put the two pieces against each other, snapping them together.

Much to her relief, nothing happened. The stones were dormant.

But the moment the stones were put together, her sliced hand started to tingle and burn as if the magic had transferred from the stone to her.

"Now, all I need is the third piece."

"All *you* need?" Chloe asked, lifting a brow. "This was your plan all along, wasn't it?"

Smug satisfaction erupted on his face. He opened his mouth to reply but then something smashed into the back of his head. He went down in a heap, landing on the ground with a thud. The two pieces of the keystone tumbled from his hand.

Behind him, Evie held a massive rock. She dropped it next to his lifeless body. Shock rolled through Chloe.

"Eve!"

"Is he dead?" she whispered, sounding horrified.

She quickly knelt and snatched up the two pieces, slipping them into her pocket. Then she felt for a pulse to put her sister's mind at ease. There was a faint one.

"He's still alive."

Evie gasped. "Your shoulder, Chlo. You're bleeding!"

"I'm fine."

She reached behind her to try to grab the arrow shaft but couldn't. She gave her sister a pointed look. Evie shook her head.

"No way!"

"You have to."

"But the arrow—"

"I know. I'll deal with that later. Yank it out."

Chloe was aware of the dangers. Removing the arrow improperly could lead to infection or—worse—her death. But she couldn't run around with an arrow sticking out of her shoulder, either.

Taking a deep breath, Evie reached for the shaft, wrapped her hand around it, and then jerked. The shaft released from her shoulder with a damp, sucking noise. Chloe clenched her jaw and grunted, proud of herself for not crying out like she wanted. Evie made a gagging sound.

"It's out. But you're bleeding. You need stitches."

"We can deal with that later. Right now we have to get out of here."

"Chlo—"

There wasn't time for bandages or finding healers or any of that. Smoke from the keep billowed upward into the night sky as more of the building caught fire. But Evie was determined. She ripped another piece of her shift, folded it, and pressed it against the wound.

"Let's go," Chloe said. She reached behind her, grabbing the cloth and pressing it against the wound in the most awkward position ever.

"What about Jamie?" Evie glanced back at the building behind her, worry creasing her face. "We can't leave him."

"We don't have time to go back for him. I have to believe he'll be fine."

She started for the open gate, pushing her tired legs to the limit. She had to admit, though, the pain in her shoulder was unbearable. Evie fell in step beside her. They were nearing the gate when the portcullis started to close.

"Hurry!"

Chloe broke into a run for the gate, trying to get to it before it was closed. Evie was right behind her, panting heavily and trying to keep up with her.

But it was no use. The gate closed as they arrived.

They were trapped.

Her breath seesawing in and out of her, Evie said, "Now what?"

"Where do ye think yer going, lassies?"

The voice boomed across the bailey behind them. They turned to see the man—their enemy—walking toward them with his great axe in his hand.

And Rory MacDonald looked irate.

CHAPTER THIRTY

MALCOLM FOLLOWED CALLUM up the steep incline. Darkness pressed all around them. An earthy pungent scent permeated his nose. All he worried about was if Chloe was safe and if MacDonald had harmed her. If he had, then he would have *him* to deal with.

Ahead, there was a glimmer of pale light, indicating they were getting closer to the postern gate.

When they arrived, Callum peered through the gate.

Sniffing, he said, "Do ye smell that?"

Malcolm inhaled. There was the acrid odor of smoke on the air. "Smoke?"

"Aye." Callum looked back at him, concern lingering in his blue eyes. "Fire?"

"Let's go." He nudged him.

Callum shoved open the gate and ran through it. He wielded his claymore the moment he stepped through. Malcolm followed. Black and gray smoke billowed into the night sky. The keep was on fire.

"God's teeth," Callum bellowed.

He bolted through the narrow passageway leading from the gate. Malcolm followed on his heels. They rounded a corner and halted, facing the bailey. Standing there at the end of Rory MacDonald's great axe was Chloe. Evie cowered behind her.

Malcolm roared, unsheathed his sword, and charged.

"Wait!" Callum called.

But he refused to listen. Blinded by his fury, the war cry ripped from his throat. MacDonald spun to face him, surprise on his face. He recovered quickly when he saw him and charged toward him.

Great axe clashed against claymore. MacDonald swung. Malcolm swerved. He fought with all the pent-up rage he'd held in the moment he learned Chloe was taken from him. The older man had difficulty keeping up with every swing of his sword. He beat him back, making him stumble over his own feet until at last he collapsed on the ground.

Malcolm pointed his sword inches from his face. His breath seesawed in and out of him. MacDonald still had his grip on his great axe as he lay on the ground, peering up at him with harsh eyes.

"Move and ye die," Malcolm warned.

"Ye cannae kill me," he said.

"I can and I will."

"Release him, MacLeod!" his son shouted from behind him.

Malcolm cut a glance over his shoulder to see Callum standing like a human shield in front of the two lassies. Behind him, Rufus had his bow pulled back taut, an arrow pointed at his back.

They were trapped within the bailey of the MacDonald stronghold while the keep was on fire. Indecision flashed through him as he tried to figure out his next move. With his gaze on Rufus, and his sword point on Rory, he had to decide if he was going to yield or continue to fight their way out.

The ground started to shake. A low rumble rippled through the bailey, making the stone walls shudder and quake.

His gaze flew to the women who had moved to stand in front of Callum. Chloe held one of Evie's hands. In the other, her piece of the keystone pressed against Evie's stone. The power burst from the two pieces put together and a bright, white light exploded from it.

"We bind the past, the present, the soul. By blood, by will, by magic

whole," Chloe and Evie chanted together.

But their voices sounded strange—as though they were controlled by the Triple Goddess herself. And their eyes—both of their eyes glowed with an ominous light.

Callum shouted his name and gave a frantic wave for him to hurry toward them. He cut a glance to Rufus, whose wide-eyed gaze was on the women. Then to Rory who remained prone on the ground, glaring up at him.

"Across the veil, our home draws near. To Dundale's keep, the way is clear."

"Malcolm, *now!"*

He broke into a run, his legs pumping hard, as a strange light split the air in two, much like the light he saw when Chloe fell through time.

"Stop them! Stop them! Stop them!" Rory shouted.

But Malcolm didn't look back. Clutching his claymore in his sweating palm as he made a mad dash for them, he watched the light engulf Chloe, Evie, and Callum. Cursing, he leapt into the light as it closed around him and winked out.

CHLOE FELT AS though she were in someone else's skin as she watched the events unfold around her. Evie urged Callum to use the tip of his dagger to slice open their hands once more. Then they smeared blood over the stones, clasped hands, and pushed the two pieces together.

As soon as they did, the magic of the Triple Goddess sparked deep inside her. In that moment, she *was* Bridget. She knew the words to speak as if they had always been inside her. As did Evie. Together, they used the stone to rip open time and space to send them back to Dundale.

Together, they stepped through to Dundale's bailey, followed by Callum. She watched as Malcolm ran toward them. He jumped through the light as the light shrank and then disappeared into nothing more than a pinprick. Then it was gone and she was back in her own skin.

When he landed on his feet, he crouched low to the ground, his sword still in his hand. His chest pumped hard as he tried to catch his breath. Chloe released Evie's hand and charged toward him, launching herself at him, relieved he had made it through the light.

When she landed against him, he grunted and fell to the ground. She perched on top of him, gazing down at those delicious sea-green eyes.

"Thank God you made it!"

Then she pressed her face against his neck and inhaled his scent. The scent of leather and musk and horse and sweat. He wrapped his arms around her, holding her tight. But his hand grazed her wounded shoulder and she winced. When he drew his hand away, his fingers were smeared with blood.

"Och, lass, yer injured."

"I'm fine," she said, ignoring the pain that flared through her. "Are you?"

"I dinnae ken what happened, but I'm glad yer all right."

"You came for me," she whispered.

"Was there any doubt?"

The shame of doubt pounded through her. Of course, he and Callum had come for them. She flushed, her cheeks warming. "I—"

"I will always come for ye. I will always protect ye with my body and sword. Until my dying breath."

"I will never doubt you again."

She breathed the words against his lips and then she kissed him. It was a fierce kiss. A deep kiss. A kiss of passion and need and want and desire. A kiss that conveyed all the emotions pounding through her.

When he pulled away, he said, "It's best ye stop that now, lass, or I cannae be held responsible for my actions."

Then he glanced down and saw the blood smudged on his tunic. She tried to hide her cut hand, but he grabbed her wrist and turned over her palm.

"Yer hand, too," he said. "And yer wrists. God's teeth, lass, what did ye do to yerself?"

She flushed hot. Her wrists were red and raw from her determination to get out of her bonds. She tried to pull away, but he held onto her with a gentle tug as he examined the wounds.

"It was the only way to get back to Dundale," she said. "It was the only way to save you." Then she thought of Jamie and bit her lower lip, the guilt slashing through her. "We couldn't save Jamie, though."

Worry flickered through his eyes. "The keep was on fire."

Another slash of guilt. The fire was her fault. If Jamie died in that fire, she would never forgive herself.

"Maybe he got out." It was her dearest hope.

But Jamie was in enemy hands. She didn't know how he would find his way out.

"We shouldn't have left him." Her voice wobbled with emotion as she clutched his tunic.

"It's all right, lass. Dinnae flash yerself about it. Jamie is resourceful. I've no doubt he will find his way home, but we can send men to look for him. Let's get ye bandaged."

But his face was pinched with concern. He shifted her off him as he got to his feet, helping her to hers, too. Evie huddled next to Callum. When they got to their feet, Evie broke from him and rushed toward her.

"Your shoulder—" she started.

"I'll be all right," Chloe said through gritted teeth.

"But you were hit with an arrow."

"An arrow?" Malcolm asked, giving her a pointed look.

Chloe shot her a look that begged her to be quiet.

"Evie pulled it out. I'm fine."

"You *need* stitches," Evie said.

Chloe wobbled, lightheaded. From the blood loss or the use

of the keystone, she didn't know which. She leaned heavily into Malcolm, who wrapped his arms around her to steady her on her feet as she groaned. Without a word, Malcolm swept her into his arms and carried her toward the keep.

"Malcolm, put me down," she protested, but she knew it was a weak one.

Truthfully, she liked being in his arms. She liked when he took charge and took care of her.

"Evie, fetch Dougal. Have him meet us in my bedchamber at once." Then his heated gaze landed on her. "And I'll have no arguments from ye, lass."

"No argument from me," she said. "Tell him to bring whiskey and a lot it."

※

CHAPTER THIRTY-ONE

CHLOE LAY ON her side in the aftermath of her shoulder being stitched. It throbbed with a deep pain that shifted through her entire body. It was a horrible experience, one she hoped never to repeat. She had known it was going to be and tried to brace herself for it. Nothing could have prepared her, though.

Malcolm remained by her side, holding her hand, letting her squeeze it as tight as she wanted. Her fingernails dug deep into his palm, but he didn't seem to mind. She clenched her jaw, refusing to cry out the entire time Dougal stitched. Before he started, she ordered him to douse the open wound with the whiskey. It was the only thing she could think of to sanitize the wound to keep it from getting infected. When he finished, Malcolm snatched the bottle out of Dougal's hand and gulped a long drink.

Now, he sat by the bed, his head on his chest as he dozed. Across the room, the fire blazed in the hearth.

It was a miracle, she thought, that he hadn't been injured during his fight with Rory MacDonald.

She had caught a glimpse of him when he entered the bailey while she stood at the end of their enemy's sword point. She had seen the rage cross his face before he emitted his fierce war cry and then charged.

She had never seen anything like that before. Her breath caught in her throat when he attacked the older man. It was in that moment she realized she would forever love Malcolm MacLeod.

Callum had skirted around their fighting as he headed right for them, his face creased with worry for his wife. He had pulled her into his arms and held her close, asking if she was all right. Then he had cut her a glance and asked after her.

"She's hurt, Callum," Evie had said. "She took an arrow in her shoulder. She needs a doctor."

"I'm fine," Chloe had said, her words terse as she kept her eyes on Malcolm. "We have to do something to help him."

Evie's gaze had followed hers to the two fighting men. "But what?"

And that's when she had gotten the crazy idea to use the two pieces of the stone together.

A soft knock on the bedchamber door roused Malcolm from his dozing. He lifted his head and jumped to his feet as he hurried to the door, pulling it open to shoo away whoever was on the other side, no doubt.

"I came to check on her." Though Evie tried to keep her voice low, it carried into the bedchamber.

Before Malcolm sent her away, she said, "Let her in, Malcolm."

He glanced over his shoulder at her with question deep in his eyes. As if asking if she were sure. But Evie didn't wait for him to grant her entrance. She slipped by him and headed right for the bed where she perched on the edge, reaching for her. Gently, she took her bandaged hand in hers.

Evie's hand, too, was bandaged. Against his better judgment, Callum had allowed them to use the edge of his sharpened dagger. The cuts were deep on each of their palms. After they arrived back in the Dundale bailey, they each had pocketed their own piece of the keystone. Chloe's now resided on the bedside table. Evie, likely, carried hers on her person.

"I'll give ye both a moment," Malcolm said. He slipped out of the room and closed it behind him with a soft snick.

"How are you?" she asked, concern flickering through her deep brown eyes.

Chloe managed a weak smile. "I'm all right."

"Dougal said you did well. He said you didn't even scream."

"That's because I clenched my jaw shut and refused to scream," Chloe said. She pushed that aside. "Evie, when we put the two pieces of the stone together, did you sense something?"

Contemplation slipped over her features as she kept her focus on their hands. "Yes."

She swallowed hard, her mouth dry. "The Triple Goddess?"

"Yes." The word slipped out on a quiet, icy breath.

"Did you sense anything else?" Though she tried to pretend it hadn't happened, it had been bothering her since the moment they touched the pieces of the stone together, the moment they used their blood to enact the magic within.

"I saw…" Evie took a deep breath, expelled it. "I'm not sure what I saw."

"I think I know," she said. "It was as though I were Bridget and you were Moira in that moment. We spoke as two-thirds of the Triple Goddess. We invoked some kind of magic that allowed us to open time and step through it."

"But how?" Evie's voice shook.

"Because you have the power of the Present, maybe," Chloe said. She thought about that for a while now, trying to work it out and understand how. "But it took the power from both of us to make it happen."

Evie shivered. "If that's true, and that is the power it possesses, I hate to think what power it has when all three pieces are put together."

She voiced what Chloe was thinking. Brianna would, eventually, arrive with her piece and they would put them all together to make the keystone whole again. What, then, would that do? What sort of magic would it bring forth?

"Let's not worry about that now," Chloe said at last.

That was a problem for when—if—Brianna showed. She tried

on numerous occasions to imagine her free-spirited sister in the medieval Highlands. Nothing about it made sense. There was something else bothering her.

"Rory's great axe, Evie. What's to stop him from coming through a portal to us again?"

Evie thought about that for a long moment. "Perhaps he can't use it more than once. He already did to kidnap us. Maybe, like the keystones, the magic needs to recharge."

That made sense. She hoped Evie was right. She had other questions about that great axe. Where did he get it and what made it powerful? She started to ask this when she noticed her sister's face was pale and fatigue lined her features.

"Are you okay?" she asked.

Evie nodded. "Tired, but I'm all right."

"The baby?"

"As far as I can tell, everything is fine."

"That's good. You should rest," she said, releasing her hand.

"If you're sure."

Chloe grinned. "I have Malcolm to watch over me."

"I know he'll take good care of you." Evie rose, standing by the bed. "He has questions, you know. Questions about what happened."

"I'll explain everything to him."

As best as she could, anyway. She, herself, still wasn't sure how that all happened. Evie leaned down and kissed her forehead.

"I'll see you later."

She headed for the door and pulled it open. Malcolm was on the other side, leaning on the door jamb. The second the door came open, he got to his feet. Evie told him goodnight as she slipped past him into the hallway.

Malcolm closed the door and returned to his seat next to the bed. Firelight flickered over his pensive features.

"Ye gave me a fright, ye ken," he said, his voice a low rumble.

She wasn't sure how to respond to that though she assumed

he referred to the use of the keystone.

"When I saw ye there at the end of MacDonald's great axe…" His gaze flickered to hers. "I wanted to murder him."

"You scared me, too, you know," she said. "Fighting him."

"The man who helped take ye will face my wrath," he said, referring to Bruce.

"When he wakes up, he'll have a hell of a headache. Evie smashed him over the head with a rock."

Surprise flashed over his face, then he laughed. "Did she now?"

Chloe told him the story then. Their time in the dungeon when Bruce stole Evie's stone from her to their escape through the mysterious secret passageway to finding Jamie captured and held in one of the rooms.

"We knew we couldn't go that way, so we continued down the passageway until we found another door." She paused, the guilt washing through her as she recalled placing the torch in the bracket under the wooden rafters. "I'm afraid the fire was my fault."

He blinked confusion as he gazed at her. She explained what happened then.

"We should have tried to get Jamie out," she said.

"Och, lass, dinnae fash yerself. I told ye. He's resourceful. He'll find his way home."

"Are you certain?"

"If I ken one thing about the laddie, it's that he'll find a way to talk his way out of the castle by chasing one of the chamber maids and gaining her confidence." He chuckled at the thought.

He reached for her bandaged hand, then, taking it gently in his. She didn't have to tell him they used the stone to get them away from MacDonald's keep. He knew.

"I didn't know how powerful the stones were until that moment when we used them," she said.

"How did you use them?"

"Blood magic," was all she said.

He seemed content enough with that answer and nodded.

"There's one thing I realized, though, Malcolm," she said.

"And what is that, lass?" His beautiful sea-green eyes met hers.

"When I first arrived, all I thought about was taking Evie and returning home. To our time. But Evie isn't going home. She's here to stay with Callum." She paused, taking a deep breath. "And I'm here to stay with you. If you'll have me."

His expression softened as he leaned toward her. "I'm glad to hear that, lass. I willna let ye out of my sight until my dying breath."

She grinned. "And how do you intend to do that?"

He leaned closer, his lips a breath away from hers. "I intend to marry ye."

Before she answered, his lips brushed hers in a sweet, soft kiss.

"I love you, too," she whispered. "Forever and always."

CHAPTER THIRTY-TWO

IT WAS A few days before Chloe felt up to leaving the bed. Fatigue hit her hard after their ordeal in the hands of the MacDonalds and then the subsequent surgery. Malcolm was by her side every moment of every day and night, bringing her food and seeing to all of her needs. It was rather embarrassing when he insisted on helping her to the garderobe but she found she didn't have much energy to get there alone.

Finally, when she was ready to leave, Malcolm fetched Roslyn to help her dress. She was looking forward to getting out of the bedchamber. Plus, she still wanted to tell Evie the good news—that she and Malcolm were going to be married.

"'Tis good to see ye up and around, lass," she said. "Yer sister has been mighty worried about ye."

"I'm doing much better, thanks. I'm ready for some fresh air."

"So long as ye dinnae overexert yerself," Roslyn warned in a motherly tone.

It struck her, then, how much the older woman reminded her of her own mother. It made the sting of loss surface with a fierceness she hadn't expected. Maybe that was why Evie liked spending so much time with her in the kitchen—because she reminded her of their mother, too.

Roslyn helped her dress, taking care with her healing shoulder. Chloe stuck the piece of her keystone in her pocket, determined to keep the thing on her from now on. The woman gathered up the rest of her clothes for washing and headed for the door.

"Roslyn, has there been any news of Jamie?"

She stopped and turned to face her, the sorrow creasing her face. "Not a word. His lordship sent several of his men back to MacDonald keep, but it was deserted. Apparently, there was a fire that destroyed most of the castle."

More guilt. It was going to take some time for her to get over that. "No word on where they went?"

She shook her head. "None. I pray he returns to us soon, though."

"I pray for that, too," she said and meant it.

She wondered if the stronghold was too damaged for them to stay. She hadn't meant to burn it down—it truly was an accident. And, as a historian, it pained her to see the fortress go up in flames by her own hand. If they did flee to someplace else, maybe they took Jamie with them as their prisoner.

Roslyn turned back to the door and opened it. When she did, Evie was on the other side. Her face was alight with excitement, her cheeks flushed pink.

"Chlo! You won't believe it. You have to come to the tapestry room!"

She rushed in and grabbed her by the hand, tugging her toward the door. She gave an apologetic glance at Roslyn as they both rushed out of the room. The woman merely grinned and gave a low chuckle as if the occurrence was not out of the ordinary.

She followed her sister's hurried steps down the stairs, through the great hall, and finally to the room they were calling the tapestry room. The door stood open. Candles blazed brightly in their holders. Evie tugged her inside and paused in front of the wall hangings.

All the images were the same as the last time she was here, but there was one in particular that was different. Previously, it had had nothing more than a faint image of a woman's silhouette, faceless with the wind blowing her hair to one side.

Now, this tapestry clearly showed the woman's face with eyes the color of a winter morning, long sun-kissed auburn hair, and golden skin showing hours of sun worship. She was tall, thin, curvy. She was beautiful with high cheekbones, pointed chin, full lips. Freckles dotted the bridge of her nose. She wore a white gown that billowed around her. Her feet were bare. She stood on the edge of a craggy hill with one hand clenched by her side.

Chloe stared at it a long moment and then sucked in a breath.

"Brianna?" she asked.

"Yes! Can you believe it?"

"No," Chloe said, and meant it. "Do you think this is right?"

"It's never been wrong." She marched to the wall of tapestries. "Before you arrived, this image appeared." She pointed to the one of her falling through time with Bruce behind her. "And this one showed me falling from the sky to the ground after I arrived."

Chloe moved toward the wall hangings to get a closer look. She glanced from the one of Brianna to the one with the Triple Goddess. The one with the three of them standing on the craggy hill with Moira's hand glowing.

"It looks like she's standing in the same place as they are." She motioned to the first tapestry. "Her hand is clenched by her side. Do you think she's holding her piece of the keystone?"

"She'd have to be, don't you think?" Evie examined the first tapestry Chloe indicated. "You're right. It looks like she's standing in the same place as the Triple Goddess."

Chloe looked closer at the one with Brianna. She thought she saw new images bleeding into the fabric next to her. As though ink had been spilled and it was slowly spreading along the textile.

"Look at this." She pointed to the smear. "What do you suppose that is?"

Evie narrowed her gaze as she stared hard at it. She shook her head. "I don't know. It looks like new images are appearing next to Brianna."

Chloe didn't want to say it but she suspected those new images next to their sister were them. Brianna represented the future. If what they were looking at was the future, then wasn't it plausible she and Chloe would be standing there with her?

"Maybe we wait and see what comes of that," Evie suggested.

"Yes," Chloe agreed. She made a mental note to return later to look at the tapestries to see if they had changed.

She decided now was as good a time as any to tell her sister her news. She reached for her hand, grasping it in hers.

"There's something I want to tell you, Eve."

She turned to her. For a moment, concern flickered over her face. "Are you going to tell me something outlandish like you've decided to go home? Because I don't want you to. I want you to stay and—"

"No," Chloe said, interrupting her. "I'm not going to tell you that."

Her brows drew together. "Then what?"

"Malcolm and I are getting married."

With a squeal of delight, Evie flung her arms around her neck and hugged her tight. "I'm so happy to hear that!" She pulled back, holding her at arm's length. "And I can't wait to start planning it."

"We haven't picked a day yet."

"Doesn't matter. Wait until I tell Roslyn. She'll be beside herself. In fact, I'm heading to the kitchen to help her," Evie said. "Do you want to come with me? She'll love to hear the news from you."

She hooked her arm with Chloe's. They started for the door.

"We can tell her later. I was hoping to go outside for a breath of fresh air. I've been cooped up for a while and I'd like to stretch my legs."

"The kitchen can wait then. I'll come with you."

Together, they left the tapestry room behind and headed through the great hall to the door. Outside, it was a cool, crisp morning. Chloe regretted not grabbing her cloak. Evie didn't have hers, either. Clouds dotted the sky with the threat of rain. There was a hint of dampness in the wind, something Chloe recognized from her time in Edinburgh—it definitely smelled like rain. Perhaps even snow.

She paused to take in a deep breath, closing her eyes to enjoy the brisk day.

A shout rose up from one of the guards on the wall. There was a rider coming.

Chloe opened her eyes to see Malcolm and Callum hurrying from the stables.

"Who is it, laddie?" Callum called.

"A lone rider, my lord," he called back. "A man. He looks injured. He's slumped over the horse headed for the gate."

"Open the gate," Callum said.

Evie and Chloe hurried over as the portcullis rose. Moments later, the rider came through, the horse at a slow walk. When he entered the bailey, he pulled the horse to a halt. He practically fell out of the saddle. Malcolm hurried over to catch him before he landed on the ground. He turned the man over in his arms.

"Jamie?" Malcolm eased him to the ground and knelt next to him.

She, Evie, and Callum were at his side in an instant. His face was dirty. His clothes torn. Dark circles were under his eyes. His breath was shallow as he leaned heavily against Malcolm.

"Are ye all right?" Malcolm asked. "What happened?"

"Tired," he muttered. "It's been a long road to get here."

"I'll fetch some water," Evie offered and scurried away.

Relief pounded through Chloe as she moved to stand next to them. But it wasn't enough to assuage the guilt of leaving him behind in a burning building.

Callum knelt next to them, concern creasing his features. "We came back for ye but the MacDonald keep was deserted."

"Aye," Jamie said, his voice rough. "With the fire in the keep, there was chaos. They left me in the chamber alone, my hands bound. But I managed to get the ropes off."

He held up his hands. His wrists were raw and red where he'd struggled to get free. There was that guilt again, banging around inside her. She felt wholly responsible for everything that happened to him.

Evie returned then with a water skin. She handed it to Callum, who helped Jamie take a long drink. When he was finished, he waved him off. When Evie saw his mangled wrists, she gasped.

"He needs medical attention," she said.

"I'll heal, lass," Jamie said, as though it were nothing more than a scratch. Then he glanced back at Callum. "I managed to find a chamber maid. Asked her to get me to the stables. I stole a horse and tried to get out, but someone shot me in the leg."

He pulled up his breeches. There was a bloody mark where the arrow lodged in the meaty part of his calf. Dried blood caked his leg. He'd pulled the arrow out, leaving behind the point. Chloe knew from her own experience how painful that was.

"So, ye were captured again," Callum said.

He nodded. "The fire was too far gone. They let it burn. MacDonald and the household headed for one of his other strongholds in the northern part of the isle. When we camped, I decided to make my move. I stole a horse and managed to get away."

He lapsed into silence, leaning heavily onto Malcolm. He blew out an exhausted breath.

"My lady wife is right. Ye need medical attention. Let's get him inside. Evie, will ye fetch Dougal?" Callum said.

Nodding, Evie hurried ahead of them to find Dougal, leaving Chloe behind. While she was relieved the younger MacLeod was home, she knew he had a long road ahead of him. He had a lot of healing to do.

And so did she.

Chapter Thirty-Three

T HE CASTLE WAS abuzz with activity.

Nearly two weeks had passed since Jamie's return to Dundale. The expectation was that the MacDonalds would try to invade but they never did. All was quiet. Mayhap, Malcolm said, it was the quiet before the storm.

Chloe was certain they would try again.

It was the day of her wedding and all worry and fear were set aside. There was a festive feeling to the air. Evie had had a glowing excitement in her face all day. She'd spent the morning in the kitchen helping Roslyn with the preparations for the coming wedding feast. But not only a wedding feast—a feast to celebrate the return of the youngest MacLeod brother. Roslyn said it was a miracle he had returned and was determined to commemorate it by making his favorite mincemeat pie.

Chloe didn't mind sharing the limelight with him. Perhaps it would help ease her guilt for leaving him behind in the first place.

When she visited Jamie while he was still convalescing, she expressed her deepest regret about that when she told him about the secret passageway and finding their way out. She did not tell him, however, that she was the one who set the castle on fire.

"Och, lass, dinnae fash yerself about that," he had said with a winning smile. "'Twas the only sensible thing to do."

"But—"

"Ye did what you had to do," he interrupted. "Ye protected

my brother's wife and my nephew."

She lifted a brow in bemused question. "Nephew?"

"Aye." Then he smiled broadly. "I'm going to be an uncle."

It made her giggle the way he was so certain Evie was going to have a boy.

Thinking of it now made her smile. She hoped Evie *did* have a boy. Maybe she'd name him after their father.

Now, she stood in her bedchamber as Evie fussed over her. Her gown was simply stunning in an ivory silk with long, flowing lines. The sleeves were bell-shaped. The bodice was formfitting to her every curve with a jeweled girdle that helped accentuate her waist. An intricate floral pattern trailed down the skirt of the gown. A scalloped hem with the same floral motif added a touch of elegance.

Chloe felt like a fairy princess as she stood while Evie buttoned up the back of her gown.

"Oh, Chlo. I wish Mom was here to see this." She sniffed and pretended her eyes weren't misty with tears.

"Me, too," she said.

She expected to feel the pang of longing for their mother on her wedding. But she wasn't the only person she wished was there. She wanted to share this day with Brianna, too.

Thinking of Brianna being there for her wedding surprised her. Despite their differences and Chloe's ill feelings toward her, for she still held a grudge for her past actions, she was still family, and blood was always thicker than water. She wanted her there.

It wasn't the first time she wondered if Brianna would accept the keystone from Moira in that antique store in Edinburgh. Which made her wonder *how* Brianna would end up in Edinburgh to begin with. What event would send her there? They hadn't spoken in years. Likely, Brianna hadn't a clue she was there on a work visa. Unless Evie had told her.

And Evie might have told her. Evie was somewhat more forgiving toward their older sister than she was.

But today wasn't the day to think about that. Today was a

day to be happy. To think about a future with Malcolm, her warrior Highlander who had vowed to protect her with his life and his sword.

A knock on the door sounded. Evie hurried to it and cracked it open. Malcolm's muffled voice was on the other side.

"It's bad luck to see the bride before the wedding," Evie stated, clearly.

"Oh, let him in, Evie. It's not like we believe in that superstition anyway," Chloe said, exasperated.

Evie cut her a glance over her shoulder and pretended to frown, but then pushed open the door to let him inside.

"You have two minutes and that's all," Evie said, her voice stern as she marched out and closed the door behind her.

Malcolm stood before her in his finery. He wore a crisp white tunic underneath his MacLeod belted tartan. It was draped and fastened on the shoulder with a silver brooch. He wore black breeches, polished, if well-worn, leather boots, his sporran, and a wool cloak. His cheeks and chin still sported that three-day growth of beard she loved.

He gaped at her as she stood before him in her gorgeous gown. She shifted from one foot to the other, a sudden awkwardness coming over her.

"Well? Do I pass inspection?" she asked, finally breaking the silence.

"I've no seen a bonnier lass then ye, love."

She flushed hot at the compliment.

He reached for her. She placed her hand in his. He glanced down to see the bandage around her hand was gone. Turning it over, he traced the silvery scar that crossed it. The burn scar from the keystone was still there, but the scar from the cut likely would never go away.

"Yer hand is healed."

"Yes," she said. "It didn't take long. I think it has something to do with the magic in the keystone."

He lifted his gaze to hers. "And yer shoulder?"

"Still sore but better."

The corner of his mouth lifted in a half grin. "Good. I promise to take great care when I tup ye later."

"Is that why you came here? To flirt with me?"

"I dinnae ken what ye mean by that, but nay. I dinnae come here for that. I came to give ye this."

He reached into his sporran and placed a small object in her hand. It was an elegant circular brooch adorned with an intricate Celtic knotwork pattern. It was made of silver with the pin extending across the back of it to secure it to a heavy cloak or other garment. Embedded within the design on each side were two amber stones polished to a high shine, winking in the light of the room.

She stared at it for a long, quiet moment. She'd seen this brooch before.

In Mystic Treasures.

For a moment, she couldn't breathe or think or move. She simply stared at it in complete and utter shock.

"I ken is no much. It belonged to my mother."

"I love it. It's beautiful," she said. "Thank you."

And it was perfect. She planned to wear it on her cloak when she walked down the aisle to be handfasted to Malcolm.

He smiled, well pleased. Seeing his smile warmed her heart and made her love him all the more.

Evie came back into the room, breaking into their moment.

"All right, you've been in here long enough. Time to get to the chapel."

She hustled him out of the room before he made any objections. As he stepped through the door, he gave her one last look. One last smile. And then Evie closed the door and turned to her, hands on her hips.

"Since when did you become a mother hen?" Chloe demanded.

"Since always."

Chloe smiled. She was right. It was since always when she

took over after Brianna left.

Her sister's eyes lit up when she noticed the brooch in her hand. "What is that?"

"Malcolm gave it to me. He said it was his mother's."

"Oh, Chlo, it's beautiful." She ran a finger over the circle in awe.

"Pin it to my cloak, Eve. It's time for me to get married."

EVIE ESCORTED HER from her bedchamber to the chapel. When they arrived, Callum waited outside the doors to walk her down the aisle. He was dressed in his Highland finery like Malcolm. His tartan was draped over him and pinned together at his shoulder.

When they arrived, Evie turned to her and kissed her cheek, her face alight with joy. Then she hurried into the chapel to take her seat near the front next to Jamie.

Chloe took a deep breath and peered through the doorway. The chapel was alight with what seemed like a thousand candelabras.

"Are ye ready, lass?" He held his arm out to her.

Nodding, she placed her hand in the crook of his elbow. Together, they walked into the chapel down the center aisle. Every seat was filled and all eyes were on her as they made their way. But her gaze was fixed solely on Malcolm, who stood at the front next to the bishop, his hand on the hilt of his sword. When they came to the altar, Callum kissed her cheek and took his seat next to her sister.

Together, they turned toward the bishop as he began speaking.

"Today, we gather to witness and celebrate the sacred union between Malcolm and Chloe. They shall be bound together in love and commitment by the rites of handfasting. They both come of their own free will to bind their love and loyalty to each other."

The rest of the ceremony was a blur for her. Their hands were bound, their vows exchanged.

The bishop announced, "As yer hands are bound together, so shall yer lives be bound as one. May ye enjoy a lifetime of love, peace, and happiness. Let us rejoice in their union. Ye may kiss yer bride."

His kiss was slow, thoughtful, and probably the sweetest one she had ever had.

Cheers went up. Evie rushed to her to hug her. Even Jamie beamed at their union.

"Two MacLeod lassies now," Roslyn proclaimed as she wiped a tear from each eye. "I cannae wait to have the hall filled with little lads and lassies."

Evie grinned and cut her a glance. Chloe flushed hot, her cheeks burning. Malcolm merely chuckled.

The crowd started to make their way out of the chapel toward the celebratory feast in the great hall. Callum wrapped an arm around Evie as they walked together. She and Malcolm followed, stepping into the cool night air. But the crush of people overwhelmed her, leaving her feeling as though she were suffocating.

"Can we wait a moment?"

"Are ye well? Ye look a wee bit flushed."

She sucked in a deep breath, the crisp air filling her lungs. "I need a bit of air."

"Something troubles ye, eh? Is it what Roslyn said about the bairns? She meant nothing by that."

She shook her head as he pulled her closer, wrapping her in his arms. She basked in the warmth of his body radiating over her, the warmth she loved with every breath she had in her.

"No. It's not that."

"What, then?"

She pushed the thought away. She didn't want to think of anything other than her husband on this night. But the worry had gnawed at her since their return to Dundale.

She shook her head. "It's nothing."

He dropped a kiss on top of her head, hugging her tight to him. She felt safe and secure in his arms.

"I ken Bruce is still alive."

"You do?"

"Aye."

"He will come back, you know."

"Oh, aye. But we will be ready for him and the rest of his ilk."

She tipped her head back to look up at him. "And if the third piece of the keystone arrives?"

"We willna let it fall into the wrong hands."

She rested her head on his chest, the steady beat of his heart underneath her ear. "I hope you're right."

He pulled away then, holding her hands in his and looking deep into her eyes.

"I make this second vow to ye here, now. Ye are my wife. A MacLeod. And ye have my name, my clan, and all the might of it behind ye." The back of his hand swept over her cheek, warm against her chilled skin. "We are one flesh."

His words rooted deep, weaving through her like sunlight breaking through storm clouds. Her chest tightened, her breath catching as she met his gaze—those sea-green eyes, endless and fierce.

"Now and always?"

"Aye, lass. Now and always."

His mouth claimed hers, sealing his vow to her. And in that strong, unyielding kiss filled with quiet passion, it was a bond nothing could break. It was a bond of forever.

THE END

About the Author

Michelle Miles believes in fairy tales, true love, and magic. She writes heart-stopping urban fantasy, young adult and adult fantasy, and paranormal romance with an action/adventure twist that will leave you breathless. She is the author of numerous series that includes everything from angels and demons to fairies, dragons, and elves.

She is a member of Romance Writers of America (RWA) and Science Fiction and Fantasy Writers Association (SFWA). A native Texan, in her spare time she loves reading, listening to music, watching movies, hiking, and drinking wine. She can be found online at Facebook, Instagram, Pinterest, and more!

Website & Blog: www.michellemiles.net
Facebook: MichelleMilesAuthor
Instagram: MichelleMilesAuthor
Threads: @michellemilesauthor
YouTube: MichelleMiles
TikTok: @michellemilesauthor
BookBub: bookbub.com/authors/michelle-miles

www.ingramcontent.com/pod-product-compliance
Lightning Source LLC
Chambersburg PA
CBHW072105300726
48975CB00003B/716